THE NIGHTMARE FEAST

TURNER PUBLISHING COMPANY
Nashville, Tennessee
www.turnerpublishing.com

Cover design: Mark Swan
Book design: Karen Sheets de Gracia

LIBRARY OF CONGRESS CATALOGING-IN-PUBLICATION DATA
Names: Klavan, Andrew, author.
Title: The nightmare feast / Andrew Klavan.
Description: Nashville : Turner Publishing Company, 2020. | Series: Another kingdom ; book 2 | Summary: "Austin Lively is on the hunt—and on the run. With a pair of hitmen on his trail in California, and an evil wizard coming after him in the Eleven Lands, Austin is trying to complete a dual quest"—Provided by publisher.
Identifiers: LCCN 2019025028 (print) | LCCN 2019025029 (ebook) | ISBN 9781684422661 (paperback) | ISBN 9781684422678 (hardcover) | ISBN 9781684422685 (ebook)
Subjects: GSAFD: Adventure fiction. | Fantasy fiction.
Classification: LCC PS3561.L334 N55 2020 (print) | LCC PS3561.L334 (ebook) | DDC 813/.54—dc23
LC record available at https://lccn.loc.gov/2019025028
LC ebook record available at https://lccn.loc.gov/2019025029

9781684422678 Hardcover
9781684422661 Paperback
9781684422685 eBook

PRINTED IN THE UNITED STATES OF AMERICA

19 20 21 22 23 10 9 8 7 6 5 4 3 2 1

ANOTHER KINGDOM

THE NIGHTMARE FEAST

BOOK TWO

ANDREW KLAVAN

This book is for Jonathan and Erica Hay,
a token of my friendship

"We shall not cease from exploration
And the end of all our exploring
Will be to arrive where we started
And know the place for the first time."

—T.S. Eliot, "Four Quartets"

Galinian Countryside
Netherdale
Ruins of Galiana

Southern Gate
Edgemond
Eastrim
Northern Gate
Wood

SO NOW I WAS A HUNTED MAN. HUNTED, HAUNTED, brokenhearted. I looked in the motel mirror. Was that really me? I was thirty years old, and I looked like death. Like death on a Monday morning after a weekend binge.

A week ago—four days ago even—I was Austin Lively, boy failure, Hollywood schmuck. A wannabe moviemaker who never made a movie. A writer who sold one script straight out of film school then faded away to become the shadow of an LA nobody. I was a reader for a crappy production company named Mythos. I was also a hypochondriacal depressive who had lost all hope of ever having the big career of his dreams.

Funny: I never thought I would miss being a dreamless hypochondriacal depressive nobody. But those were the days, all right. Now? My life was gone. My job was gone. My friends were gone. The cops were trying to pin a murder on me. An all-powerful billionaire, Serge Orosgo, wanted me dead. My family—my mom, my dad, my brother—were all in Orosgo's pay. Only my kid sister Riley was above suspicion, and guess what? She was nuts. Plus she'd gone missing. Even her insane conspiracy videos had vanished off the internet.

And all that trouble I was in? That was just in this world, the real world.

What other world was there? Glad you asked. Galiana. The Eleven Lands. A magical, mystical brain tumor of a hallucination I seemed to walk into without warning from time to time. Could happen any time I went through a door. And if things were crap here, believe me, it was nothing compared to the way they were in that lunatic fantasy. The woman who loved me there—Lady Betheray, the woman I was supposed to defend and protect—was dead, murdered. Her husband, Lord Iron, the tyrant of the country, and Curtin, his pet wizard, wanted to capture and torture me. I was supposed to be on a quest to find the emperor, Anastasius, who would restore the wise queen, Elinda, to her throne. I know—it sounded ridiculous to me too. But ridiculous or not, it was a job for a knight in shining armor—"a fighting man of brave heart and right belief"—not some SoCal dickhead in a cheap motel.

That's where I was now. A motel so cheap they let me pay in cash. A run-down hole on a small highway just south of Salinas. I was waiting for darkfall there so I could finish my run to the Bay Area. It was too dangerous to try it in daylight. The cops might be on the lookout for me. And Orosgo's bald-headed thug—the guy I called Billiard Ball—was almost certainly on my trail as well.

But somehow I had to get there. Had to find my sister. Had to find the manuscript she might or might not have, the novel called *Another Kingdom*, which seemed to have some power to connect this crazy world to that crazy other one.

I turned away from the mirror. I looked around the room. Room Six in the Shangri-la Motel: a cinderblock rectangle. The cinderblocks were painted urine yellow. The carpet was sewage brown. There was a double bed with a floral bedspread that was mingled green and red, sort of like vomit. There was a particleboard dresser with a lamp on it under the mirror. There was a TV and a cheap table and a couple of cheap chairs. There was a locked door that I guess connected to the next room over.

Beside the table, there was a small window. It looked out onto the parking lot and onto the rest of the one-story, U-shaped, barracks-like motel. Through the misty veil of the privacy curtains, I could watch the light dying over the drab highway.

As soon as dark came, I'd be on the road again.

I moved to the bed. I lay down on the vomit-colored bedspread, my hands clasped behind my head. I looked up at the ceiling. My heart felt like ashes. That was the odd thing about Galiana. It was an acid-trip of a fantasy world filled with ogres and centaurs and fairies and the like. It couldn't be real. But when you came back, you brought your wounds with you, and the wounds were real. And so was your grief.

My hand went to the chain I wore around my neck, down to the golden locket that hung on the end of it. It had belonged to Betheray. I pulled the chain up over my head and held the locket up in front of me. I pressed the clasp and the locket opened. There was a portrait inside, a miniature painting of Queen Elinda. I gazed on her serene and regal and exquisitely feminine face. Engraved on the locket's other half was a coat of arms—a sword across an open hand—and the queen's motto: *Let Wisdom Reign and Each Man Go His Way.*

I reread the words. I could hear my mother's arch response: "What's wisdom, I wonder."

I had no idea.

As I lay there gazing at the picture, I thought I felt a strange heat coming off the metal of the locket, a strange power. It seemed to grow heavier in my hand, heavy as a stone.

Quickly, on instinct, I snapped the locket shut and held it tight.

And something happened. Something weird. For a moment, I lost myself in a kind of rapt otherness. The motel room disappeared from around me. I was in a different place, a place I knew: the house where I'd grown up in Berkeley. The living room. I could see it. I could hear a child crying—not just crying—screaming—hysterical—terrified. It was so real, so startling, I loosed my hold on the locket and let it drop to my chest.

At once, the otherness—the image—the memory—whatever it was—vanished. I was back in the motel, back on the bed. When I tentatively picked up the locket again, it wasn't heavy anymore, no power came off it. The experience was over. It had lasted only a second. It was easy to convince myself that I had imagined it. Just nerves, that's all.

So I lay there, holding the locket, thinking of Betheray, missing her, blaming myself for not being man enough to protect her. I watched as the shadows in the small room shifted, as the evening came on outside.

Then, finally, it was dark. Time to go. With the locket still in my hand, I rolled off the bed. There was nothing to pack; I had nothing with me. I'd ditched my phone so no one could trace me. I'd stopped at an ATM near LA to stock up on cash. I couldn't use credit cards. They could trace those too. I'd dismantled the GPS in my car. No internet. No social media. I was invisible—and I was utterly alone.

I crossed the shit-brown carpet to the door. I opened the door onto the night outside.

There was Billiard Ball.

He stood gigantically on the threshold, framed in the doorway with the parking lot lights glaring behind him.

Before I could react, he jabbed me in the neck with a stun gun. The electric blast sent me reeling—back into the room—convulsing—down to the floor.

2

I DROPPED TO THE CARPET, JERKING AND SHUDDERING. My muscles were locked up, immobile. All I could do was lie there and judder and watch as Billiard Ball stepped calmly into the room and calmly shut the door behind him.

His enormous shoulders were packed into a leather jacket. His muscles bulged through the thin sweater he wore underneath. He looked down at my quivering body without a smile, without a sneer, without any emotion at all. He hardly seemed interested in what he saw.

He reached into his jacket and slid the little stun gun into his left inside pocket. Then he reached across into his right inside pocket and drew out a small leather case.

Terror exploded inside me as I watched him unzip the case and deftly remove a syringe.

I made a horrible, helpless gurgling noise in my throat as I battled to get control of my body. It was no use. My muscles had been severed from my will. Billiard Ball was going to poison me, kill me, and I couldn't do a thing to stop him. They would find me in this crappy motel room, dead of what seemed like natural causes. My mother and father would pretend it was a tragedy. My brother would tell himself it couldn't be helped. The police would lie. No one would ever know that Orosgo had had me murdered to preserve his crazy plan to establish The Orosgo Age, a utopia on earth. I had to move. I had to run. I had to—but I couldn't. My muscles were strung out tight.

Billiard Ball knelt at my feet. He laid the syringe on the carpet. He calmly untied my right sneaker. He calmly removed my sock. Like a mother undressing a toddler. He was going to inject me between the toes where no one would find the needle mark.

I gurgled. I struggled. I made a high-pitched screech of useless effort. I could not move anything.

And then I could. A little. My hand, the fingers of my right hand. By focusing all my effort, all my will, into my fingers, I could stretch them out even as they went on trembling violently. I could bend my right wrist—just a little. That horrid, helpless noise kept spitting out between my teeth as I battled to shift my forearm.

Meanwhile, Billiard Ball finished taking off my sock. He set it down on the floor by his left knee, next to the sneaker he'd already removed. It was all very neat, very efficient. He wanted to be able to find the sock and sneaker quickly so he could put them back on my corpse after I was dead.

I moved my hand across the carpet. A little. Half an inch.

I touched something. Something cold. The locket! Betheray's locket. I had dropped it when I fell. I fought to close my fingers around it. It was like bending bars of iron. My whole body shook violently with the effort, my spine thrumming like a bowstring. But slowly, slowly, slowly, my fingers closed.

Having set my sock down beside my sneaker, Billiard Ball now turned to pick up the syringe lying on the carpet by his right knee.

I closed my hand. I gripped the locket in my fist. Like an explosion, I felt that odd power radiate off the metal again. The power pulsed into my flesh. Flashes of vision interrupted the reality of the moment. The house where I grew up. The living room. A child screaming somewhere. I fought to stay focused on the real world, the motel, my swiftly approaching murder . . .

The power of the locket flowed into my hand, my wrist, my arm, giving me more strength. I lifted the locket from the floor. It felt heavy, as it had before. Heavy as a rock.

Billiard Ball sniffed absent-mindedly as he lifted the syringe in his right hand and held it upward, needle pointing at the ceiling. Working in a deadpan, business-like manner, he used his left hand to pry my big toe away from the toe beside it, to make a space where he could inject me. He brought the syringe's needle down toward my foot.

I flicked my arm and threw the locket at him.

It was a good throw. Or maybe his head, leaning down over his homicidal work, just gave me a big target. Or maybe there was some Galianan magic in the locket itself. I don't know. But the locket—the locket with its extra heavy load of bizarro energy—smacked hard into the thug's temple.

The blow knocked Billiard Ball's head to one side. Both of his hands flew up into the air reflexively. He let out a cry of pain and surprise: "Ah!"

He dropped the syringe.

It fell onto the carpet to the left of me. With a great shout and a mighty effort, I threw my arm across my body, my shoulder lifting with the motion. I found the syringe and grabbed hold of the barrel.

All this took less than a second—but long enough for Billiard Ball to recover from his surprise. A flicker of annoyance crossed his face as he saw me go for the syringe. He reached out and clamped his hand around my wrist in a grip of steel. He held me fast. There was no way I could get the syringe anywhere near him.

So I shifted my hand in his grip, bent the wrist, aimed the needle at him, and pressed the plunger down with my thumb.

Whatever poison was in the tube squirted out in a thin, steady stream. I pointed the stream at his face, then bent my wrist further and slashed the stream across his nose until it hit him smack in the eye.

Billiard Ball let out a monstrous roar of pain. He let me go and clutched at his eye with both hands. His huge body fell sideways against the bed.

My muscles were still stiff and half frozen. Grunting loudly, I managed to turn myself over onto my side, then my belly. I dropped the empty syringe and pressed both palms into the carpet. I pushed myself up. It felt as if there were a huge block of cement on my back. I crawled a few inches, just trying to put some distance between me and the killer in that tiny room.

I reached the particleboard dresser. I could hear Billiard Ball cursing in pain behind me, but I didn't look back. I grabbed the dresser, the drawer handles. I dragged myself up to my knees. Letting out another shout of desperate effort, I grabbed hold of the dresser top and hauled myself to my feet. My legs felt like spaghetti under me. I had to will the strength back into them.

I saw my image rise into the mirror as I rose. A face like a corpse, three days buried.

I heard a noise behind me. I saw Billiard Ball in the mirror too. He was rising too, clawing his way up the vomit-colored bedspread as he got his feet on the floor beneath him. His eye streaming, his teeth gritted in fury, he hoisted his torso onto the bed.

The room was so small we were barely a foot apart. No way I could get past him to the door. I needed a weapon—now. The lamp on the dresser. It was all there was. I grabbed hold of it. It was heavy. The wire ran over the side of the dresser and was plugged into the wall behind. I looked over my shoulder at Billiard Ball. He looked at me. His one good eye was aflame with rage. His jacket had fallen open to expose the holster under his arm.

Oh God, he had a gun! Of course he did.

I lifted the lamp—no more than a few inches. The cord held it in place after that. I yanked the lamp as hard as I could. It didn't come free. I yanked it again.

Billiard Ball reached into his jacket for his gun.

There was a pounding knock at the door. It startled us both into a moment of inaction. We both looked at the door. An old woman's voice came through it. It was the woman at the front desk: the bent, nearly humpbacked old woman who had checked me into the motel.

"What's going on in there? Stop it, whatever it is! I called the police! They're on the way!"

She pounded on the door again. *Bang, bang, bang.*

My face twisted in strain, I yanked the lamp with all my might. The cord broke, snapped away from the plug, spitting orange sparks.

Billiard Ball worked himself up into a sitting position on the edge of the bed. He drew his gun out of the holster.

Bang, bang, bang at the door. "The police are coming!" screamed the motel lady.

Billiard Ball aimed the gun at me and pulled the trigger. I swung the base of the lamp at him as hard as I could. It smacked him in the side of the head, full force. The gun went off. The noise in that small room was like the end of the world, only louder. I thought I felt the bullet whistle by my ear. The mirror shattered behind me. Billiard Ball wobbled where he sat, stunned by the blow from the lamp.

When the deafening gun blast subsided, everything seemed muffled and far away, weirdly quiet and dreamlike. Was the old lady still pounding on the door? I didn't know; I couldn't hear. Was Billiard Ball making some sort of noise through his contorted features? Maybe; I wasn't sure.

But I could see—see through a hazy daze—that the thug was coming to his senses, bringing the bore of the pistol around to point at me again.

If there was any advantage to my time in Galiana, it was this: I had learned how to focus and how to fight. On this side of my existence—here, in what I laughingly called the real world—I had always been a nerd, a wimp, the sort of guy who knew how to smile and snigger and shuffle on by without getting noticed by anyone who would do him harm. But in Galiana . . .

. . . in Galiana, I was a knight in armor. I had battled for my life. I had dueled with expert swordsmen and watched them die on the point of my blade. I had learned that I could clear my mind. I had learned that I could focus even through panic. I had learned that I could kill. What little skill I'd acquired—what little skill and what little courage—I had brought back with me, here to California.

So now, as Billiard Ball turned the gun on me again, I didn't flinch. I just went at him.

Gripping the neck of the desk lamp, I swung the base at him again, at his gun this time. As I brought the lamp around, the lampshade snapped off and fell, leaving the bulb bare. The heavy base hit Billiard Ball's hand. His gun went flying. It dropped to the floor. It spun a few inches over the carpet and came to rest by the door.

I rushed for it—or tried to. As I went to get past him, Billiard Ball lunged off the bed and tackled me. I fell on my back. He fell on top of me. He wrapped his hands around my throat and closed them tight. I couldn't breathe. I tried to swing the base of the lamp up at his head, but I couldn't get any leverage. I couldn't put any force into it. And now, Billiard Ball shifted his massive body and drove his knee into my bicep, pinning it to the rug.

And all the while, he went on strangling me. I gagged. My mouth came open. My tongue stuck out. I could feel my eyes bulging. Blue spots floated in the air around me. The spots turned black.

Billiard Ball's enormous bald head leaned down toward me; his twisted face filled my field of vision. I was still deaf from the gunshot. Everything around me seemed far away and dreamy. I was sinking toward unconsciousness, toward death.

I shifted the lamp in my hand. I bent my elbow. I stabbed the lamp upward, hard, driving the bare light bulb into Billiard Ball's face.

The bulb exploded on impact. I closed my eyes as glassy dust spilled down over me.

But I felt Billiard Ball's hands fly off my throat. I felt his weight fly off my body. I sucked air into my lungs as I squirmed away from him, as I turned over and tried to rise, the glass pouring off my face in a sprinkling sheet.

On my side, I opened my eyes and looked. I saw Billiard Ball sitting with his back against the dresser. He was clutching his face. He was rocking his body. Blood was pouring out between his fingers.

I still held the lamp in my hand, the broken bulb now just a jagged shard of glass sticking out of the socket at the end. My ears were beginning to clear. I could hear something. A siren. More than one. Police cars approaching from who knew how far away.

I had to get out of here. I knew the police could kill me just as quickly as Billiard Ball could—and they would if they were in Orosgo's pay. I rose to my knees, grunting.

Billiard Ball dropped his hands. His face was a mass of blood, with one blood-streaked eye and his gritted teeth showing white through the scarlet. He let out a wild roar of rage and threw himself at me, his hands reaching for my throat again.

Reflexively, I jabbed the lamp at him like a bayonet. The force of my movement and the force of his combined, and he was impaled. The broken glass of the bulb sank into the side of his neck and part of the metal socket followed it. He was pinned in midair. As he fell back, the lamp dropped out of him and the blood spurted after it, dousing my face and shoulder. Billiard Ball dropped to the floor in indescribably awful paroxysms.

I stared in open-mouthed horror as he thrashed and died in a shower of gore.

A MOMENT LATER, BILLIARD BALL LAY STILL. THERE WAS blood everywhere. I was covered with it. So was the rug. There were red streaks on the bedspread and the walls.

I could still hear sirens. They were louder now and growing even louder fast.

Gasping, I pulled myself up onto the bed, then rolled off it onto my feet. I stumbled to the table, to the window. I looked out.

Through the white haze of the privacy curtains, I could see the flashing red lights of police cars racing into the parking lot. My silver Camaro—my sister's boyfriend's car—was parked right outside, right beside the door, but there was no way to get to it with first one cop car, then two, bounding over the sidewalk ramp and shooting across the lot toward me. A moment later, the first car braked, tires screeching. Two officers leapt out, their guns drawn. A third uniform stepped out of the second car even as it swerved to a stop.

I had to get out of here.

I looked around me. There was only one possible exit: the locked door that led into the next room over.

Fighting down the urge to puke my guts out, I forced myself to head across the room. Squinting through the blood on my face. Weaving like a drunken man.

Billiard Ball lay sprawled across my path, splayed in the narrow aisle between the bed and the dresser. His head was propped against the dresser so that his still-open eyes, white in his red-drenched face, seemed to stare at nothing. His gun lay on the rug near his motionless right hand. Betheray's locket lay right beside it.

I stepped over him, trying not to look. But I had to bend down to retrieve the gun and the locket. As I did, those dead eyes of his stared right into mine. It sent a chill through my entire body.

I straightened, the gun in my fist, the locket chain dangling from my fingers. I slipped the chain over my head as I walked unsteadily to the back of the room.

Behind me, still somewhat muffled in my blown-out ears, I could hear a fist pounding on the room door. I could hear a voice shouting: "Police! Open up!"

I reached the other door, the locked door. It had no knob, just a deadbolt protruding from the wood. I lifted the gun and slammed the butt of it down onto the mechanism. Once, then again.

It was all cheap stuff. The deadbolt came loose on the first blow. On the second blow, it fell from its hole and dropped to the floor.

The police went on shouting: "Open up or we're coming in!"

They pounded on the room door again to make their point.

I pushed on the inner door. It rattled in its frame. Using what little was left of my strength, I lifted my leg and kicked it, just beneath where the deadbolt had been. The door gave way, flew open.

I gasped aloud.

There was Galiana, right in front of me: the hazy ghost of another country, a fantasy of night and distance shimmering on the far side of the threshold. This was a new magic. It had only happened once before, earlier that day in the police station in Los Angeles. There, for the first time, I had seen the veil of transition from this world to the other before I stepped through it. It was as if my mind was adjusting to the bizarre reality of my impossible double life, as if it were beginning to get some control over the seemingly random passages back and forth.

Or maybe my brain tumor was just advancing to the point where the hallucinations seemed more real than they had before. Who knew? Not me.

In any case, when I kicked the door in, I saw Galiana: the dark and starry landscape outside the walls of the town of Eastrim. From where I stood in the motel, I could even hear the faint noises of battle as the freedom fighters of the Forest King Tauratanio fought against Lord Iron's oppressive armies.

I hesitated one more second, panicked, half-mad. I was standing there, bathed in blood with a dead man on the floor behind me and the police about to come bursting through the door, their guns blazing. And yet, even so—even so—I felt a weary sadness wash over me as I contemplated going back into that other world, that world where I had failed in my duty so entirely, where I had left my lover dead and where my heart had been broken.

But the pounding of fists on the motel room door grew louder and more insistent. The shouts of the police grew angrier, more intense: "This is your last chance! Open this door or we come in shooting!"

I took one last glance around the blood-soaked room.

Then I stepped through the veil into another kingdom.

OF ALL THE strange things about Galiana, the strangest might have been this: I could not hold on to my sense of its reality. When I was back in LA, I could not believe in it at all, not truly. No matter how many scars I returned with—no matter how much grief or what memories—I felt my adventures there must have all been a dream or a hallucination.

But then—then—the minute—the very instant—I stepped across some threshold somewhere and returned to the castles and enchanted forests and wasted plains—then, suddenly, it was all as solid and alive as any place I had ever been. Then there could be no question about its substance. It was as there as there could be.

That's how it was now. A moment ago, under siege in my cheap motel outside Salinas, this kingdom seemed no more than a symptom of some brain dysfunction. A split second later, after I walked through that door, here I utterly was, astride my black stallion in an open field, galloping into the autumn night.

The mist of the ancient Eastrim graveyard, where the great battle had been waged, where the emanations of the dead had fought over the souls of the fallen, where Lady Betheray had died in my arms while her spirit rose and vanished into the upper atmosphere—that mist was gone. The air was thin and chilly and clear as a bright new windowpane. The stars were strewn across the sable sky like diamond dust. At my back, centaurs, bathed in the rainbow light from swirling hordes of fairies, battled against human warriors while peak-capped trolls fought to keep the city gates open in order to allow Tauratanio's army of forest creatures to retreat and escape.

No, really! That's what was happening right behind me!

But I couldn't stop to watch. All I could do was take advantage of the melee and confusion and spur my stallion in a hot gallop over the fields toward the deeper darkness of the forest in the far distance.

I RODE AND rode hard. Soon the woods surrounded me. The still, black trees stood like still, black sentinels, watching me pass. Their tangled branches hung above me, silhouetted against the stars. Their dried and dying leaves chattered in the wind.

I rode and rode and, finally, slowed, then stopped. For the first time, I became aware that I was exhausted. The battle here . . . the death of Betheray . . . the fight with Billiard Ball back in California . . . they had sapped all my strength. My body felt a like dead weight. Even my mind seemed heavy as lead.

I slid off my horse like human gelatin. I plunked down on my ass on the forest floor, open-mouthed, staring, still holding the reins in my hand. I was panting, wheezing. I couldn't catch my breath. I was dazed with shock and weariness. Waves of emotion passed over me. Flashes of memory. Betheray sagging lifeless in my arms. My escape from LA in the speeding silver Camaro. Billiard Ball thrashing on the motel floor, spewing blood, as the police sirens came closer, grew louder. All of this had happened within the span of a few hours. I felt used up, hollowed out, as if there were nothing left inside me.

I dropped onto my back with a heavy sigh, dead leaves kicking up around me as I fell. I lay there and stared stupidly up through the darkness, up at where the stars winked out from behind the branches.

I began to weep.

I know. Wimpy. But I couldn't help it. It was Betheray. It was my failure to protect her. It was the dead man in the motel and the cops coming after me. They'd still be there pounding on the motel door whenever I got back. If I did get back. It was the despair. It was the loneliness. It was everything.

I mean, after all, what was I? Just some guy. Just some gormless schmoe who'd been trying to make it in the movie business without much success. Another Hollywood wannabe circling the career drain. In a few more years, I'm sure I would have given up the whole enterprise. I would have gone back to school like my parents wanted. I would have gotten some teaching job at some college somewhere. Married some girl. Had some kids. From time to time, I would have reminisced about my wild and crazy years in showbiz. The toxic sting of failure would have faded to a dull throb. I'd have gotten over it. Sure I would have. Not everyone's dreams come true.

But instead, it was this. I was here. In the dark woods with the branches creaking, with the leaves chattering and God knows what animals making God knows what noises off in the tangled blackness of the night. I could almost hear the voice of my friend, the mutant squirrel-woman Maud—I could almost hear her weird buzzing screech telling me: *Be a man, Austin! Be a man!*

But I couldn't do it. I couldn't be a man. I lay there on my back on the dead leaves and cried like a baby. Waah, waah, waah. Some hero!

I DON'T KNOW when exactly my eyes sank shut. But the next thing I knew, the sun was slanting low across the earth in misty beams all around me. The cheery birds were tweet-tweet-tweeting in the trees. The red and green and yellow leaves were dancing in the air above me.

I sat up. I remembered the night before. The sobbing. I shook my head in self-disgust and cursed myself for a weakling. Then I climbed to my feet.

I was ready to begin my quest.

I WASHED MY FACE IN A NEARBY RILL. I KNELT ON THE bank and drank the clear, quick water from my cupped hands. I stood and pissed in the leaves beneath a maple tree. Then I mounted my stallion again.

I rode.

Here was the deal, the quest: I was wearing a talisman around my neck, a golden pendant on a golden chain. It had an S-shaped bolt carved into its center. It was a gift to the good Queen Elinda from her fiancé, the emperor Anastasius. Anastasius was currently fighting a war on the far side of the Eleven Lands, wherever the hell that was. My mission—my quest—was to bring this talisman to him as a signal that Elinda was in danger. Then he and his armies would drive out of the east to defeat Lord Iron and restore the queen to her throne.

Let Wisdom Reign and Each Man Go His Way.

That was our password—we of the queen's party. Our password and our battle cry. That was the sort of world we were supposed to be defending.

Now it probably goes without saying, I had no idea how I was going to accomplish what I was supposed to accomplish. My friend Maud had instructed me to keep the North Star on my left shoulder and follow the rising sun. Eventually, she said, the emperor Anastasius would call to me . . . somehow.

So that was the plan, such as it was. I saw the fiery disc of the sun burning white through the farthest trees, and I headed toward it. After a long while, I broke out of the forest. And I just kept riding toward that yellowing fire.

GALIANA WAS A country with a blasted gothic beauty. Sere fields, abandoned towers, impoverished shacks, and dark, forbidding woods. There were people here and there along the way, but no one I would have stopped and spoken to. They were, all of them, hungry and feral-looking, their eyes baleful, their lips white, their bodies tense and jittery, as if they were getting ready to pounce and devour you.

I'm told when the good queen reigned, it was all different here, all lush and serene and joyful. But now, even in the bright fall morning, it looked to me like an old black-and-white horror movie, everything slanted and gloomy, vaguely haunted, vaguely strange.

Still, it was autumn, harvest time. There were fields here and there with gleanings left on them, ears of corn my horse and I could peck at, some peppers and the like. I even found an apple tree with a few ripe apples left. That kept us going for a while.

I rode until dark, then slept in a rickety shed, then mounted and rode again, then slept, then rode.

Toward dusk, the third day, I felt a change in the atmosphere around me. It began with a thin stream of fresher, cooler air that smelled like springtime. It curled alluringly beneath my nostrils like the aroma of baking bread. Weary as I was, I sat up straighter on my horse. The air grew even cooler, even fresher. My heart stirred and rose.

I came to the top of a ridge and looked down on the view spreading out below me. I knew right away I had come into a different country.

The grass was green here. Wild flowers, yellow, purple, and white, were scattered everywhere. Great white clouds sailed like mighty ships across the deepening blue of the twilit horizon. Chalky hills rose in the distance. And at their feet, in the midst of freshly harvested fields, there was a village.

It was a jolly-looking little place. Not fancy or anything, just a cluster of little buildings with the hills looming over them. But the houses were all clean and attractive. Their thatched rooftops were decked with brightly colored pennants. Their walls were whitewashed and decorated with newly painted beams. All in all, it was a welcoming, homey, neighborly sight.

Hungry, lonely, weary, I spurred my stallion and started down the slope toward the village. As I approached, I could make out men and women going about their business, hauling sheaves into red barns, driving oxen and their ploughs through fields of golden stubble. The sun, sinking toward the horizon behind me, blanketed the entire scene with a warm orange glow.

But as I came near the village, the people stopped whatever they were doing and stood watching me. People in the fields and among the buildings too—they all stopped where they were and stood and stared at me with expressionless faces. There was no sound of voices. There was no breeze. Everything was suddenly motionless and quiet. It felt odd. More than odd.

Well, I shrugged it off. They weren't used to seeing strangers here, that's all, I told myself. Why else would they be gawking at me like that? There was nothing particularly weird about me. I had cleaned the blood off my face and hands. There were still bruises on my neck from where Billiard Ball choked me—I had seen them in my reflection in some pooled water a while back—but how strange were bruises? They couldn't be gaping at those, could they? And it couldn't be the magic sword at my side or the liquid armor that would sometimes cover me. They were invisible. They only appeared when I went into battle. No, I was dressed in plain brown clothes, like a stablehand. And if I was a bit grimy from travel, what about it? None of that explained why they were just standing there, just staring at me like that.

Yet they were. All of them.

I reached the village and came among the buildings. No one moved. Every single person I could see had stopped dead in his tracks and was gazing my way. I tried nodding to a few of them. I even smiled. But there was no reaction. No one smiled back. They just kept staring. It really was downright eerie.

In fact, close-up like this, I saw the people themselves were kind of bizarre-looking. I wasn't sure what it was about them at first. Then I realized: they all looked sort of the same somehow. I mean, they were all different enough at first glance. There were short ones and tall ones, fat and skinny, blonde, brunette, redhead. But they were all dressed in the same rough brown cotton shirts. And more than that, their faces, their features, their eyes, noses, mouths, they were all so similar, small, and vague, like they were pinched in putty. Doll-like. Like the features of something fashioned rather than someone born.

I spotted a tavern at the center of the town. *The Invisible Woman*—that was the name on the sign dangling from a post above the door. Out on the dirt street in front, there was a hitching rail with a drinking trough like the ones I'd seen in movie westerns. I dismounted and threw the stallion's reins over the rail like I'd seen the movie cowboys do.

My horse whiffled and lapped at the water. Aside from that, the village was absolutely silent. The villagers—all the villagers, every single one—just went on standing there, standing and staring at me, without making a sound.

I stared back, turning my eyes from one to another of them.

And I thought suddenly: *no children.* That was strange too. Wasn't it? Shouldn't there be children here? But there were none.

I let out a long breath. I turned away from those staring, samey faces. I walked to the tavern door. I pushed inside.

Like the town, the tavern seemed a nice enough place to look at. At first. At first, it seemed warm and welcoming. Big windows let in lots of the day's last sunlight. A chandelier with burning candles cast a dancing glow. So did the burning torches in sconces on the wall. A great big blaze in the great big fireplace spread its heat across the whole room, wall to wall. It all seemed very bright and cheery.

There were two men standing at the long bar. Each had an ale in one fist. Each had one foot up on the wooden rail. They were looking over their shoulders at me. There was a young man and a woman seated at a rough wooden table to my left. There was an older man and an older woman at a table to my right. They were all silent. They were all turned my way. They were all staring. Their doll-like features were all the same.

I was starting to feel truly creeped out by now. But I was starving too. I needed something to eat. I walked up to the bar.

A woman was standing there, her back to me. She was round as a ball. Dressed in the same brown shift as everyone else. Round-headed, round-bodied, no shape to her but round. Just as I stepped to the bar, she turned and faced me. My breath caught. She had the same face as all the others, the round version of the same small-featured face. Not a woman's face either. Not a woman's and not a man's. Sexless. And the eyes were pinched and suspicious, weak and afraid, like she had a secret and she was worried I'd find it out. They all looked like that.

The barkeep was holding a beaker of beer in her fist. She set it down on the bar top with a whapping bang. My eyes went to the frothing head, and I felt my mouth begin to water.

"It's on me," came a voice at my back.

I turned and saw another woman, just coming in. She was very tall, very broad shouldered, with long brown hair that fell to the curve of the large breasts shaping her brown shift. She wore a bright white ribbon slantwise across her chest. I guessed it was the mark of an official position. Other than that, she looked . . . Well, she looked like everyone else, like the bartender and the drinkers—and also like the people who were now slipping in through the door behind her.

"I'm the mayor of this city," the woman said. She stepped toward me, expressionless but with her hand outstretched. "Mayor Adriana."

I shook her hand. Her grip was powerful, not like a woman's grip at all. Come to think of it, it was sort of surprising to see a woman serving as mayor in these medieval surroundings. Not that I was a scholar of history or anything. It just seemed like a medieval female mayor was the sort of thing you'd see in a fantasy movie or a novel, not in real life. But then was this real life? Who the hell knew, right?

All the same, if I was creeped out before, I was more creeped out now. A sense of actual horror was growing in me. But why? I wasn't sure.

Meanwhile, more and more villagers were pushing in through the door behind the mayor. One after another, they spread out across the tavern, slowly filling the large room. As each one found a spot for himself, he would stop there—stop and stare at me silently. A growing crowd, standing there, staring, silent. It really was getting on my nerves.

I said, "Well . . . thanks. For the beer. That's nice of you. Thanks." And, uncomfortable under her strange gaze—under all their strange, silent gazes—I looked away. And my eyes were caught by something on the wall behind her: an empty space, a large rectangle paler than the wood around it, and with a nail sticking out near the top. It seemed a picture had hung there and had only recently been taken down. Sure enough, when I lowered my eyes, I saw it in the corner, a large framed painting leaning against the wall, facing the wall so I couldn't get a glimpse of it. What was it a painting of? I wondered. Who had removed it? And why was it just leaning there like that?

The mayor gave a high, trilling, ladylike laugh that somehow didn't suit her. It seemed put on. Fake.

"It's just my way of saying welcome," she said. "Welcome to you, Austin Lively."

I straightened as if an electric bolt had gone through me. It was always a little strange to hear my name spoken in this otherworldly world—as if I were a character in a movie I had never seen. But to have it spoken here, after three days' ride from any place I knew, in an obscure little village in an obscure little valley in a country I had never heard of or been to, well, that was downright spooky—supremely spooky—shocking, really. I mean, what the hell was going on?

And all the while, the bar was filling up with villagers, and the villagers with their sexless, doll-like faces just looked at me, just stared, saying nothing.

"You know me?" I said to the mayor. "How do you know me?"

"Your fame has spread," she said, with a friendly wink of one small eye. Then she gestured at the bar behind me. "Help yourself."

I was about to ask a question, but at her gesture, I glanced over my shoulder, and as I did, I was struck full force with a smell that made my stomach growl like a beast. The round woman behind the bar was just now setting a meat pie down beside the beaker of beer. The aroma was rich and delicious. And I was ravenous after my long ride.

Licking my lips, I nodded my thanks at the mayor. "That's very kind of you. Really. Would you mind if I . . . ?" I swallowed hard. "I haven't had a meal in days."

"Please," said the mayor in a peculiarly bland tone. "Dig in."

I probably should have heeded my sense of unease or horror or whatever it was. But I was just too damned hungry to care. I stepped back to the bar. There was a spoon by the pie plate. I grabbed it by the spirally metal handle and dug into the pie. When the spoon's tip broke through the crust, steam came up to my face—oh Lord!—steam filled with that rich, warm, meaty smell. I lost all reticence and began scooping the thick confection into my eager mouth. I ignored the villagers, ignored the staring eyes that I knew were boring into my back. I forgot all about them. I ate and ate.

Only when I was halfway through the pie, only as the ache of my hunger began to subside, did I try to carry on the conversation.

"What is this place anyway?" I said to the mayor through a succulent mouthful. I grabbed the beaker and washed the food down with ale. "Am I still in Galiana?"

The Mayor had not moved from where she stood. I had to turn sideways so I could see her and stuff my face at the same time.

"No," she told me. "You left Galiana miles back. You have entered the Eleven Lands. This is the village of Newfell in the country of Edgimond."

"Seems like a nice place," I went on, scarfing pie, swigging beer. "It has a whole different climate. A whole different feel. It's almost like it's a different season here."

"Yes. Spring. It's always spring."

"Really? That's a neat trick. Is it the mountains that do that? Do they create some kind of microclimate or something?"

"The mountains? The mountains? Why, no." When I glanced at her again, I thought she was examining me, tilting her head and studying me, measuring me, as if she were judging my looks or my physical condition or something. The rest of the villagers were as they had been, just standing, just staring. "It is the work of our nation's governor," said the mayor. "We are under his protection. He guards us against the consequences."

"The consequences," I said. "Of the revolution in Galiana, you mean?"

When the mayor didn't answer, I glanced up from the ruin of my meat pie and saw her smiling—smiling as if to herself, with a distant, dreamy look of satisfaction in her eyes. Whatever she'd been searching for in me, she'd obviously found it.

"What consequences?" I asked again.

"What? Oh. All of them," she said. "Revolution. Winter. Tragedy. None of them happen here."

I laughed nervously through my growing unease. "Wow. Good deal. Who is this governor of yours? God?"

She laughed right back at me. "God?" she said. "Hardly God. God is all consequences." And she shifted her pinched doll eyes away from me. She looked down at something else. The painting maybe, the painting leaning against the wall. Hard to be sure. Hard to see anything but the villagers, their faces. They were everywhere now. The room was packed with them. Plus, night had fallen at the windows, and while the chandelier and torches and firelight filled the tavern with a deep orange glow, it was darker than it had been. There were deep, wavering shadows in every corner.

I blinked hard to clear my head. The pie . . . The ale . . . I had been so hungry, and now I was so full . . . A thick, sated feeling muddied my mind . . . and yet I wanted more, to eat more.

"How . . . ?" I said thickly, scooping out another spoonful of meat. "You never answered my question: how did you know my name?"

Slowly, the mayor lifted her gaze back to me. "It came to us," she said. "It came to us upon the fabric of the air, whispered by the spirits of the inferno that stretches across all universes and all dimensions. It became part and parcel of the identity with which our master blinds and blesses and rules us all and will one day rule the very framework of eternity."

I had lifted my spoon halfway from the pie plate to my mouth—and there my hand froze.

"Uh . . . what?" I said.

The mayor's tone of voice had changed. All at once, it was hollow and empty and weirdly musical, the voice of a ghost calling up the cellar stairs. Her eyes were suddenly bright—I mean scarily bright, lantern bright. Even worse, even stranger, everyone's eyes were suddenly bright, all the villagers were now staring at me with white bright eyes, their little mouths curling up into sharp, nearly V-shaped grins.

"Wha— what did you say?" I asked again. But I could barely get the words out.

The spoon fell from my slack fingers. It dropped onto the pie plate with a soft, nauseating splash. I was dizzy. I was swaying. I gripped the edge of the bar to hold myself steady.

There was a noise. There was motion. I looked around me. It was even harder to see now than it had been before. Was it the nightfall? Was the fire dying? The room seemed sunk in shadow, the shadow seemed distorted by a wavery mist, as if the whole place were suddenly underwater.

Through that oscillating atmosphere, I saw that the villagers had begun to move. Bright-eyed, grinning, they were stirring from their places as if they had just awakened from some sort of standing coma. Some were reaching up to take the long wigs off their heads. Some were reaching inside their blouses to remove and withdraw bra-like contraptions containing fake breasts. The mayor herself was sliding her long hair down the side of her face. It gave the strangest impression through the gathering fog: it looked as if her head were melting.

I widened my eyes, trying to clear my vision. I stared at her, squinting through the gathering gloom.

Except she wasn't a her. The mayor. She wasn't a woman at all. She was a man in dress-up.

I turned and looked around the room. It was the same with all the women. They were all men in dress-up. Once they removed their wigs and fake breasts, once all the villagers revealed themselves to be male, they all looked even more alike than they had before. They all had the same bland brown-colored hair now, and their features—what I could make out of their features as they went in and out of focus—their features, which before had seemed androgynous—had become clearly the features of men—dead-hearted, feminized men. It was as if I were standing in a room full of eunuch zombies. A whole village full of eunuch zombies.

By now, of course, I realized I'd been poisoned. The fog in the tavern was really fog inside my mind, and it was growing thicker by the moment. All those faces, those identical, grinning, bright-eyed, malevolent faces, were blurring and slurring together. My mouth was hanging open, and I somehow couldn't gather the strength to close it. I lost my grip on the bar, and when I tried to grab it again, I knocked the pie plate off. I heard its wobbly clatter on the floor as if from far away.

I sensed more movement in the room. I turned toward it—turned painfully as if my neck had rusted on my shoulders. I saw two men, one of them still with a woman's figure. They were lifting the painting that had been leaning in the corner. Lifting it up above the heads of the others. Lifting it until they could hang it on the nail at the top of the pale rectangle on the wall, back where it had been hanging until just before I came in.

As my consciousness began to swirl down and down like the water in a flushing toilet, I squinted hard to see through the congealing miasma. I saw the face of the figure in the portrait. A short man wearing a robe of deepest indigo that flowed around him like liquid night. His face was shriveled and wrinkled and yet somehow ageless. He had a tuft of gray hair on his head and another on his chin. His eyes were small, but they burned and boiled with a lava-red intensity of malignant power.

I knew him! Curtin. The evil wizard who had helped depose the queen of Galiana. He was the one who had manipulated the minds of the people, made them believe they were building a utopia even as they transformed their country into a hellhole. The queen's justice gave to each what he deserved, but Curtin had promised to give all to everyone. It was he who had turned that once free and lovely nation into an oppressive wasteland. Lord Iron ruled there, but Curtin was the real power.

And he was the guardian of Newfell village, it turned out, the governor of the land of Edgimond, the leader who protected these people from the consequences—all the consequences. And he had turned them into what they were, whatever that was.

I tried to speak his name aloud. I couldn't. My legs buckled under me. I clutched desperately at the bar, trying to stay on my feet.

Had they killed me? Was I dying now?

Helpless, I tumbled to the floor.

WHAT FOLLOWED WAS DREADFUL.

I couldn't move, but I was wide awake. I could see everything, but I saw it through that distorting druggy haze that gave it all a confused, unreal quality. I watched, powerless, as they came for me.

The room filled with a low, muttering chant. All the villagers in the tavern—all the Eunuch Zombies—were chanting together in some language I could not understand. The sound had a deep, heavy, ritualistic quality to it, like some ancient prayer. The first thought that came into my mind was that the villagers were making ready for a sacrifice. The second thought that came into my mind—the realization of who exactly the sacrifice was going to be—filled me with such raging terror that I wanted to scream at my body to move, to run. But I couldn't scream. I couldn't run. I just lay there crumpled on the tavern floor like a marionette with cut strings.

Shuffling with slow ceremony, the villagers gathered around me. The mayor stood at my feet. He lifted his hands in the air as if in supplication to some unseen being.

"Earth is earth, and water is water," he intoned. "We are flesh, and you are power. Every son will be your daughter. Every death will be your hour."

These were the only words I understood. The rest was gibberish.

My eyes, the only part of me I could control at all, darted wildly from one villager to another. In my up-spiraling panic, through the wavery fog that filled my mind, their faces seemed to morph and liquify. At one moment, they all had the same bland, doll-like, castrati features, but in the next, the air seemed to ripple over them, melting their flesh until they appeared like cadaverous monstrosities risen half-rotten from their graves. Then they solidified into villagers again, and so on, back and forth.

As the mayor led them in their incomprehensible chant, four of them squatted down next to me, two on each side. In my brain, my speechless brain, I was grunting with horror at their shifting, changing faces. I was urging my body to writhe away from them. But I could not move.

The four Eunuch Zombies lifted me into the air. The others gathered around them, chanting. The mayor turned his back and, with his hands still lifted, led the parade to the tavern door, which two of the other zombies held open.

"Earth is earth, and water is water," he said again.

Chanting, they carried me out of the tavern.

Full night had fallen. A gibbous moon was rising to one side of the chalk hills. The moonlight was very bright. It washed the sky starless. My panicky gaze turning everywhere, I saw that the village, like the villagers themselves, seemed to shift and change behind the wavering curtain of the atmosphere. At first, the houses and shops and outbuildings all remained the same, but then the air shifted and the facades melted away to reveal the ruin and the death beneath. The buildings were charred and broken. The fields in the moonlit night were white with rot. The crops were crawling with devouring insects, insects so large they were visible even at a distance.

And my stallion? Where was my black stallion? Gone from the hitching rail outside the tavern. My thoughts were so scrambled and hysterical in my powerless body I imagined for a moment they had killed the beast and butchered him, served him to me in the pie. But that was impossible. Wasn't it?

The procession moved away from the tavern, down the street toward the edge of town. The mayor led the march. The four men carried me like a corpse to burial. The rest of the Eunuch Zombies swarmed around us, chanting in those dreadful, deep, toneless voices.

We passed through the stubble fields. The moonglow lit the swarms of gigantic mantises so I could see them crunching at the rotted gleanings with their enormous mandibles and nearly human eyes.

I was carried along in the maddeningly slow procession for what seemed like forever. We were outside the town now, beyond the fields, approaching the chalky hills that looked almost white in the light of the low-hanging moon. At the foot of those hills, I saw an opening in the earth, a wide crevasse or sinkhole. Some greenish steam was rising out of it. The steam made the slimy vegetation curling over the crevasse's rim stir and tremble as if it were animate. When the smell of the steam reached me, I gagged. The steam was full of rot and sulfur as if it had blown up from hell by way of the grave.

The Eunuch Zombies laid me in the dust and weeds at the edge of the opening. The rotten steam wrapped itself around me until I felt I would suffocate in the stench. The mayor looked down at me complacently with his white-bright eyes and V-shaped grin. Two other men knelt beside me. The two men held a harness tied to a heavy rope. They worked the harness over my shoulders and under my arms. My heart was beating so hard I thought it would explode in my chest.

With all the villagers still chanting, four of them lifted my limp body again. Two men held the rope and braced their feet in the dust. The others lowered me into the crevasse. The hot stinking gas enveloped me until I could barely see anything but green steam everywhere.

They fed the rope into the hole and I descended through the miasmic darkness, deeper and deeper into the abyss. The chanting up above grew dim, then faded to silence. My arms began to twitch. Whatever potion they had given me was wearing off, and my muscles were beginning to work again. And still I went down. After a while, I lost all sense of movement. I just seemed to dangle there in the curling steam.

Finally, my toes and then my feet touched bottom. The tension of the rope slackened, and I crumpled up like a cloth dummy and fell to the stony earth, facedown. Above the hissing sound of gas, I heard myself groan—it was the first noise I had made since I'd collapsed in the tavern. The rope came coiling down out of the upper darkness and plumped heavily on top of me.

My whole body was shivering now. I gritted my teeth and tried to move. I did it. I rolled over onto my side. God, what a relief it was to feel my body responding to the call of my brain!

I craned my neck to get a look at my surroundings. It was strange: I could see down here. This far beneath the surface, it should have been pitch black, but there was a sickly yellowish glow coming off the surrounding walls. At first, the green fog was so thick I couldn't make out anything except its twisting skeins and complications. Then, though, a draft from above swirled over me and the miasma drifted and cleared.

Oh, what I saw then. What horror.

I was in a cave filled with corpses.

Beneath the narrow opening of the crevasse, the rock room opened up around me in a nearly perfect circle. In the unnatural light coming off the stones, I saw the bodies everywhere. They were piled along the walls and on the floor and close beside me. Women.

Dead women. All women, some of their bodies incomplete, some torn, some rotted to broken skeletons with only a hank of hair or the remnants of a dress to show what sex they'd been. They were piled up in haphazard mounds. Their limbs were stretched out toward me. Those that had faces seemed to be screaming in agony and fear.

Groaning again, I managed to push off the stone floor and sit up a little. I brought my hands to the harness around me and slowly worked it over my head. I tossed the thing aside. It dropped down onto the pile of dead women next to me.

I lifted my gaze, trying to see whatever I could see through the fetid air.

I saw the crevasse above me, a narrow slit leading up and up to the nearly invisible night. Were the villagers leaning over the rim up there, watching me? I didn't know. It was too far to see, too dark.

I lowered my eyes. My gaze passed over the piles and piles of corpses. I looked at the walls. They were smooth and greasy and gave off that dull yellow light. The stenchy steam was drifting up through pores and cracks in the floor. It hissed as it rose. It caught the light and glowed.

There was a small opening in the wall to my left, like a mousehole for an enormous mouse. And there was another much larger opening to my right, a broad archway that led into a rocky corridor. Was it an escape route? I thought it might be.

My eyes returned to the dead. This, I understood now, was where all the village women had gone—the women and the girl children too, judging by the sizes of some of the bodies. They had been lowered down here and then—then they had been slaughtered. Torn to pieces. I could see that some of their corpses had been partially eaten.

So I was right. This was a place of sacrifice. But sacrifice to whom? To what?

What awful creature was down here with me?

The very second that question entered my mind, the answer came. The earth shook underneath me. I heard a thunderous pounding from deep within the foggy corridor to my right. One reverberating thud, and then another, and then another after that.

It was the sound of footsteps, the footsteps of something monstrous.

And, whatever it was, it was slowly coming toward me.

6

ANOTHER MOMENT, ANOTHER HEAVY FOOTSTEP, AND I saw the beast through the yellowish light. I saw the shape of it at least—a hulking, crouched, and lizardy shadow, black and gigantic against the luminous mist.

A noise escaped my throat, a choked and whimpery whine of fear. Once again, I could hear Maud screeching at me in my mind: *Be a man!* And I thought: *Screw you, squirrel girl! You're not the one about to be devoured!*

But she—this Maud of my imagination—had a point. My body still felt helpless and dead, a suit of concrete flesh hanging on the weak framework of my paralyzed muscles, but one look around me at the heaps of torn female corpses, at their skeletal, half-rotten faces frozen in their final expressions of terror, and I knew I had to do whatever I could to avoid their fate.

There weren't a lot of options. With the walls so smooth and slippery, I couldn't climb back up the crevasse. I couldn't go down the corridor where the beast was approaching either. That meant there was only one way out—through that narrow little mousehole on the far wall.

I didn't know if I could reach it. I didn't know if I could fit into it if I did reach it. I didn't know if it would lead anywhere if I did fit into it. It didn't matter. I had to go for it. What other choice was there but to sit and wait for this thing to get me?

I tried to stand. I couldn't. I was too weak. I fell back onto my butt. The thunderous footsteps moved faster down the corridor. The shadow of the beast grew larger and larger through the mist. The cave floor trembled under me with every move the creature made.

Grunting with exertion, gagging on the stench, I began to crawl for the mousehole.

I reached out and grabbed hold of half a dead woman. My fingers sank into the decomposing substance of her hip. I pulled myself up over the ruin of her and grabbed some bones and pushed with my rubbery legs and tumbled over a face frozen in its final scream to spill down the far side of the charnel pile. All the while, the cave shook more, the footsteps resounded louder. And now—now a howl filled the cramped space—a howl that sounded dreadfully like a chorus of shrieking women. I sobbed with terror at the sound and pulled and pushed myself another yard and then another, climbing over more bodies, coming closer—inch by slow, painful inch—to the narrow aperture in the far wall.

But I was growing stronger as I went. The potion was wearing off and enough adrenaline was pumping through me to bring even a dead man back to life. I started moving faster.

The beast behind me shrieked again, a thousand women shrieking. Its footsteps grew even louder, the sound exploding through the little space of the cave. The world around me was shaking so hard it seemed that it would shake itself apart. But somehow, I made it: I was at the mousehole. A woman's body sat beside it, propped against the wall. I could feel her staring at me—which was bizarre because she had no head!

I reached out and grabbed hold of the opening in the stone. I dragged myself toward it. The next roar was so loud I was sure the creature would be on me any second. On instinct, I looked back over my shoulder.

Just then, gigantic, the beast broke through the mist and came charging out of the corridor. I saw it. Lit by the yellow light from the walls, shaded by the miasmic green, it was a thing so dreadful it made my mind go blank. My brain simply couldn't handle it, couldn't take it in. I could not let myself see what I saw or I'd go raving mad.

I panicked. Gibbering wildly, my eyes wide, I scrabbled and scraped my way into the mousehole, tearing at the rock walls with my fingernails. I could hear the beast's footsteps coming after me as I pulled myself deeper into the passage, moving as fast as I could. The corridor was low and small, so tight I could barely draw myself through it. But my fear propelled me on. And when, straining, I lifted my chin, I could see a little way in front of me: there was a wider opening. I could feel a fresher breeze blowing to me. There was a way out! Not far. A few yards away.

I thought: *I can make it!*

Then, the beast grabbed me.

It had reached into the mousehole behind me. I screamed in terror as its fingers wrapped around my leg. I screamed in pain as its claws sank into the flesh of my calf.

I tried to keep scuttling through the hole to the exit, but the great paw held me in place. Then it began to drag me back through the hole, back into the cave from which I'd just escaped.

The one glimpse I'd had of the thing—the one unbearable sight of it—flashed in fragments in my mind as I clawed at the rocky floor, trying to pull myself away from it. It was no use. The beast's grip was too powerful. As desperately as I fought to go forward, I slid back, back and back across the stony corridor, trapped in the creature's clutches.

Then, in one swift moment of shattering terror and despair, I came flying out of the mousehole—and in the snap of a finger, I was in the motel again, in the motel outside Salinas, dashing through the door into the next room over, with Billiard Ball dead on the floor of the room behind me and the police bursting in out of the parking lot, hot on my trail, shouting at the top of their lungs.

7

I COULD NOT THINK. I RACED ACROSS THE MOTEL ROOM to the front door, Billiard Ball's gun in one hand, my other hand digging in my pocket for my car keys. My wounded leg was burning with agony. My mind was like a jigsaw puzzle that had been blown apart by a bomb. Pieces—images—thoughts—half-shaped mental cries of fear and pain—flew every which way across my brain, randomly flashing into bright focus. One mental picture and then another lit up in my consciousness—the piles of dead women, Billiard Ball staring through his own blood, the beast. I couldn't hold on to any of them, to anything except my shrieking sense of urgent danger.

I could hear the police shouting to one another in the room I'd just left.

"Where'd he go?"

"This one's dead!"

"The shooter went through there!"

"Check the bathroom!"

"Go slow! He's armed!"

I plunged forward through the dark motel room, ignoring the searing ache in my calf where the monster's claws had sunk into me, ignoring the images in my mind of the unimaginably horrible beast that would be dragging me into its maw the moment I found myself back in the nightmare land of Edgimond. I ignored everything—everything but the fact that the police were about to come through the door of the room behind me. Half crazy with panic, I rocketed forward.

One second, maybe two, and I was at the door to the outside. I paused only a second to throw Billiard Ball's gun onto the bed behind me. The last thing I wanted was to run out into a crowd of cops with a gun in my hand.

Then I ripped the door open and hurled myself out into the parking lot.

Sirens were blaring through the cool autumn night. Lights were flashing. More police cruisers were bounding over the ramp of the sidewalk, careening into the lot under the motel's neon sign.

But the cops themselves—the ones who were on foot—had all gone rushing into my motel room. For a moment, one moment, the path to my Camaro was clear.

I could feel the blood spilling out of my leg, dampening my jeans, but I didn't look, I didn't pause, I just ran.

I pressed the button on my key to pop the Camaro's door lock. I seized the handle, yanked the door open, and tumbled inside. Any second, the cops would come out of my motel room or out of the room I'd just escaped from or out of the cars that were even now screeching and skidding to a stop in the parking lot. The second after that, they would open fire.

I jammed the key in the ignition, twisted it until the engine roared. In one coordinated motion, I pulled my legs inside and shut the door and threw the car into reverse and jammed my foot down on the gas. The car lurched backward through a noxious cloud of burning rubber. I threw the car into drive and shot forward, away from the oncoming cop cars, toward the far edge of the lot.

Over the engine noise, I heard a policeman shout. The Camaro bounded over the curb, through the air, into the street. It landed with a jouncing jolt. I spun the wheel. The car screamed and turned. There was a gunshot. One rear window snapped and went foggy behind a web of cracks. I practically stood on the gas pedal.

The Camaro shot down a side road and into the shadows under the trees.

The cop cars came after me, sirens screaming.

I reached a crossroad. I glanced up frantically into my rearview mirror. The police weren't behind me yet. I turned the car hard, trying to get out of sight before they saw which way I'd gone. I hurtled down a residential street between two rows of parked cars. I reached a corner, turned again in a spitting cloud. Anything to keep ahead of the police.

I could see now: I was in a grid of residential streets, flying past one- and two-story houses, one after another on its little square of lawn. The night was loud with sirens, and the air flashed red around me. I turned another corner and then another, trying to keep out of the law's line of sight.

Then, up ahead, I saw the main drag. Streetlights, a gas station on the corner, a glow from other businesses, bars, and restaurants. I knew the freeway ramp was near, but then what? Once I was on the freeway, it would only be a matter of time before the cops chased me down and surrounded me.

But as I came to the corner, I glimpsed, from the corner of my eye, a small, dark house. A garage with the door open. No cars inside. No one home.

I was almost past the driveway when I jammed my foot down hard on the brake and wrenched the wheel over like a ship's captain fighting high seas.

I held my breath as the Camaro's rear end spun out behind me. Dust and smoke flew up around me. The headlights shone into the empty garage as I jammed the gas pedal down to the floor again. The car leapt forward into the driveway—over the driveway—into the garage.

I braked. The tires screamed again. I cursed as the car skidded toward the garage's rear wall. Then it jolted to a halt just inches from a crash.

I cursed again. I killed the lights. I killed the engine. I shouldered the door open and rolled out, grimacing in pain as the wounds in my leg flared up again.

With the sirens screaming louder and the red lights from the cruisers growing brighter, I rushed, in a limping hop, to the garage door.

I reached up, grabbed it, and dragged it shut with a bang.

EXHAUSTED, I PLUNKED down onto the garage floor, out of breath. I sat there in the dark, staring at nothing. I listened to the sirens howling in the night outside like hunting hounds.

What was in my mind then? Not much. A fog of fear. Lights blinking through the fog: thoughts, images, half-formed cries, and wordless terrors.

The sirens grew louder. I couldn't think. I couldn't move. I just sat there, staring at nothing, listening. They were right outside the garage door.

Then all at once, the sirens shifted tone. They started fading. Their wild cries swiftly grew dimmer. The cruisers had sped past the garage. They were heading for the freeway. Soon, I heard other sirens joining them. They all seemed to blend together. The whole world outside the little garage now sounded like a single enormous wolf keening for its prey.

Long moments passed. I went on sitting there, panting, staring, my thoughts in disarray. The sight of that beast in the cave—that obscene glimpse of it—it haunted me. What would I do when I opened some door somewhere and found myself once more at the bottom of the crevasse, back in the creature's clutches, yanked helplessly out of the mousehole and toward its fang-filled maw?

The sirens continued fading. The night beyond the garage grew quiet. I don't know how much time went by. I don't know how long I would have gone on sitting there like that if the pain in my leg hadn't broken through my daze.

I looked down at myself. I saw the blood: it had soaked the bottom quarter of my left trouser leg and turned the blue denim the color of rust. The top of my sock was cold and dank. The idea broke into my shock-dulled brain: I ought to check my wounds.

I leaned forward, reached out, and pulled up the cuff of my pants leg. The sight of my mangled flesh sent a chill from my crotch to the nape of my neck. That creature in the cave had been no dream. The wounds left by its giant claws were far too real. In some spots, the talons had merely sliced the skin. But in two places, they had gone in deep. The black blood was still burbling out of the ragged holes like oil from the earth.

I dropped back against the wall. My heart felt sour. The skills I'd learned in Galiana—the tricks of the fighting spirit, the power to feel fear without allowing fear to overcome me, the power to battle when there was no chance to win, the power to win for no other reason than that my soul was indomitable—all this seemed to have deserted me. These past hours . . . Billiard Ball . . . the cops . . . the Eunuch Zombies in the village . . . the piles of dead in the cave . . . the monster . . . It was too much for me. I was overwhelmed. I could not think anymore. I could not gather even enough energy to figure out what to do.

Sitting there, slumped, my back to the wall, my head hanging, my hand went to my chest, to the locket there, Betheray's locket. I felt again that strange, warm power radiating off the metal into my flesh. I closed my eyes. I closed my hand around the glowing gold.

It happened again. That flashing transport back into my own past. That's where I was, all right: my unremembered past. For a moment—a longer moment this time than before—I was in my home again, the home I had grown up in. I could hear that hysterical child, crying, screaming. Upstairs. In her bedroom . . .

I recognized that cry. It was my sister! It was Riley. Riley as a little girl. My parents—my professor mother and my professor father—were in the dining room with my brother. They were talking as they always did, with their snooty, lockjawed tones and their big words and their complicated ideas—all of which, as I now knew, were really Serge Orosgo's ideas, his blueprint for a perfect world.

But I did not know that then. Back then, in this immersive memory, I was sitting in an armchair in the den. I was reading a graphic novel, some adventure story about a knight and an elfish woman in an enchanted wood. I couldn't concentrate with my sister screaming like that. She was so upset, and no one was going to help her. She screamed and screamed, and my mother, my father, my big brother—they all just went right on talking, as if they didn't hear her, as if they didn't care. Why didn't anyone care?

Now I was on my feet—in this locket vision I was having. I was on my feet, laying the graphic novel aside. I was moving to the stairs. Up the stairs. Moving toward the sound of my little sister's hysterical cries. Why did it always have to be me? Why was I the only one who would go to her, the only one who would make the effort to comfort her?

I saw myself entering her little bedroom. Sitting on the edge of her bed. I saw her looking up at me with her big, sad, trusting eyes shimmering with tears. I picked up her favorite book from the bedside table. *Nobody Listens.* A drawing on the cover of a little girl running through the streets, shouting a warning. I lay down beside her, ready to read until she calmed down and fell asleep . . .

And then, with a sort of mental flash, the connection broke. I was back in the dark garage again, sitting on the floor. The locket had gone cold. I slipped it back inside my shirt. I ran my fingers up through my sweaty hair.

Strange, I thought. The way the locket took me back to that specific moment. And the way the past was still there inside my mind even though I hadn't remembered it before. It was kind of the same as being in Galiana: like being in a story about myself that had somehow begun before I got there, a whole life already lived that only came into full existence as I experienced it.

And I thought: *Riley.* Poor little Riley. Gone missing. Her boyfriend, Marco, run off in a panic, leaving me his car, begging me to find her.

She needs you! They're trying to kill us!

It was all because of her series of online videos. *Ouroboros: Dark Dreams of Reality.* As crazy as they were with their tales of a world-conquering conspiracy among space aliens and Templars and God knows who else, they seemed to have contained enough truth to make Orosgo want her silenced—just as he wanted me silenced now too. And so, she—and the videos and maybe the manuscript of *Another Kingdom*—was gone. And she was in trouble. If she was still alive, that is. I could imagine her, hiding somewhere, afraid, weeping, as she had been afraid and weeping that night in her bedroom so long ago. And just as on that night, there was no one to go to her. No one but me.

Nobody Listens.

Slowly, grimacing with pain, I gathered my legs beneath me. I took hold of the garage walls and pulled myself to my feet.

I rolled the garage door up. Peeked out at the suburban street. All the cop cars were gone, and all their sirens too. The night was quiet.

And yet I could almost hear Riley crying for me.

I hobbled to the car.

I had to find her.

8

I TOOK THE LONG WAY NORTH. YOU WOULDN'T BELIEVE how long. Two-lane roads through wooded nowheres. Spidery thread-like lanes through half-abandoned towns. Long winding climbs up desert mountains. Dusty wilderness trails past scraggly trees. I had to get some maps at a gas station to find the way. Maps! I know, right? Paper maps that fold up and everything. Who uses those anymore? I had to stop at three places before I could even find some. But a GPS could be traced, and I needed to stay invisible. Because there must have been a million cops looking for me out there in the great spaces of the autumn night.

It was late, almost ten o'clock, when I cruised into Walnut Creek. It was a leafy, suburban town, not far from where my parents lived in Berkeley. My sister had a job here, if you could call it that. She was a part-time "actress" at the nearby Happy Town Theme Park. She played a rag doll at the souvenir stands there or a farm girl at the petting zoo or sometimes something scary at the Halloween Horror Walk. I had seen a billboard for the Horror Walk along my journey: a picture of a frightened woman looking over her shoulder as she stepped unwitting into the clutches of a waiting witch. The witch—that would be Riley. That was how she paid her rent and financed her videos—that and borrowing money from our reluctant parents.

The town was quiet. Not much traffic. Everyone indoors, I guessed, getting ready for bed. It made me nervous to be the only car on the streets. Surely the police would have put my license plate out on their networks by now. If I passed even a single cop car, the red lights and siren would come on and the chase would start again.

I had never visited Riley at home before. I had never seen her apartment. But using my maps, I made my way there on the back roads. I came to a depressing cul-de-sac near a bunch of office parks, skyscrapers abandoned for the night. On one side of the little road, there was a long wooden building painted some unnameable shade of brown with dark brown shingles on the roof. It seemed a drab and sorrowful place.

I was afraid to park, afraid to leave my car on the street, lest a passing policeman spot it and come after me. But driving around behind the apartment building, I found a long macadam lane that ran past a series of garages with closed doors. It looked as if the doors would open at the touch of a remote-control button. On a guess, I reached over and opened the Camaro's glove compartment. Sure enough—what do you know?—Marco had left me a remote control, buried under some papers. Not just a remote control either. There was a set of keys in there as well.

I drove slowly down the lane behind the apartment building. I pressed the button on the remote each time I passed one of the garage doors. On the third try, a door groaned and rolled up and open. I drove into the garage and closed the door behind me. Here was a safe place to park where the police wouldn't see the car.

ONE OF MARCO'S keys let me into the building's stairwell. I limped up the stairs, clinging to the cold metal bannister. My wounded calf was throbbing. Every few steps or so, I left a small streak of blood on one of the carpeted stairs.

Riley's apartment was on the third floor, the top floor. I cracked the stairwell door and peeked out to make sure the hall was empty. It was—though I could hear some thumping music coming through one of the doors at the hallway's end.

I slipped out of the well. Stepped quickly to the second door on my left. Luckily the hallway runner had a dark floral pattern. If I made any more bloody footprints here, they didn't show.

I opened the door and hesitated. The last two times I had entered fantasy land, I had seen it through the doorway before I made the transition. But would that always be the case? If it wasn't—if I went through a door and suddenly passed back into that other kingdom unsuspecting—I would have only a single second before the beast in the cave drew me to itself and ripped my head off.

Well, all the same, if I was going to find Riley, I had to go in. I held my breath, stepped across the threshold and shut the door behind me. I felt for the light switch in the darkness. Turned on the lights.

My breath came out of me in a long hiss. I leaned against the door, still holding the knob behind my back. I looked the place over. I recognized the space from my video calls with Riley. But it had never looked like this.

Someone had ransacked the apartment. Some of Orosgo's thugs, no doubt, searching for *Another Kingdom.* I didn't know why the billionaire wanted the book, but I knew he did. I knew he was willing to kill for it.

The studio was a mess. The TV screen was smashed. The bedside radio likewise. The rest of Riley's electronics—phone, computer, and so on—were nowhere to be seen. The mattress had been pulled half off the bed. It had been slit open. Handfuls of the inner foam were lying on the floor beneath it. All Riley's books had been pulled off the shelves, strewn on her writing desk or on the carpet. Some of them were mangled, their spines broken, their pages torn or crumpled into balls. Her clothes—those ripped jeans and T-shirts and frilly peasant tops that made her look like she was still a little girl—had been pulled out of the closet and out of the dresser drawers. Some of the blouses had been ripped, some of the dresses cut into pieces. The child-like underwear she wore on her boyish figure had been shredded.

I had been afraid before, anxious for Riley's safety before, but now, my anxiety flared up, wild. The scene was so violent, the damage so viciously done, it made me wonder: had my little sister escaped these goons? Or had they dragged her out of here and done the same sort of violence to her?

I tried to calm myself. I told myself that Riley had sent Marco to find me, so she must've escaped. She must still be alive. She must be.

Taking a deep breath, I moved away from the door. I stepped carefully through the wreckage, eyeing the brutalized clothes and furnishing. I was looking for—something—I didn't know what. Clearly, if the pages of *Another Kingdom* had still been here when Orosgo's thugs arrived, they would have found them. I guess I was just looking for some clue—hoping Riley had left me some clue—to where she'd gone.

I tiptoed around among the ruined clothes and the gutted books. I didn't see anything useful. Not at first. But then, I spotted a large volume lying on its face, its aqua blue binding spread eagle, its pages ripped out and scattered on the floor. It was one of Riley's crazy conspiracy books: *Are Aliens Already Among Us?* But that wasn't what caught my eye. It was the little triangle of laminated paper sticking out from underneath it. Something seemed familiar about it.

I bent down and lifted the blue book. Underneath it was another book, small, thin, an old paperback children's book with a drawing on the cover: a little girl running through the streets, shouting a warning.

Nobody Listens.

I gazed down at it. That book. That same book I had read to Riley the night she was crying, that night I had forgotten until I touched Betheray's talisman and it returned to my memory.

Either this was a coincidence or there was magic in it. I had to bet on magic.

I tossed the aqua blue book aside and picked up the smaller volume.

I hoisted the eviscerated mattress back onto its frame. Sat down on the edge of it. I thumbed through the pages of *Nobody Listens.* In the quiet, I could hear the thumping music from down the hall coming through the walls.

Now, that long-ago night came back to me again—not like before—not through the magic of the locket, but just through the familiar touch of the book's laminated cover, a visceral trigger to my memory. I remembered how Riley's screaming subsided the moment I appeared in her bedroom doorway. I remembered her little girl smell as I bent down to kiss the top of her head, her wispy, straw-colored hair.

I'll read to you a while if you stop your crying, Riley.

She forced herself to stop with a pitiable sniffle.

What's the matter anyway? I asked her. *Did you have a nightmare?*

She gave a mournful nod, her eyes still running, her lips pulled down in a childish frown.

Was it because of Uncle Rusty?

Uncle Rusty. Yes. I remembered now. He had been a friend of my parents, the chairman of the Psychology Department in which my father worked. He was one of the few academics who had been kind to us children or had noticed us at all. And he had recently killed himself, poisoned himself. Rusty Winkelman, that was his name. My father had been the one who found Uncle Rusty's body. It was an ugly scene, apparently. He had described it to my mother in disgusting detail. Riley wasn't around when he told the story. But you never knew about Riley. She had a way of overhearing things, of knowing things she wasn't supposed to know.

But she had shaken her head when I asked her about it. It wasn't that.

The movie scared me, she said.

What movie?

She wouldn't answer me.

Read me the story, Aus. That was all she said.

Sitting there now in the ransacked room, I read the book again. It was a picture book about a little girl named Susie who liked to make up stories. She made up so many fantastic tales that no one would believe her when she came downstairs one day to tell her mother there was a dragon under her bed. But there was a dragon, there really was.

Nobody Listens.

One corner of my mouth lifted. It was ironic. Riley had grown up to make her kooky *Ouroboros* videos, her outlandish stories of aliens and humans working together to take over the world. Nobody had listened to her because the stories were so obviously false. But maybe they were false and true at the same time, a false version of the truth, like a parable.

As I scanned the book, I remembered reading it to her in her bed. I remembered the big blue eyes in her round face, eyes trained not on the pictures on the pages but on me. I guess it must have comforted her to see me there, because by the time I got to the end of the book, she was asleep.

I sighed. Holding the book open on my lap, I looked up at the mess of her apartment. My heart felt hollow. I loved my sister. I always had. She was broken now, crazy now, lost. She was so wrapped in her fantastic conspiracies it made her careless and selfish. She wasted her girlish romantic fervor on jerks like Marco. But I loved her anyway. And I felt for her—pitied her in retrospect for how scared she had been that night and how no one had come to comfort her but me, no one ever came to comfort her but me. *Where was my mother to mother her?* I thought to myself angrily. My mother—that indifferent and brittle woman, all theories and ideas and words, words, words and not so much as a kiss on the forehead to warm a child's heart. Where was she when Riley needed her?

And where was Riley now?

I glanced down at the book, still open on my knees. That's when I spotted the drawing.

It was made in pencil, scribbled lightly on the upper righthand corner of the page. I hadn't noticed it before because it wasn't any recognizable shape. But now that it caught my eye, I saw that it wasn't a mere doodle either. It was carefully made, an intricate design. I turned the page. There was another design on the corner there, and another design on the next page.

I realized then what it was.

There was this trick, a trick I'd taught my sister when we were young. If you drew different parts of a scene on the corner of each page of a pad, when you flipped the pages quickly, the full scene would appear: an optical illusion. It was hard to do, because it wasn't like a normal flip book, merely imitating motion. You had to make it just right—and flip it just right—and the observer would think he was seeing the whole image at once.

I pinched the corner of the book's pages between my thumb and forefinger. I flipped through them quickly. It took me two tries before I could do it fast enough to get the trick to work. Then it did work. It created the illusion that I was walking up a path to a house. That was the trick at the end: the way you could see the whole house even though she'd never drawn the entire structure on any single page.

It was my parents' house, the house I grew up in. There was no mistaking the eccentric shape of it. I gazed down at the book, thoughtfully chewing on my tongue. Had Riley made this image for her own pleasure? Was it just an absentminded game she'd been playing? Or was it a message—a message left specifically for me?

Impossible. Right? How could she know I'd come here? Search the place? Find the book? Find the drawing?

But then how could Betheray's locket have reminded me of that night I'd forgotten? And how had the locket come to me? It had been handed to me on the streets of LA by a woman who looked exactly like Elinda, the exiled Queen of Galiana.

For a moment, my throat tightened, my eyes filled with emotion. Riley was so desperate. And I was so alone. But was it possible that here—even here in this world of wickedness and murder, of conspiracy and corruption, of the mad, cruel arrogance of controlling power—was it possible that a nobody like me and my little lost sister were receiving some secret help from another kingdom?

I would go to my parents' house then. That was what Riley's drawing meant, right? *Go to our house, Aus.* There must be something there she wanted me to find.

I set the book aside on the mattress. I got up and limped into the bathroom. It was a tiny space, littered with Riley's girl things. The ransackers had hurled them all over the floor. I searched among the scents and makeup and hair doodads and found some antibiotic cream and some gauze.

I closed the toilet seat and sat on it. Rolled up my pants and went to work on my wounded leg. I washed the wounds clean with a damp cloth and spread the cream on them. I bound the ugly mess with the gauze. I needed stitches; I knew that. But this was going to have to do.

All the while I was bandaging myself, I was thinking: if Galiana and the Eleven Lands were a fantasy or a hallucination or the symptom of a brain tumor, where the hell did these wounds come from? How could they be so real?

When I was done, I limped back out into the studio. As I crossed the threshold, my eyes roamed around the room. I saw where Riley's desk drawer had been pulled out and tossed aside. The contents were scattered in an arc amid her torn clothing. I spotted a key.

I went to the place. I squatted down—the motion made my calf burn. I picked up the key and twirled it in my fingers. It was the key to Riley's Volkswagen. Good—that was good. She'd mentioned the car once or twice, but I'd never seen it, so I hadn't noticed if it was parked in the garage. She might have taken it when she escaped Orosgo's thugs. But if she had been clever enough to leave the car behind, I could use it. The police would be looking for the Camaro, not a Volks.

I stood. I took one more look around. I could not see anything else that would serve as a clue to Riley's whereabouts. Well then, like it or not, I was off to see my parents.

I went to the door. Pulled it open—and reeled back in shocked dismay.

"Oh God!" I groaned aloud.

Through the door, through a liquid haze of light, I saw that other world: the cave in Edgimond where the monster had me by the leg, where it was dragging me toward its jaws and an unbearably hideous destruction.

One second after I stepped across that threshold, I would be meat for the beast.

SHUDDERING, I SHUT THE DOOR QUICKLY. MY EYES flicked here and there in a sightless panic.

What do I do? I thought over and over again. *What do I do?*

I fought the panic down. I took a deep breath. I used my Galianan powers to silence my mind, to focus past my fear.

I remembered: I had a sword. In the fantasy kingdom—or hallucination or whatever the hell it was—I had this magic sword that appeared whenever I began to fight. Queen Elinda had left it in Shadow Wood as a gift for her chosen hero—who turned out, absurdly, to be me. The King of the Wood Tauratanio had given me the sword—and a suit of magical armor to go with it. The liquid mercury-like armor would pour out of my skin and cover me head to toe during a battle. It wasn't impenetrable. The beast would almost certainly bite right through it. But it would offer me some protection. Maybe.

What if—I thought—what if I could reach the sword before the beast ate me? What if I could strike at the creature? Use the speed with which it was pulling me to add to the force of the blow?

I nodded to myself. Good idea. Encouraged, I opened the door again. The magical passage into the Eunuch Zombie Cave of Female

Sacrifice was still there. I shut the door. I had a better idea: *Don't go back there, asshole. What are you, crazy?*

Right. There had to be another way out of here. Even jumping out the window would be better than stepping back into that cave like a world-class idiot. A three-story fall might break my leg, but that was nothing compared to being bitten in half and having my remains dumped among the slaughtered female population of Newfell.

Drawing another deep breath to keep myself steady, I looked around, searching for an escape route. The little studio had two windows on one wall. Both faced the back of the building, looking out on the macadam lane that ran along the garages. I tried to remember what the building looked like from the outside. Was there a way to climb down?

I went to the window, kicking through the debris on the floor, flinching at the stabbing pain that still went through my leg with nearly every step. I unlocked one of the windows and lifted the lower sash. I stuck my head out into the night.

What I saw gave me a strange, double feeling—two feelings superimposed on one another: a thrill of hope and a twinge of nausea at the same time. Yes, there was a way out, but it seemed nearly as dangerous as the passage back to Edgimond.

The face of the building was smooth. There was nothing to hang onto, no path I could climb down. But one apartment over, there was a balcony—and two more balconies under that one—a line of balconies with waist-high railings around them and with glass doors that led into the other apartments. If I could somehow jump over to the nearest balcony, I might be able to go into one of those apartments or maybe climb down from balcony to balcony until I reached the ground safely.

At first glance, the odds I could make such a leap without breaking my neck did not seem good. At second glance, they seemed even worse. The jump to the balcony wasn't very far—just a couple of yards at most—but there was no way to get into a good position for the leap. Riley's window had no outer sill, nothing to balance on. I would have to climb out and try to swing over somehow. But when I thought of the alternative—stepping through that door, feeling those claws digging into my leg again, having that unimaginably horrifying creature devour me . . . well, a broken neck did not seem so bad.

A cool autumn breeze swept over me, chilling the sweat that had now broken out on my face. I steeled my nerves and climbed out.

It was awful. I put one leg through the window, then my torso, then the other leg. And the next moment, I was dangling there with my fingers gripping the windowsill for dear life. I only had to glance down to picture myself lying below on the front lawn, helpless, writhing in pain until the police came to take me away.

Hanging there, I eyed the balcony sidelong. It was only now I realized how nearly impossible it was going to be to get the traction I needed to make the jump across the gap.

But I had to try.

I had to try fast too. The sill was sharp, digging into my fingers. My hands were sweating, making my grip slippery and unsure. I only had about thirty seconds before I lost my hold and fell. Panting with fear, I shuffled over as far to the right as I could go, as close to the balcony as I could get. Even so, the railing seemed about a mile away, and about two miles too high to reach.

Grunting, I bent my knees and pressed my sneaker toes against the smooth wall of the building, trying to engineer whatever leverage I could. My fingers were slipping. I had to do it. I had to do it now.

I leapt. I reached out for the railing.

I missed it completely.

I plummeted downward through the empty air. For a second that seemed to last forever, I was in freefall, my hands clawing wildly at nothing.

A second later, my fingers touched iron. It was the railing of the next balcony down. Desperate, I grabbed hold of it. I kept falling, then jolted to a halt. Sheer zany terror gave me superstrength. In an instant, I hauled myself up and scrambled over the top of the railing. I tumbled down onto the wooden floor of the balcony and hit with a thud.

Still soaring on adrenaline, I jumped to my feet at once. How was I? Was I hurt? No, I wasn't. What now? My brain was buzzing, thoughts flying so fast I could barely think them before they were gone.

The balcony doors, the glass doors into the apartment—were they locked? The curtains inside were drawn. The apartment beyond was dark. If I could just get in, I could get back down to the garage.

I stepped to the doors, seized the handle, pulled it to the side. There was no lock, just a flimsy latch. A harder tug and the door slid open. Huzzah. I could do this. I could get out of here. I could get away.

I slipped through the curtains into the shadowy apartment.

The lights went on. A young woman in a thigh-high nightshirt stood in the bedroom doorway, staring at me, mouth agape.

I held my hands out toward her. "Don't scream!" I said.

She started screaming. She put her hands over her mouth. She shook her head so that her long brown hair swung back and forth.

"Stop screaming!" I shouted.

She didn't stop. She went on screaming. She was very good at it.

"I'm leaving!" I shouted, moving toward the front door. "I'm already leaving!"

"Get out!" she screamed.

"I am getting out! Just let me go! Stop screaming!"

"Why are you even in my apartment?" she screamed.

"I can't explain!"

"I'm calling the police right now!"

"Don't call the police! I'm leaving."

She ran back into the bedroom to get her phone. I ran to the door. I grabbed the knob. What if the passage back to Edgimond was here too?

"My God!" said the young woman. She was in the bedroom doorway again, the phone to her ear. "You're covered in blood! I need help!" she screamed into the phone.

"You don't need help! I'm leaving! Stop screaming!" I shouted.

I pulled the door open. No passage into fantasyland. Just the hallway. I raced out.

Doors in the hall were opening. People were peeking out to see what all the screaming was about.

"Look at the blood!" one man shouted.

"Call the police!" shouted another man.

I shouted at everyone. "Don't call the police!"

Everyone had a phone. Everyone was calling the police.

I took off. I ran like a demon in the Demon Olympics. I reached the stairwell door. Dragged the door open. Only at the last second did I think to hesitate, to look through, to make sure I wouldn't be thrown back into the Eunuch Zombie Cave of Female Sacrifice. But no. It was just the stairwell.

"Grab him!" someone shouted behind me.

"I'm calling the police!" shouted a woman.

This was going incredibly badly: the worst escape ever. I raced through the door. I bounded down the stairs, taking three steps at once, ignoring the pain that knifed through my leg every time I landed.

I reached the garage floor. I pulled open the door—another door—so many doors—doors everywhere—but here too, thank God: no magic passage. I dashed into the garage. I saw my car, my Camaro, but that's not what I wanted. I dug hurriedly in my pocket. I brought out Riley's Volkswagen key. I pressed the button.

The Volks—a ratty little gray Passat, dented all over—blinked its lights in the garage's far corner. I rushed toward it. Pulled the driver's door open, looking over my shoulder to see if anyone was chasing after me. No one.

Gritting my teeth with determination, I slipped through the Volkswagen door.

I only saw the magic passage at the last second. Too late. I was already falling in behind the wheel.

The next moment, my calf exploded in searing agony as I felt the monster's claws sunk deep into my flesh again. I was dragged out of the mousehole and back into the cave and lifted swiftly toward the creature's drooling jaws.

10

I DIDN'T THINK. THERE WAS NO TIME TO THINK. I WAS lifted in the air upside down. Spinning helplessly, I caught glimpses of the unimaginable beast, that terrifying sight that had made my mind go blank the first time I saw it. The daggers of its teeth. The blackness of its maw. The horror of its shape . . .

The cave filled with that roar that was so dreadfully like a hundred women shrieking.

I drew my sword.

The idea had occurred to me back in Riley's apartment—that's why I was able to act so quickly, without a thought. That's why I was not paralyzed with fear and blinded with disgust as I had been before. I had had time, back in Walnut Creek, to process the madness of this moment, and so now, with only a single second of life left to me, my hand was steady and swift, acting almost before my brain could tell it what to do.

As the magic mercury armor poured out of my skin and covered me, I whipped the sword in a vicious arc and slashed out wildly toward the monster.

Green-black blood sprayed everywhere. The whole cave echoed with that hideous shrieking chorus of a roar. The beast lost its grip on me. I fell.

I would have cracked my head on the raw stone below, but the rotting bodies of the women broke my fall. I tumbled off the rancid pile amid a shower of clattering bones. I rolled—only hoping, in my confusion, that I was rolling away from the shrieking monster.

I jumped to my feet. The green glow of the slimy walls lit the swirling yellow gasses seeping up through the floor. My lungs were filled with the nauseating miasma. I turned and faced the creature.

What a thing it was. What an awful thing. A beast like a dragon—but by some ghastly magic, its body was covered not with scales but with fragments of its victims. It had become an abominable amalgam of the people it had killed.

Each piece of it had been a woman once, a piece of a woman, the slab of a thigh, a wobbling breast, a torso. Worst of all, here and there along its flank and up its serpentine neck, there were faces, dead faces, dead women gaping at me with slack mouths and open eyes. These fragments made, altogether, a patchwork thing, a nightmare quilt of mutilated humanity woven together into one great dragon-like behemoth. It roared with all their ghostly voices. It reared so high its head nearly scraped the ceiling of the cave.

I stood beneath it, quailing in my heart of hearts. But, clothed in liquid armor and gripping my sword in one sweaty hand, I braced myself for battle—for the simple reason that I had no choice.

I saw where I had wounded the thing. I had sliced a part of its forearm that had once been a human leg. It was slashed and bleeding black. The creature had recoiled from the pain of the blow but even in that moment as I watched it, it recovered. It drew itself up for a fresh assault.

Its snaky neck whiplashed back, and I understood the beast was preparing to strike at me, jaws first. It meant to snap me in half with a single clamping bite of its enormous teeth.

I peered at it through the green mist. All my pain and all my fear were channeled into radiant awareness. I had to time this next move perfectly.

The creature struck. With stunning speed, its head snapped out of the foggy upper reaches of the cave. Its open jaws, its dripping teeth, filled all my vision.

I spun to the right—full circle—out of its reach. I felt the thing's head blow past my back. I saw the green smoke swirling crazily in its wake. I came around and struck at it, a backhand blow. The gleaming silver blade cut hard across the side of the dragon's throat. Horribly, the shining edge lanced through what had once been a woman's face, cutting it in half so that it spat green-black blood at me.

God, the noise, that shriek, the shriek of a hundred voices. The whole cave trembled with it as the beast snapped backward in pain. I, still turning, stumbled on a dead body at my feet. I staggered. Tripped over another corpse. I reached out for the cave wall and only just managed to keep myself standing. The dragon, meanwhile, wheeled around to find me and strike at me again.

I saw its eyes flare. Huge, fiery black eyes. Blood flowed from the bisected face on its neck, down over the body parts that formed the front of it. Blood dripped from the leg in its wounded forearm too. Its shrieky roar was an angry babble: it sounded like a mob of female ghosts rioting on some haunted street in hell.

It swiped at me with its claws this time, claws like scythes. I stumbled against the cave wall and swiped back with my blade. We both missed. But I, in my light armor, was faster than the unwieldy dragon. I stabbed at it before it could fully retreat. This time, I wounded the female arm on the back of its paw.

The dragon snarled, its eyes burning. It reared above me again, its huge teeth bared. I crouched, gripping my sword hard in anticipation, trying to gauge which way it would come at me. I was tiring. I couldn't fend the creature off much longer. The inevitability of my own death seemed to close over me like nightfall. My heart thundered so hard in my chest that my whole body pulsed with it.

But then . . . then something happened. I wasn't sure what. The beast breathed deep, a low growly breath. It glared at me with what looked like real rage, glared as if it hungered not so much for my flesh as for revenge and my destruction. But at the same time, its hot stare changed focus. It seemed to be listening to something, some secret voice I couldn't hear.

The next moment, the dragon retreated, one heavy step. The cave floor shuddered with the impact. The rotting bodies trembled with it. A skull was jarred loose from atop a pile of corpses. It rolled down to the ground where its lower jaw cracked and broke away.

The beast began to turn. Its face remained toward me another second. Its eyes remained on me with that same baleful glare, on fire for revenge. When it growled again, I thought I heard those phantom women's voices speaking. I couldn't make out the words, not really, but I felt sure the beast was telling me: *We'll meet again.*

And with that, it swiveled away. With surprising lizard quickness, it stomped off into its high corridor, into the green mist, into the far shadows, and out of sight.

I watched it go, amazed. Was that it? Was the battle over? It seemed to be—for now, at least. For now, the creature seemed to have decided—or to have been told by that voice I couldn't hear—that the risk of further battle was too high, that we would fight another time, in another place, where it would have another, better chance at me.

I lowered my trembling sword hand. The darkness of death lifted from me, and I breathed a sobbing sigh of pure relief. I sheathed my blade. It vanished into nothing, leaving my hand empty. My armor slowly melted back into my flesh.

I stood there in the green mist, in the yellow light, in the cave filled with women's corpses. My very bones were aching with weariness, and the wounds in my leg had begun to torment me again. I looked down at them. The gauze I had put on my gashes back in Riley's apartment was gone, of course. My pants leg was torn ragged, and I could see my blood flowing freely through the tatters.

Still stunned that the fight was so suddenly finished, I glanced over at the mousehole. That was the only exit left to me. I didn't know where it went, but I was going to find out. Right now.

Limping, wincing with pain at every step, I went to the opening. The headless dead woman was still sitting there, propped against the wall. I tried not to look at her as I climbed back into the hole.

I dragged myself along on my belly through the narrow space. Again, as before, I saw the opening widen—saw it by the green glow of light that came in behind me from the Eunuch Zombie Cave of Female Sacrifice. Again, as before, I felt the cool air reach me—and again, my spirits lifted to think there must be a way out, a way back to the world above.

But what then? My stallion was gone. And after days of travel on horseback, I was still only in the first of the Eleven Lands. How could I ever finish my quest and save Galiana? I wasn't even sure I could get out of Edgimond, cursed, as it seemed to be, by the wizard Curtin.

The passage had widened enough now that I could crawl along the rough stone more quickly. I could still feel the cool outside air washing over me. But when I looked ahead, when I saw the place beyond the reach of the green light, there was only darkness, and more than darkness, absolute pitch blackness, so much blackness slowly folding over me that when I reached the end of the tunnel, I couldn't even see I was there. I just felt my hand slip over the edge into nothing.

I waved at the emptiness trying to gauge how deep a drop it was. I couldn't tell. I couldn't see a thing.

It was hard work, but I managed to turn myself around in the narrow space. I cautiously slid my legs out over the edge. I found a crack in the rock and dug my fingers in and held on as best I could. I cautiously lowered my legs and slid my torso over the edge of the corridor until I was hanging by my fingertips. How crazy it would be, I thought—how crazy to escape that dragon and then die in a fall.

I let go of the rock and dropped.

I hit the ground almost at once. The impact sent lancing bolts of pain up my wounded leg, but the fall was nothing, two or three feet. I stumbled and then regained my balance.

I squinted, staring. Nothing. I was absolutely blind. I had heard the expression: *I could not see my hand in front of my face*. Well, I couldn't. I stood still, confused and overcome by so much darkness.

And all at once, a hand reached out of the dark and seized my wrist.

11

I LET OUT A HIGH-PITCHED SHOUT AND JUMPED ABOUT three feet into the air like some wimpy character in a second-rate slapstick comedy. I tore free of the gripping hand, but even before my feet touched down again, it occurred to me the hand had not really felt all that scary. It was small and soft: a child's hand.

"Don't be afraid," came a little boy's whisper from the darkness. "It's only me."

It took me a second or two to catch my breath. Then I said, "Okay. Who's 'me'?"

For answer, the child slid his little hand into mine. Instinctively, I took hold of it.

"I came here looking for my mother," he said. "They took her away. They took all the mothers."

I nodded. "I saw."

"They took my sister too. And I was looking for them. Then the monster came and I had to run away. Did you see the monster?"

"Yeah, I sure did."

"It was scary."

"It sure was."

"I had to run away," he repeated sadly. Then he asked me: "Did it hurt you?"

"Yeah. My leg, a little. It clawed me. How about you?"

"No. I was too fast. I got into the hole and crawled through." After a moment of thoughtful silence, he added: "I know a place. There's a pool in the forest. The crying man lives there. He makes the water magic. It will make your leg feel better."

I stared down in the direction of his voice, but I still couldn't see him, not even the shape of him.

"Do you know the way out of here?" I asked him. And when there was no answer, I said, "Are you nodding?"

"Yes."

"I can't see you. I can't see anything. Can you see?"

"Yes. My eyes got used to the dark."

"Why didn't you find your way home then?"

"I don't want to go home. I don't like home anymore. Now that there are no mothers there."

"Right." I let out a long sigh. My leg was killing me. If there really was a magic pond where I could get some magic medical care, I wanted to magic over there in a big magic hurry. "Well, lead the way, kid," I said. "Let's get out of here."

The boy's tiny fingers closed around the edge of my hand. I felt him tug me forward. I began to walk.

"Go slower," I told him. "I can't see. Ow!"

I had brushed the top of my head on a low ceiling of rough rock.

"Watch your head," said the little boy.

"Thanks."

We walked on, me blind. The path went uphill. After a while, I could feel the cool air of the outdoors coming to me, stronger than before, damp and heavy as if wet with rain. But here, there was no light, none at all. I had to keep my free hand held up in front of me for protection. I had to shuffle very slowly to keep my balance.

"What's your name?" I asked the boy as we went.

He didn't answer me at first. Then he said, "I don't remember now. My mother knew."

"You don't remember your own name?"

"No."

"How long have you been down here?"

"Long."

"A week?"

"How long is that?"

"Seven days. The sun rises and sets seven times. That's a week."

"I don't know 'seven.' "

"It's the fingers on one hand, then another finger, then another."

"Oh no. I've been here much longer than that."

"How do you live?" I asked him. "How do you eat?"

"I just do."

This wasn't getting me very far. Either the kid was living like an animal, on mindless instinct, or he was hiding something from me. But I had to keep trying. There were things I needed to know if I was going to get out of this cave—and out of this country—alive.

On we went, on and up. I was about to ask him another question when, in the distance, I heard a low, throaty growl. I stopped in my tracks, holding the boy back.

"What was that?" I asked him.

"Just thunder."

"Are you sure?"

"Oh yes," he said.

I wasn't. I wasn't even a little sure. And it occurred to me to wonder: should I really be following this kid? Was he really on my side? Was he really a little boy at all? I couldn't see him. He might have been some demon agent of the evil wizard imitating a little boy's voice so he could lead me to my death. I mean, how did he live down here? And how the hell could he see when there was no light? It didn't make any sense.

The child urged me to start moving again. "Come on!" He tugged my hand. "It's only thunder. It can't hurt you. Don't be afraid."

I thought of resisting him but what then? I couldn't stay here, and I couldn't find my way out of this darkness alone.

I followed his tug and shuffled forward, flinching at the pain in my leg.

"Tell me something," I said to the kid. "What happened in your village? It wasn't always like it is now, right? I mean, it must've been different before they took the mothers away."

"Oh yes. It was different then. Before the wrinkled man came."

"The wrinkled man. Curtin. The wizard. The man in the starry robe."

"Yes," said the boy. "In the starry robe."

"What was the village like before he came?"

I stopped again. I thought I had seen something. For a split second, I thought I had seen a flicker of light up ahead, a dim silver flicker. But it was gone so fast I couldn't be certain. And then there came another low growl.

Well, I thought, maybe the kid was right. Maybe that flicker was lightning and the growl was thunder like he said. I relaxed a little, my suspicions fading. We continued to move. The air grew fresher. I thought we had to be approaching the mouth of the cave.

"It was regular," the boy said then.

"What?"

"At home. Before the man came in the starry robe. It was just regular."

There was another flicker. It lit up the stone in the distance for two quick instants. A few seconds later, the growl repeated. Lightning. Thunder. We were definitely getting close to the outside.

"There was snow and rain," said the boy. "Sometimes it was winter. In the spring, invaders came, and the men had to fight them or they would take the mothers and sisters away and our food too. Sometimes there was no food because the weather was bad. The men prayed for protection from the invaders. They prayed for good weather and food. But God didn't help us. So they prayed to the wizard instead."

For all I'd been through—the hideous monster back in the cave, the cops after me, Billiard Ball, and all the rest—there was still something unnerving about listening to the boy's tale. Something about his dreamy, hypnotic voice wafting up to me in the dark. It sent a chill through me. It was like listening to a ghost story by a campfire in the dead of night.

"Go on," I said to him. "The men prayed to the wizard, and—what?—the wizard came?"

"Not at first. But then they made shrines for him. They made statues of him and put them all around."

"How did they even know there was a wizard?" I asked.

The boy hesitated a moment. Then he said, "I don't know. They just knew somehow."

"Okay. So they built shrines and statues for him. What happened then?"

"They gave him one of the sisters," said the boy.

I shuddered in the dark as we trudged along. "You mean they sacrificed one of the girls?"

"I don't know. They took her away. She was crying. She never came back."

"And then the wizard came?"

"Oh yes. After they gave him the sister, he came. He came and told us there would always be food and never invaders anymore."

It took me a moment to follow the logic of this, but then I got it. "Sure," I said. "If the men got rid of the women, there'd be no mothers and children. No mouths to feed. And nothing to draw the invaders. Without women and children, there'd be plenty of food. And peace in our time. Was that it?"

"They took my mother and sister," the boy repeated tonelessly, as if reciting something he had memorized for school. "I climbed down here to find them. But then the monster came."

"My God," I whispered. "So the prayers brought the wizard to Edgimond. And then he went on from there to Galiana."

The boy didn't answer, but that had to be right. Curtin drew his magic from the minds of men—that's what Tauratanio, the King of Shadow Wood, had told me. That's why the wizard thrived in cities: the more people he had around him, the stronger he became. After the idiots in Newfell conjured him out of whatever nightmare world had spawned him, he took over Edgimond and then moved on to Galiana. He'd seduced Lord Iron there, twisted the minds of the people, ousted the queen and staged his revolution.

"He won't stop there. He must be planning to take over all the Eleven Lands," I murmured, more to myself than the boy.

The light flickered on the cave walls again, and this time I was certain: it was lightning, all right. And when the thunder rolled right after it, I could tell by the sound that we were very close to the mouth of the cave, the exit. I peered hard into the darkness to see if I could make out at least the silhouette of the boy beside me. But so far, no, the darkness was still too thick.

The boy tugged on my hand and his soft ethereal voice floated up to me. "You'll hear the man crying. In the Children's Forest. That's where the pond is."

"What?" I said.

And just then, my hand, held up in front of me, touched raw stone, a wall. Had we reached a dead end?

The boy tugged me to the right. "This way."

I followed him a few more steps. Then thunder and lightning struck almost simultaneously: first the flickering lightning, then the thunder and the lightning both at once in a long, muttering, twinkling flash. By that light, I saw the cave exit.

Thrilled to find the way out of this awful place, I turned to the boy. I was still holding tight to his hand.

The lightning struck again and the cave lit up bright around me.

I was alone. There was no one with me.

I leapt back, letting go of the hand, or whatever the hell it was I was holding. The dark settled over the tunnel again. Not full dark now. There was some dim moonglow coming in through the cave mouth.

I looked around. No boy. No one. Just me.

And yet then, from the emptiness, the boy's voice came again. "You'll hear the man crying. In the Children's Forest. That's where . . . "

But then the voice faded away into silence.

I stood there gaping like a buffoon at the place where the boy should have been. What was he? I wondered. A ghost? Had he died when he came down here looking for his mother? Was he cursed to wander in the dark of the cave, speaking to the rare visitor who escaped the dragon?

Or was he something weirder, worse, more sinister than that?

My heart beat hard with fear. Bumps rose on my skin. A whistling wind blew in through the cave entrance. It stirred my hair and chilled me. I swallowed hard. I wanted to get out of here—now.

I limped quickly to the cave mouth. What a relief it was to step through, out of that darkness into even what little light there was. The sky was now covered with thick clouds. The stars were gone from view, but the bright moon still illuminated a swirling patch of thunderheads. The faint glow spread out over the long grassy plain beneath.

I cast my eyes around and saw the dark line of a forest in the distance. I figured that was the forest the ghost boy—or whatever he was—was talking about. The Children's Forest.

A harsh noise startled me. Frightened, I turned toward it quickly.

I laughed out loud.

My stallion! I could make out the shape of my black stallion standing not a dozen yards away from me. He reared and lifted his forelegs into the air and whinnied loudly in greeting. It was as if he had just been waiting for me to find my way to him. How the hell had he managed that?

But who cared how? There he was. And man, I was delighted to see that horse. He wasn't much of a conversationalist, but just his presence made me feel a little less lonely in this terrible country. Plus I didn't think I could travel another three steps on my throbbing, bleeding leg.

The horse came up close to me. I pressed my face to his and we nuzzled each other.

"Let's blow this funhouse," I whispered. I stepped into the stirrup and hoisted myself up into the saddle.

"Ride," I said.

12

WE RODE.

Over the dark land toward the darker forest. In the roiling sky above, the lightning struck again and the thunder followed. I could feel the rain gathering in the air.

It wasn't long before the first trees were all around me. A short while after that, I reached the edge of the woods. A tangled depth of darkness stretched away into the distance.

But I knew I couldn't go on much further. My leg hurt too much, and the terrors of the cave had exhausted me. I needed rest.

I scanned the night, searching for shelter. In the next flash of lightning, I saw what I was looking for: a lean-to—a low log structure about as long as a man—just a little ways off along the tree line. I headed for it.

It wasn't much to look at—three log walls, a plank floor, and a shingle roof—but it would keep me dry till daylight. I pulled up beside it and lowered myself off the stallion, careful not to land too hard and jar my leg. My wounds were really hurting now. The pain was dull and deep, and all the skin around was stiff and thick. I felt like I was coming down with a fever too. The gashes must have gotten infected. Damn monster probably never washed its claws.

Tired, sick, I limped and stumbled into the lean-to like a drunken man. I practically fell onto the plank floor. My eyes began to flutter shut immediately.

Then the lightning struck again—and there was the wizard, Curtin, standing over me!

I shouted and leapt to my feet, stumbling back in terror until I hit the low wall. The wizard just stood there, silent and motionless. I caught my breath as the thunder rolled and the lightning struck again. But in the fresh flicker of light, I saw that, no, it was not the wizard. It was just a painted wooden statue, standing in the lean-to corner. It was a good likeness though: the raisiny face, the malevolent eyes, the tufts of gray hair on his head and his chin, the starry robe—they were all carved and painted to perfection.

They made shrines for him.

That's what the ghost boy had said. This place must have been one of their shrines.

My stomach rolled over. I gagged, disgusted. I couldn't sleep here, not with that thing staring at me. One of us had to go.

I limped over to the statue and grabbed hold of it. It was heavy, but not too heavy. I rolled it on its base over to the edge of the plank floor. Then I shoved it out of the lean-to.

The moment the statue hit the earth, it exploded in a great white flash. My stallion whinnied and backed away.

"Whoa!" I said, raising my hand to shield my eyes from the sudden brightness.

Blue-white flames rose out of the icon. It burned so hot I had to retreat to the back of the lean-to. But after a few more seconds, the wooden image crumbled to black cinders. A moment more, and it was ash, then gone.

Breathing hard, I limped to the edge of the lean-to and gazed down through the dark at the black spot in the grass where the thing had been. The stallion snorted and cautiously returned to sniff at the place.

"And stay out," I muttered to myself.

Then, with a sigh, I lay down on the planks again.

"This country sucks," I whispered.

It did. It was terrible here. Black magic and red danger in the very air. I never thought I would miss Galiana, but I did. I never thought I'd miss Los Angeles, but—well, I almost did.

My breathing steadied. My eyes sank shut. I fell asleep.

A CRASH OF thunder woke me. It was dawn, a green-gray dawn, still not raining. My stallion stood just outside the lean-to, pawing the ground impatiently. I rolled over on my back and groaned.

I did not feel good at all. I had a full-blown fever now. My mind was muzzy. My head was hot. The pain in my calf had spread over my whole leg. When I finally worked up the nerve to look down at it, I saw my entire calf had turned dark purple. The claw wounds were swollen and suppurating, pus seeping from the blackening edges of the gashes. If I didn't get to the magic pond soon—or to a modern hospital in Walnut Creek—I was going to lose the leg—lose the leg and then die.

The stallion snorted at me, pawing the earth.

"Yeah, yeah, I'm coming," I said.

I had to reach up and grab hold of a log in the wall to pull myself to my feet. My leg would barely support my weight. I hopped over to the stallion. He looked down at my wounds. Insofar as I could read the expression on his horsey face, the expression said, *oh shit.*

"I know," I said.

I cried out in pain when I hoisted myself into the saddle. I glanced up at the sky. The thunderheads were growing darker by the second, sickly green and full of rain.

It was going to be a bad day.

THUNDER ROLLED AS the black stallion and I plunged into the woods. Quickly, we were surrounded by a thick, gloomy, eerie forest, entangled branches like witches' arms swaying in the wind around obscure depths of shadow. The wind was strong and brought the scent of rain. Fallen leaves whipped up around the trunks of trees and into the twisted vines. The trees swayed and their wood cracked. The high branches whispered and whistled.

My fever grew worse. I had to fight to keep my eyes open, and when they were open, my vision was wavery and unclear. Somehow I managed to feel nauseous and hungry at the same time. I kept sinking forward in the saddle, consciousness fading.

After a while, I lifted my heavy head and peered into the tenebrous thicket on every side of me. What had the ghost boy said? *You'll hear the man crying in the Children's Forest.* I reined in the horse and sat still and listened. All I could hear was the rattling, cracking, whistling, whispering wind.

And then, for just a moment, the wind subsided. And I did hear something. Someone. A man's voice, lamenting in the distance.

I turned toward the sound and, as I did, I straightened, startled. There was a child there. A child, just standing in the woods. A little girl in a brown dress. She had long blonde hair around a face that was so white it seemed bloodless. She stood on the duff between two scrawny elms and stared at me without expression. Then she turned and slowly walked behind one of the thin trees. Somehow, narrow as it was, the trunk obscured her completely. When she didn't appear on the other side, I spurred the horse to step around so I could see where she was hiding. She wasn't hiding anywhere. She was gone.

Okay, I thought, *that was spooky*.

Confused, feverish, I blinked hard and searched the woods for her. I turned to the right—and cursed. I saw another child there. At least, I thought I did. There was a little boy, grimy and small. Staring at me, blank-eyed. The moment I spotted him, he shrank back into the shadows beneath the branches of a spreading maple. He blended with the shadows until, like the girl, he was just gone. Spookier still. And when I turned to the left, damned if it didn't happen again. A girl, a different girl, staring. She sank into the surrounding gloom and melded with it and vanished.

The Children's Forest. What the hell?

There was a long, throaty rumble of thunder like a growling beast. I raised my eyes and saw patches of sky through the high branches. It had grown even darker than before, the clouds even heavier with rain. The air around me was turning that strange green color you get just before a mighty storm.

The thunder died away—and once again, I heard the sound of a man mourning in the distance.

I spurred my horse and rode slowly toward the sound.

It was a long ride—a long, scary-as-shit ride. I traveled deeper into the woods, through twisted shadows. My fever bedeviled me, confused me. Every few minutes, I saw another child, staring at me, watching me pass. But whenever I looked back, the child sank away and became one with the forest obscurity and was gone. Truly creepy. Maximum creepy. It felt like the whole forest had eyes and was watching me. And who were these children? What did they want? Were they dead? Alive? Were they the wizard's demons or just harmless phantoms of my fever?

I pushed on through the forest with their fading figures all around me.

And all the while, the man in the distance wept. I was getting nearer now. I could make out his words.

"My love!" he cried. "My only love!"

I followed the sound. The cold, wet wind of the oncoming storm swirled around me and the leaves swirled and the trees squeaked and groaned. I swayed in my saddle, fighting to stay conscious as my fever grew worse, as the sickness closed around my head like a cowl of damp cotton.

Who knows how much more time passed before, through the thunder-dark forest, I caught sight of a glint of dull silver? Water. A pond. I prayed to God it was the magic healing pond the ghost boy had told me about.

The stallion and I passed through an arc of pine trees into a little grove. There was the pond at the center of the clearing, a large circle of dark water rippling with the wind.

I blinked hard, sick, groggy. Of its own will, the horse carried me toward the edge of the pond. From all the tree trunks all around me, children peeked at me and then ducked out of sight. But the crying man had stopped crying. The forest was quiet except for the wind.

We reached the water. The stallion nosed it. Drank it. Then lifted his head and nodded and whiffled: it was okay. I slid out of my saddle. I was too weak to hold on, and I made a hard landing, crying out in pain as the impact went up through my leg, which was now stiff and swollen well over the knee. Gripping the leg and wincing, I limped to the pond. The spectral children watched me from the woods.

I went on limping until I stepped off the edge of the earth, lost my balance, and fell into the water shoulder first. *Splash.*

The water seemed suddenly to seize me. I cried out once, then it dragged me down beneath the surface and swallowed me whole. It surrounded me. Clutched me. Held me and sucked at my body like some gigantic leech. It was agony. It was rapture. I let out a bubbling scream and thrashed and clawed to the surface and was dragged back down again. The pond sucked at my body, hard. I could feel the deadly toxins being torn out through my pores. Which was great, but in the meantime, I was drowning. I gargled and choked and thrashed back toward the surface.

And with that, the water suddenly let me go. I don't know how else to describe it. It just released me. I bobbed up on top of the pond like a cork, gasping and sighing and laughing and crying too. Weakly I swam to the shore and pulled myself onto the ground. I fell on my back and lay there, spent, staring up at the wind-whipped pines. I shouted, "Oh!" and laughed again and lay there, taking stock of my body.

I felt better. The fever was gone. The pain in my leg was gone. The swelling: gone. When I could finally gather myself, I lifted my head and looked down at the shredded bottom of my pants leg. My skin was clear. The wounds had vanished. I was healed.

I fell back against the ground. The stallion bent over me and nosed my face.

"Wow!" I said to him. "That was amazing!"

For a moment, I had forgotten about the ghost children all around me. I had forgotten about the lamenting man.

I turned over and crawled to the edge of the pond. I leaned down and took a drink from my cupped hands. It was cool. It was good. I gazed into the water. The wind died. The pond grew flat and reflective. I saw an image form on the surface: the image of a face.

But it was not my face.

It spoke to me.

"Run," it said. "Run for your life."

"YAAAAH!" I REMARKED. I SCRAMBLED BACK FROM THE water's edge. Even the stallion was startled. He leapt sideways to get away from the pond.

I mean, what the hell, right? That was supposed to be my reflection, but it wasn't. And whoever it was, he was talking to me!

Crouching, afraid, I stared wide-eyed at the pond. The water stirred unnaturally and lifted in a little wave.

And in the wave, I saw a hand rising.

But then the water—and the hand—fell down with a splash.

A silent second passed. Another. Then, slowly, warily, I crawled back to the edge of the pool. I peered into the still water.

The face peered back at me. Not my face.

It was the face of a man in his twenties. He had thin, narrow, aesthetic features, the features of a scholar or a saint. He had short black hair and a thin, prominent nose and sensual, sensitive lips, a poet's lips, a lover's. He looked worn—worn by sorrow and care. I knew at once that this was the man I had heard lamenting.

He looked up at me out of the water. He was made of water for all I could tell, at one with the water, inseparable from it. He groaned quietly, a hollow, wavering, liquid sound.

"My love," he said. "My love."

"Who are you?" I asked him—or tried to ask him. My voice had turned to dust.

The thunder rolled above us. Lightning flashed. And when the wind ruffled the water, the man's face disappeared in the ripples. It only formed there again when the water grew still.

The man searched the surface, looking for me. Then he saw me, squinted at me as if it was hard to make me out above the pond.

"Get away from here," he said in a somber, hollow tone. "Out of the forest. Out of Edgimond. Quickly, man. Before Curtin finds you and curses you like he did me."

At that, I heard a noise behind me. I looked over my shoulder. I saw a boy staring at me. He pulled back quickly behind a tree and disappeared.

I faced the pond, faced the face in the pond. "Are they his children? Are they Curtin's?"

He shook his head mournfully. "They're mine. All I could preserve of them."

"Are they dead? Are they ghosts?"

"No. They were never born."

I looked around again, my lips parting. I caught glimpses of the children peeking out from behind the trees, then gone.

"Never born," I whispered.

I turned back to the man in the pond.

"They were all I could save of the women," he told me. "Their children."

I understood. "The children they didn't live to have."

"Run," he moaned. "Run for your life from this terrible place."

"I will, I will," I promised him. But somehow, I couldn't run. Not yet. I needed to know more. I had this sense, this instinct, that it was important for me to hear his story. "Tell me who you are first. Then I'll go."

"I am Natani, the magician."

"Magician. Is that like a wizard?"

"No. It's a learned power. Power over the shapes of things—things seen and unseen. Healing too."

"The water," I said. "That was you."

"I am the water now."

"Is that what you meant about how Curtin cursed you?"

"My love," he lamented in that watery voice.

My heart seized in my chest as a whip-crack of thunder shook the branches and lightning lit the green-dark day.

"Go," said Natani from the pond. "Go now. He's far off, but he senses your presence. Just like he sensed mine. He *will* come for you."

I knew he was right. I could feel it. This country belonged to Curtin and the wizard could feel me here. He was angry too. His anger was in the storm somehow, somehow his anger and the storm were one and the same.

And the storm was getting closer. I had to get away from it fast. And yet . . . and yet, I couldn't. I needed to know more.

"Tell me what happened to you and I'll go," I said.

"He moves in the wind," said Natani the magician, speaking from the substance of the water, through the water. "In the wind and across dimensions, place to place. That's how he saw us together."

"You and your love."

"My love," he echoed. "She was so beautiful. And she was mine. The power of my magic fed on her love and grew stronger. He hated that. He feared it. So he stole her from me."

"Curtin."

"He drew her to a lonesome tower while the purge was going on in the villages."

"While they were feeding the women to the beast, you mean."

"He tricked her. That's how his magic works. He tricks his way into your mind and takes it over."

I had seen that, back in Galiana. Curtin fed his magic on weakness and desire. He used Lady Kata's loneliness, Lady Betheray's jealousy, Lord Iron's ambition, to seize control of them. He took power from their minds and turned it against them.

"He came to her in a shape like a hero's," Natani went on. "Handsome and brave and strong. He tricked her into sin."

"Into sin? You mean she fell in love with him?"

"She was afraid—and I was gone. I should have stayed to protect her, but I went on my quest instead. She was alone in Newfell when the sacrifices began. She escaped into the woods. But Curtin saw her. He drew her to the tower. He told her she'd be safe there. That they would not find her. They would not throw her to the beast in the cave. When, in her fear, she locked the door, he put a spell on the lock. And she was trapped."

I shook my head. "What an evil bastard."

"My fault, my fault. I left her alone. I was on my quest, moving through the villages, you see, doing what I could to save the children, the children who would not be born. I gave them shapes and hid their spirits here in the forest in case any of the women escaped to claim them. Too late I realized Curtin had seized upon my absence to seduce my love." His pale, aesthetic, poet's face took on a new expression of determination. "I saw then what a fool I'd been. How wrong I'd been to leave her. I returned. To find her. To set her free. To take her away to safety across the Eleven Lands."

A thought was teasing at the edges of my brain now. *A sin. A quest. A curse.* I had heard these words before.

Natani continued. "I draped myself in shadow so Curtin wouldn't see me. I found the tower. I climbed to her room. I called to her through the door and she came back to herself, came back to me. Our love made my magic strong again, and the lock was broken. Oh, my love, my love."

The wind swirled angrily down from the sky and up from the earth again, carrying the dead leaves in a chattering tornado. Now, when the thunder growled and grumbled, when the lightning flickered and the green-black clouds seethed, I felt the wizard's anger in them. I felt him moving across the dimension of space, coming toward me in the wind, as fast as the wind and twice as terrible.

I knew I had to run. I knew I had to get out of the forest. But still I lingered.

For a moment then, with the wind making the water seethe, Natani's face disappeared beneath the agitated surface. But I spoke into the ripples anyway.

"What happened next?"

And sure enough, his voice came up to me, rippling like the water. As the water grew calm once more, his face reappeared.

"We ran," Natani said. "My love and I. Into the woods to get away from him. But he was coming. Closer and closer on the storm just as he is coming now. There was no hiding from him, no escape. I tried to cover my darling in magic. I made a mantle of my love for her. But . . . " His voice broke. "But he had gotten inside her head and she could not free herself. I couldn't protect her. I knew when he reached us, he would destroy us both. So I did the only thing I could think of . . . "

The lightning flickered above the trees and the thunder crashed so loudly and so angrily that the forest seemed to shake with fear. The wind rushed over us and I could feel the rain inside it. My stallion stirred and whinnied, as much as to say to me: *Hurry, Austin! Hurry!* Curtin was near. The storm was about to break.

"I changed her shape so he wouldn't know her. I used all the power of my magic to turn her into a creature of the woods—so she could slip away, you see, and elude him even as he swept into the forest searching for her." He was speaking quickly now. Hoping to finish his story so I could get the hell out of there in time. And I—I was staring down at him, my mouth open, my mind racing, the thought repeating as he spoke, a thought I couldn't believe and yet couldn't quite deny. *A sin. A quest. A curse.*

"She ran. I made her run. She escaped—I saw her escape. But where? Where did she go? I never knew. I don't know now. I don't know how far or whether she's alive or dead . . . " His voice sank to a watery moan. "And once she was gone, all my magic was gone with her. Alone—alone, without my love, I was no match for Curtin. He found me and came into my head and drove me mad. I threw myself into this pond, hoping to drown myself before he used my own magic against me, used it to transform me into something abominable. But he would not let me die. He seized on my despair and forced me to change my own shape into the element of water."

With that, the lightning flashed, the pond went white, the thunder struck again, so near, so loud, I could hear nothing else for a moment. Then from the roiling water, the magician's gargling voice cried out to me, "Run. Run for your life. Run now."

But I lingered one more second. *A sin. A quest. A curse.* I tried to speak. I couldn't. I tried again.

I said, "Maud? Was it Maud? My friend? The squirrel girl? Maud?"

And from the depths of the now-churning pool, Natani's churning voice rose up to me.

"Maud. Maud. Maud. My love, my love."

The storm broke. The rain fell. The wizard was almost upon me. I had to run for it.

I ran.

14

I RUSHED TO MY STALLION. WITH MY LEG NOW HEALED, now strong, I stepped quickly into the stirrup and swung myself into the saddle in a single motion. The clouds burst and the rain washed over me in a torrent. The force of the downpour was incredible. It whipped my face. It stung my cheeks and nearly blinded me. Leaves were torn from their branches. They dropped down hard. The thunder cracked again and again, and the great clouds above the treetops flashed blackly with the lightning inside them.

Through the hellish noise, I shouted toward the pond. "She lives, magician! She's alive! I've seen her! She sent me on this quest. She sent me—and you healed me—and so help me, I will bring her back to you! I'll find the emperor. We'll free these countries. And so help me . . . "

But the thunder roared so loudly and the lightning struck so near, my voice was drowned and my courage failed, and I dug my heels into the stallion's side and shouted: "Hah!" The last I saw of Natani was a wave lifting wildly on the wild, wild wind with his hand inside it as if to bid me go. Then the stallion reared and ran.

We dashed through the rain, beneath the trees. The leaves swirled up from the ground and slanted out of the sky at once. The wind drove a dark mist between the flailing branches. Through those leaves and through that mist and through the sheets of rain, I saw the never born children running in terror, fading in and out of being in the tempest-tossed obscurity. I went on, battling my way through the maelstrom. Lightning struck a mighty pine and severed its trunk like the blow of a giant axe. Sparks flew and the stallion halted and whinnied as the tree toppled over in front of me, its branches flaming. I shouted at the horse again and snapped the reins. The stallion leapt high and we cleared the fire and rode on.

I was searching for the tree line, for a trail, for any way out. But the forest just grew deeper as the storm grew worse. The wind was now so strong, the horse could barely make headway against it. The lightning was striking fast on every side, flash, flash, one strike after another. All around me, trees were going up in yellow flames even as the rain washed down and drenched them. Trunks were crashing through the branches, thudding to the ground. Flaming branches were sweeping past my face. Each new obstacle and danger forced me to turn and turn again until I had no idea which direction I was facing, which way I should go to get out of this forest. The rain lashed me. The wind buffeted me. Fire flared around me.

"Damn it!" I shouted in frustration. But my voice was swallowed by yet another crash of thunder.

Then, for just a moment, the storm lulled, the way storms will. And in the sudden, unnerving quiet, there was the steady whisper of rainfall—and a voice, a soft voice calling to me.

"Over here!"

Desperate, soaking, breathless, I turned and saw a woman standing among the trees.

She was wearing a hooded robe, a peasant's robe, but even at a glance, I could see she was not a peasant. Beneath her cowl, she had elegant, lovely features and red, red hair spilling out from the rough cloth to fall around her cheeks. The ghosts of unborn children flitted past her and vanished among the trees all around her in the black mist and the gray downpour. She beckoned me urgently with one hand, clutching her robe closed around her with the other.

"Hurry! Over here!"

I didn't know what to think. Was she real? Was she friendly? Had I crossed the border out of Edgimond and escaped the wizard's domain? Or was she a creature of his, some sort of demon or illusion? I just didn't know.

But the storm was already rising again. The next time the thunder struck, it was so loud, it scattered my thoughts. The lightning lanced out of midair and cut another pine in two and sent the pieces flaming to the earth. The wind swirled, full of wet leaves. The leaves and the wind smacked into me and nearly knocked me from my saddle.

Squinting through the downpour, I saw the woman beckon me again. She shouted to me, but the noise of the storm swept her words away.

I decided I had to trust her. Alone, unguided, I would never get out of this tempest alive. I pulled the reins to point the stallion toward her and spurred the horse on. The motion brought the wind to my back. The wind gave me speed.

As soon as the red-haired woman saw me coming, she turned and started hurrying through the forest. I could see she knew the way. Amid all the massed undergrowth and the fallen wreckage, she moved smoothly and swiftly as on an open path. When I followed in her footsteps, I also passed quickly among the swaying trees.

We broke through the tree line into a broad clearing—and there stood a house. Not just a house, a grand mansion. Brown and white like the brown-white wood around it, it seemed almost to grow up out of the ground, stables and gables and bay windows and peaked roofs surrounded by birches and autumn maples, lashed by the storm.

I pulled up, staring, startled, amazed. Who built such a grand house here? The woman was up ahead of me, running for it. She turned as she went and beckoned again, more urgently.

I hesitated only another second. I felt a sourness in my heart: doubt, distrust. Who was she? How had she come to be here?

But looking around, I saw the whole forest bending and groaning under the force of the tempest, patches of flame rising and falling here and there as the lightning struck and then struck again.

I was going to die if I didn't get shelter. Me and the stallion were both going to die.

I rode on, following the woman.

She was at the stables now. With an effort, she slid open the large, heavy door. She stood back to let me pass. I rode into the structure, ducking low to clear the lintel.

IT WAS A huge relief to come in out of the weather. The stallion shook himself beneath me, throwing off water. I slid out of the saddle, exhausted. If I hadn't been gripping the reins, I think I would've toppled into the hay.

Breathing hard, I turned to the woman. She pushed the rain-blackened cowl off her head.

My breath caught. I nearly gasped aloud. She was even more beautiful than I had realized at first. So beautiful. Mesmerizing. Her red hair flowed lushly around an oval face of small, neatly sculpted features. Even in the shadows of the stables, I could see her gleaming cobalt eyes, tender and caring and warm. She did not look like anyone I knew—anyone I had ever seen anywhere—and yet there was something about her—something about the kindness and gentleness in her expression—that reminded me of someone, I could not place who it was.

"Who are you?" I said.

"My name is Hamarta." Her voice was also warm, also kind. It seemed to pour over me like a soothing balm.

"What is this place?" I asked.

"It's all right. You'll be safe here. I'll take care of you—until the storm is over. After that, you can make a run for the border."

"The border. We're still in Edgimond then."

She nodded unhappily. "We are. But *he* can't find us here. I promise. I'll protect you." He. Curtin. She didn't have to say the name. She gestured toward the black stallion. "Come on now. Unsaddle him. I'll brush him down."

While I worked the saddle off, she took a brush from a peg on the wall. She stroked the horse dry, murmuring sweetly to him as she worked her way across his flank. I stood in my soggy clothes and watched her. Couldn't take my eyes off her. I was a city boy. I didn't know a thing about horses. But she seemed to wield the brush with a sure hand as she kept whispering to him, "There's a good boy, there's a good boy." She really did remind me of someone, but I still couldn't figure out whom.

"You seem to know what you're doing," I said.

"You've got to get them fluffy again or they can't get warm." She glanced at me. Smiled—a smile like her eyes, like her voice, infinitely gentle, womanly. "Oh, look at you, you poor thing. You look so worried. Don't worry. I'll take care of him. And then—that smile again. "Then I'll take care of you. Go fetch a bale of hay so he has something to eat now."

There were a few bales stacked against one wall. Not many, I noticed. Why not? Where were the other horses? My black stallion was the only one here.

I hoisted a bale and carried it over to the stallion and set it down for him. It made me realize—now that I was well, now that my fever and nausea were gone—how incredibly hungry I was.

Hamarta finished the brushing. She hung the brush on the wall again. She wiped her forehead with one wet sleeve. "All right now, sweetheart," she said to me. "Come along. I'll feed you."

She flashed another sweet smile and gently patted my cheek. The warmth of her touch went right through me, knife meets hot butter. Then she pulled her hood up over her flowing hair and moved to the door. I stood by the stallion, watching her go, mesmerized by her. Such a beautiful girl. And so kind. Almost wifely. Almost maternal. *I'll feed you. I'll take care of you. Sweetheart.* But what was she doing here? A woman in Edgimond where all the women were dead. And this house . . . Even in crazy Austin-is-having-a-hallucination Land, there was something about this situation that did not add up.

Sliding the stable door open again, Hamarta turned to me, framed against the backdrop of the storm. She saw me hesitating and gave me yet another of those charming smiles. I realized then whom she reminded me of. Jane. My friend. The girl I loved back home. Jane Janeway. It was *her* smile, *her* tenderness, *her* feminine sweetness that seemed to reach out to me from this stranger that seized my heart here as it always did back in the real world.

"Come on then, darling," Hamarta said to me, as if she were coaxing a reluctant child. "It'll be all right. Come on."

She pushed out into the rain and I, mesmerized, trailed after her.

The tempest was still running high. The whole forest was seething with wind and rain. The trees around the clearing bent low and slashed up straight again as the fallen leaves tornadoed. The boiling clouds above us exploded over and over with white-black lightning. Clutching her cowl tight around her face, Hamarta raced for the mansion's front door. I raced after her.

She went quickly up the three front steps, pulled the door open and hurried inside. Eager to get out of the rain again, I leapt up the steps after her and dashed across the threshold. As I did, just as I was crossing over, I caught one quick glimpse of her, one glimpse of Hamarta standing in the front hall, waiting for me there. Her bright eyes now seemed brighter, weirdly bright, and her sweet smile suddenly struck me as wrong, creepy, and unpleasant.

I thought to myself, *I've made a terrible mistake.*

But the next thing I knew, I was through the door—and in the garage at Riley's apartment house, just sliding behind the wheel of Riley's Volkswagen.

For a moment, I was too dazed by the transition to understand what the hell was going on.

Then I did understand: I was back in Walnut Creek. I was trying to escape. The people in the building were calling the police. For all I knew, in minutes, squad cars would come swarming onto the scene, sirens blaring.

I was on the run again.

SOMEHOW, DAZED AS I WAS, I MANAGED TO SWITCH THE engine on and snap the Passat's gearshift into reverse. I backed out of Riley's parking spot and swung the car around, tires screeching. Then I rolled forward to the garage door, which rolled open automatically as I came. A moment later, I was out on the street, back in the city, driving past the empty office parks, their towers lit up bright and hollow in the misty night. I wound around them on the broad curving boulevard, then fired like a rock from a slingshot out into the darkness of the side streets.

I was heading to Berkeley, to my parents' house. Heading home.

There was no GPS in the ancient Volks, but it didn't matter. I knew the way from childhood. I left the straight path as soon as I could and traveled on lesser byways. I hoped the police would not guess that I had switched cars, but I couldn't count on it, so it was best to keep out of sight as much as possible.

It felt strange to be rolling lonesome through the dark like that. It was hard to process the vastness of my disconnection. No phone, no internet, no media. My isolation was like a hunkering presence, a stone gargoyle glowering on my shoulder. When had I ever been so solitary?

I stared through the windshield at the headlight-lit two-lane. My mind was reeling, images sluicing in and out of memory like scary faces in a carnival horror ride. I saw the storm-tossed woods of Edgimond, the magician's poetic features lamenting in the pool, the monster in the cave, the mansion in the forest...

I thought of Hamarta—that last glimpse I'd had of Hamarta's face. A glimpse is all it was. It had lasted less than a second. But in that flash, she seemed to me—what was the word I wanted?—*malevolent*. Yes. Had I imagined that? Had I mistaken what I saw? Or was that the truth about her? Was she some creature sent by the wizard Curtin to draw me into a trap—as he had drawn Maud to the prison tower where he locked her away?

Maud . . . That was the next thought that came to me. Maud, the mutant squirrel girl, my friend. It was strange to think of that stern, unruly creature as fully a woman, and a woman in love, and in love with such a pale, poetic type as Natani. I wondered if I would really be able to keep my promise to him, to find some way to bring them back together. I tried to think it through as I guided the Passat through the California darkness—but as always, when I was back here in modernity, I found it almost impossible to fully believe in that other semi-medieval fantasy-novel world. Curses, spells, wizards who wormed their way into your will . . . They were so real when I was fighting them for my life, but once I was back in a car on a modern byway . . . Well, how the hell was I supposed to think of them as anything but crazy dreams?

Maybe that's why my fears about Hamarta and my worries about Maud faded as I was driving, fell away from me like a shed skin. After all, here I was on a lonely road, winding up from the depths of a deserted canyon. And as I crested the ridge, I looked out through the window, through the trees, and saw the familiar lights of Oakland spread out below me—and my mind just naturally returned to the troubles at hand: Billiard Ball dead and my crazy sister missing and my entire family conspiring with Serge Orosgo to do I didn't even know what.

Reality: what a depressing thought.

I so did not want to be doing this. I did not want to go home and see my parents, not at all. It was bad enough back in the old days—last week—when I only had to contend with their disdain for my artistic ambitions, when I only had to swallow my envy at their worshipful admiration of my successful older brother. Bad enough then, but now? Now when it turned out that they *and* my brother, all three, were agents of a lunatic billionaire who killed anyone who got in his way—who was trying to kill me, their own son, and Riley, their only daughter. Not that they cared.

My right hand moved to my throat, went into my shirt, touched the locket around my neck. My fingers brushed the gold and felt the warm energy coming off the surface of the metal. But I didn't need any magic to remind me of Riley—little Riley as a child—her hysterical, frightened cries from her bedroom and how no one went to her, no one but me.

Which made me think of my mother. It made me think about her prim, bloodless lips and her passionless eyes and her dry intellectual drawl. Trading academic patter with Dad and Richard while Riley cried. *Oh, go see about Riley, Austin, would you?* A word of tenderness in that woman's mouth would have died of loneliness.

Which made me think, in turn, about Jane Janeway. About the passion I'd felt for her back in LA, the passion I still felt for her whenever I was calm enough to feel anything at all besides fear. My desire for Jane wasn't some pale, polite, tepid, modern yearning. No. It was more than her company I wanted, more than her body, more than sex and even love—though God knows I wanted all that too. But when I thought of Jane, really thought of her, I wanted to reach right through her flesh and grab the soul of her, drag her to me by her soul, and press my soul into hers, lips first. I wanted to plant my children inside her like founding a city on fertile soil. You know how feminists used to complain that men wanted to keep women barefoot and pregnant? Well, hell, I was willing to let Jane have shoes—I guess—but other than that, I wanted our children falling out of her like fruit from a tree.

That's how I felt, and to hell with anyone who didn't like it. I could see a whole future with her, daydream the whole thing from our wedding day to my funeral. But now—now as I drove—I began to doubt myself, to doubt even my own desires.

Which brought me back to Hamarta. Her womanly sweetness, her maternal kindness, so like Jane's. How quickly she had hypnotized me, drawn me in. Was it like that with Jane too? Had a childhood with such an unmotherly mother simply left me so hungry for feminine care that it was as if I had a yearning ghost inside me, a spirit boy like in the Children's Forest, desperate to be brought to life by the first motherly maiden who came along?

Riley's Volkswagen curled down out of the night hills, and I finally joined up with the freeway, coming into the bright cities from the south. It was after midnight now. Not much traffic. I skirted the campus on Shattuck Avenue and climbed into the wooded hills of the Northside until I arrived at my parents' house.

I will say this for Mom and Dad. Whatever dastardly deeds they'd been doing for Serge Orosgo, they hadn't got rich off them, not so far as I could see anyway. Their house was the same odd and ramshackle place where we had lived when I was growing up. Big, husky, weatherworn. A rambling storybook illustration of a place with lots of shingled roofs and fanciful curves and hidden crannies, even a sweeping stone staircase that rose from the lawn to a stunted tower. It was set back from the steeply climbing, sharply winding road, amid a cluster of drooping beech trees and stunted redwoods, all of them turned to eerie silhouettes by the night.

I pulled into the driveway and shut off the engine. The house was quiet, dark. Either my parents were still down in Los Angeles or they were asleep. Asleep, I wagered, seeing their Mini was in the garage.

I stepped out of the Volks into the night. I stood and breathed the fresh, cool air and listened to an owl whoo-whooing somewhere in the nearby trees. I scanned the street. No sign of cops. Changing cars, covering my tracks, I'd lost them. I supposed it was possible they'd think to look for me here. Hell, it was possible my folks would turn me in if they saw me. But I didn't plan to stay that long. I didn't know what Riley had left for me here. I didn't even really know if she had left anything. But if she had, I knew where I would find it.

I trudged reluctantly up the rising front path. I was in no hurry to step back into my childhood home. I never had been, but especially not now, now that I knew what I knew. I approached a redwood on the sloping front lawn. The spare key was still there in the water tray beneath the hummingbird feeder. I used it to let myself in the side door and entered the kitchen. I turned off the alarm by poking my brother's birthdate into the keypad.

I stood in the darkness. Even the smell of the place depressed me, the smell of my past. I'd never liked it. Had I always known what was going on here? Had I always been aware, deep down, that something in this house was terribly wrong?

I knew I ought to start searching right away, but I suddenly realized again how hungry I was. Very hungry, just as I had been back in Edgimond. I checked the refrigerator. Typically austere parental fare. I slapped together a sandwich of cheese and artisanal bread plus some sort of brown relish for flavor. I sat at the kitchen table in the shadows and chomped on it. My brain kept telling me I ought to hurry. I ought to search the place and get out before I was discovered. But much as I disliked this house, it was home. I was comfortable here. I was losing my sense of urgency.

When I was done eating, I dusted the crumbs from my hands and stood up. I swayed, unsteady on my feet, touching my forehead, closing my eyes. Man, I was tired. I trudged out of the kitchen into the living room. A pleasant room—I could make it out in the shadows: lots of warm wood and floral furniture. Like the rest of the house, it had the homey but manufactured charm of a country inn. From there, I slowly climbed the stairs to the shabby hall off the second-floor landing.

I meant to head straight to Riley's room. I did. But as I shuffled along the burgundy runner, I reached my own boyhood cubicle and paused in the doorway. There was my old bed in the shadows. Inviting. I was so tired. And this was home. If I could just lie down for a few minutes . . . Not to sleep, just to rest.

Fully dressed, I settled on my back on top of the bedspread, my hands folded on my chest like a corpse. My gaze moved over the dark walls. Oh, don't think for a moment the room had been tenderly preserved to remind my parents of my treasured childhood. Ha. The sci-fi movie posters had been stripped from the walls, the superhero models swept from their shelves. It was now a spare, mostly bare, and yet somehow pretentious little guest room decorated with wan prints of—I don't know—Provence or some similarly fashionable place.

Nostalgic misery settled over me like the darkness. Another second and I was fast asleep.

I SHOT UP, awake, thinking: *Shit!*

It was morning. White sunlight streaming in through the window. What had wakened me? My mother.

Shit! Shit!

She'd been holding the door slightly ajar, peeking in on me, silent. I had seen her through half-opened eyes—just for a second. The look on her face! Like Hamarta's look: malevolent. Then she'd withdrawn and shut the door again.

Shit! Shit! Shit!

Quickly, I rolled my legs off the bed and sat up on the edge of the saggy mattress. I rubbed my fingers through my hair and shook my head, doing my best to bring myself to full alertness.

All right, I thought, trying to calm myself. *All right.* There was no seizing back the lost time. I just had to stay solid inside. Do my thing and get out of here. Keep chill. Chilly. Chilliest.

Shit! I thought.

I got up. I remembered: the last time I'd been here, about three months before, I'd left a change of clothes. I'm not sure why. Maybe just to remind my parents I existed. When I checked the bottom drawer of the bureau, the clothes were still there. Fast as I could, I changed into them. It was nice to get into some fresh underwear, jeans, and a sweatshirt. I left the bloody old clothes in their place.

As I was walking downstairs, I heard my parents talking to one another in the kitchen. *Murmuring* to one another is more like it. And the tone of their voices sent the proverbial icy finger up my proverbial spine. It was nothing I could describe exactly, nothing I could really give a name to. But I can say this: theirs was not an oh-joy-our-darling-son-is-home sort of murmur. More like oh-crap-what-are-we-going-to-do-now.

Well, what else could I expect? The last time I'd seen the dear rents—just a couple of days ago down in LA—they'd been telling me why I had to lie to the police and cover up Orosgo's murders for him. They were all too disappointed when I refused, and they seemed perfectly gratified to listen to Richard threaten me with the destruction of my life and reputation and what I'll laughingly call my career. So I couldn't exactly hope they were going to be thrilled to see me. Still, you know how it is: Mom, Dad, all that. You always keep hoping for a little love and approval from them, even when you know better, even when you're pretty sure they're conspiring with a power-mad lunatic to destroy the known universe or whatever the hell they were conspiring to do.

They must have heard me coming because they shut down their conversation about two seconds before I pushed through the swinging door.

"Well, well, well," muttered my father as I walked in, "what have we here?" He was an owlish man with close-cropped salt-and-pepper hair, narrow glasses, and a distracted gaze.

"What a nice surprise," said my mother. She was angular where she existed in fleshly form at all.

It was the worst imitation of a parental welcome I'd ever heard, and I'd heard more than my share. My father had been reading something on his device before I entered. I caught the word "*motel*" and knew that Billiard Ball's death had made the news. Dad quickly pressed the button to make the screen go blank. Then just as quickly, he raised his coffee cup to his lips and sipped innocently, smiling thinly around the rim.

The silence then was so awkward it was nigh on unbearable. I busied myself by going to the coffee machine and pouring a steaming mugful. Behind me, my father finally came up with something vaguely father-like to say.

"So . . . what brings you up this way?"

I turned to him and leaned against the kitchen counter. Beams of morning sun were shooting in through the window above the sink and if you had taken a picture of us just then—Mom and Dad at the table, me sipping joe, the bright yellow daisies on the walls and the message magnets on the fridge—you would have captured us looking exactly like the happy, all-American family we had never been.

I snorted into my coffee. "What brings me up this way? How about the fact that my little sister is missing? Your daughter, Riley. Remember her?"

"Oh," said my mother with a little frown. "I hardly think she's missing, Austin. Don't be so dramatic."

"Drama—never helps anything," my father muttered, as if musing to himself. He was a musing mutterer, my father was.

"Okay, so she's not missing," I said. "Let's just say her own boyfriend doesn't know where she is . . . "

"Well . . . Marco!" said my mother, rolling her eyes.

"Her videos have vanished from the internet."

"Those videos!" said my mother, rolling her eyes.

"Her apartment's been ransacked, and the last time I heard from her, she was afraid for her life."

"Ransacked!" said my mother, rolling her eyes. "I wish you wouldn't use overblown words and phrases like 'ransacked.' 'Afraid for her life.' Really, Austin."

"Drama, drama," my father said in a singsong mutter. He wagged his finger at me.

Then Dad sipped his coffee and Mom stirred her tea, and the silence was unbearably awkward again. Who the hell were these people? I asked myself. I mean, really. Were they inhuman monsters willing to let their cult leader slaughter their own children in order to bring about "The Orosgo Age," as he called it? Were we nothing compared to that bastard's utopia?

There were plenty of things I thought of asking them then, plenty of information I would have liked to know. For instance: Orosgo had told me a strange, dreamlike tale about a cowled man who had sat with him through the night in his dacha back in Russia many years ago. Somehow, in Orosgo's mind at least, he had made some kind of deal with Cowl Guy, and now Cowl Guy had shown up to collect his end of the bargain. Orosgo needed to find the manuscript *Another Kingdom* or suffer some sort of consequence. That was the gist of the story anyway, as far as I could make it out. It was all pretty unclear.

Did my parents know anything about this? Did it refer to anything real or was it just an old psychopath's paranoid fantasy? I would have liked to ask, but somehow I couldn't get the words out. I didn't have the energy to stand there listening to them lie and mumble vague inanities that trailed off into another awkward silence just like this one. What was the point?

I cut my losses, took one more slug of coffee, then set the mug on the counter with a clunk.

"Well . . . " I said.

"Going so soon?" said my father hopefully.

"Let me just wash up and I'll be gone," I said.

The rents exchanged an unreadable look at that.

"Well, I should probably head up to my study and do some work then," my father muttered. But he didn't move.

And my mother said, "Yes, I really must write some emails." But she didn't move either.

So I moved. "Well . . . " I said.

Then I walked out of the kitchen to search the damned house.

16

I WENT STRAIGHT TO MY SISTER'S BEDROOM. HER presence, like mine, had been all but erased from the childhood manse. Her room, like mine, like every room, had been scrubbed of personality and redecorated with the homey but faceless charm of a bed-and-breakfast. The only original furniture that remained was her bed and the old bureau with its big mirror on the opposite wall. I peeked under the bed and rummaged briefly through the bureau drawers, but I knew there would be nothing there. And I knew exactly where to look next.

When she was little, Riley had had the odd habit of climbing into the odd house's odd storage closets and crawlspaces. She would go in there with a doll or by herself and do I never knew what and eventually—unnervingly—reappear in a different room, because some of the spaces were connected to some of the others through vents and such. I'd gone into one of these passages once to see what the attraction was, but it was dusty and cramped and unpleasant and made me claustrophobic, so I never really explored the whole network. Anyway, as Riley got older, she stopped going in as well.

I knew there was a nook in her closet, so I started there. I opened the door and found that my mother had appropriated the space for her own use. A lot of her old dinner-party dresses were hanging from the rod. As I pushed through them to the back, I caught the musty smell of her clinging to the cloth. The smell of Mom: it surrounded me. And yes, if you want to know, it made my heart hurt. All those warm memories I didn't have of a childhood I had never lived came back to me as if they were more than mere longing.

On the other side of Mom's dresses, at the back of the closet, down low, there was a little storage nook about the size of a suitcase. I got on my knees, then down on my stomach, and squirmed in. Sure enough, at the back, there was a narrow passage into the wall. I stuck my head in, then my hand. Then, grunting, I went in all the way.

It was as I remembered: unpleasant; claustrophobic. I could just barely squeeze my shoulders through the gap, and I had an immediate, panicky urge to squeeze right out again, if only to make sure I wasn't going to be stuck in there forever. But by the light filtering in from behind me, I could see that the passage went on quite a way. And I thought, if Riley really had left something for me, if I wasn't desperately kidding myself, this would've been the place for her to hide it.

So on I slithered. It felt like being back in the mousehole passage out of the monster's lair in Edgimond: fighting through the cramped corridor, sweating, grunting with exertion, breathlessly frightened of getting stuck. In a few more yards, I reached a crossroads where an air duct intersected with the crawlspace. The duct was larger, and it had vents that let in air and light, which was a relief.

With an effort, I craned my neck. I looked down the duct one way and then the other.

And I'll be damned. There it was.

There was a flat I-didn't-know-what lying on the duct floor near the second vent. The sight of it made my pulse quicken because, whatever it was, it seemed to have been positioned intentionally:

close to Riley's room, in a lit spot that made it easy to see. Riley had placed this thing where I might find it but where no one else ever would.

It was no easy business to maneuver my body around the corner into the duct, but I managed it. I crawled to the second vent and picked up the package.

It was an old DVD case—ancient, Jurassic. On the cover, there was a fuzzy picture of a haunted house silhouetted against a full moon and a tree branch. *Horror Mansion*—that was the title. Some low budget piece of crap, obviously. I snapped the case open. The DVD was still inside—and Riley, or someone, had scrawled some numbers on the shiny surface with a marker: a phone number.

I paused there a moment, thinking. *Horror Mansion*. The title seemed vaguely familiar. I felt I had seen the movie once, a long time ago. In fact, a scene came into my head. A small bedroom. A shelf. A lantern. A dead bird. That was all I could remember. If this was the clue Riley had left for me, I could not for the life of me fathom what it meant.

I had an idea then. I thought maybe I should touch the locket around my neck. It had reminded me of that night Riley was crying hysterically in her bed. That had led me to the book in her apartment. So maybe now it would remind me why I knew this movie, why Riley might have left it here.

My hand moved to my throat, but before I touched the locket, something happened. I heard something. Voices. My parents.

Well, this was weird. Extremely weird. I was upstairs. The vent looked out on the second-floor landing. I was pretty sure my parents were nowhere nearby. They had both said they were going to do some work. My father's study was in the queer little tower part of the house, and my mother's was down the hall from the kitchen. And yet—this is the weird part—their voices were as clear to me as if they were standing right next to me, speaking in my ear. It was one of those aural tricks. You know: the air duct, this part of the air duct, was in one of those hot spots where sound congregates from all over. It occurred to me that that explained why, when she was little, Riley always seemed to know stuff she wasn't supposed to know. She could climb in here and listen to us talking wherever we were.

"It's no use pretending there's a decision to make," my mother said. And this was also weird. Her voice was different than it usually was. Less vague. More sharp, more certain. "All the decisions were made long ago, Charles. It's the consequences we're dealing with now, that's all. And isn't that what a decision is, really, when you think about it? It's a commitment to the consequences."

"No doubt. No doubt," my father muttered. He sounded the same as always: distant, musing. "I was just remarking on the difficulty of it, that's all."

"Oh, I know. We're not unfeeling. Austin's a dear, dreamy fellow in his way. And we are his parents."

"Yes, there's all that. But I meant the wait, more than anything."

"Oh, well, the wait, yes. Waiting is always the worst part of everything, isn't it? But it won't be long. They should be here any minute."

"It's best this way, likely."

"Of course. Of course it is. We've worked so hard."

"The boy's going to get himself killed if he keeps on like this."

In response, my mother just said, "Mm."

Now by the time I got to that "*Mm,*" I was already plenty scared, but that "*Mm,*" that really terrified me. I mean, the moment I heard my mother talking about what a "*dear, dreamy fellow*" I was, I understood that she—that both of them—had sold me out. They had called Orosgo's minions to tell them I was here. That phrase "*they should be here any minute*"—that told me exactly how little time I had to get the hell out of there before the thugs arrived.

But when my father said I was likely to get myself killed? And when my mother answered with nothing but that "*mm . . .*" The impression I got was that Dear Old Mom knew something about what was going to happen next, something that Dear Old Dad hadn't quite figured out yet. Dear Old Dad may have been in denial, but it was pretty obvious that Dear Old Mom knew the truth: namely, Dear Old Me was about to go missing for good.

So much for coming home. Time to hit the road.

I STUFFED THE DVD box into my waistband. The duct was too narrow for me to turn around in and backing up seemed too slow, so I crawled forward, hoping to find an exit up ahead.

I did find one—but not soon enough.

I scrambled along the duct to the end of the landing. Took a tight turn there into an empty storage space. In the empty storage space, I found a trapdoor. I pushed the trapdoor and it creaked open a crack. I was able to work my feet around and press them down and kick the trap open the whole way. I lowered myself to the landing. The second my feet touched the floor, I took off, running.

I reached the stairs and grabbed the newel, swung myself around and went thundering down. But the moment I reached the living room, I knew my time was up. Through a window onto the front of the house, I saw a great big dark blue Cadillac Escalade pull to the curb and stop. As I peered out, two large men exited the car, one from each front door. It was the driver who caught my attention.

Yeah, he was a bad man, a dangerous man. I could see it at a glance. His whole bearing spoke of competence, professionalism, and a blithe indifference to human suffering. The way he walked, the little smile on his lips, the way he casually pulled his jacket shut and buttoned it to hide the gun in the holster on his belt—everything about him told me he had done terrible things and done them well and done them for a living. Slick, I named him in my mind, because that's what he was. Tall, lean, fit, with a long, cruel, handsome face.

His sandy hair was combed back but dry as if the wind were blowing it. His suit was blue like his Cadillac, and his tie was red like blood. He wore tinted glasses but they weren't dark. You could see his eyes through them. They were witty eyes but mean.

The guy with him was black, mustached, broad-shouldered, tall, and thick like a football player. He was the muscle. It was Slick who would do the thinking for both of them.

They hadn't parked in the driveway, so if I could get to Riley's Volks, I might still be able to escape. I'd have to run out the back door and sneak around to the front but with a little luck, I might pull it off.

I dashed to the back of the room. Just as I reached the archway at the far end, I heard the rap at the kitchen door, metal against glass, a ringed finger rapping the door's sidelight. Slick was knocking.

"Coming," my mother sang out—sang out casually as she went to open the door for my executioner.

That casual sing-song tone of hers: it went into me like a dagger. My mother! Dazed with the implications, I left the living room and stumbled down a single stair into a mudroom. The mudroom door led to the backyard. I seized hold of the knob and ripped the door open.

And I let out a strangled curse. And froze. Because there—wavery through a fantastical haze—there was Hamarta waiting for me in the foyer of the mansion in the forest of Edgimond—waiting with that strangely bright smile that had made me believe she was luring me into a trap.

Behind me, I heard my mother open the kitchen door.

17

"WELL, YOU MADE VERY GOOD TIME," I HEARD MY mother say. She sounded as if she were greeting a dinner guest, instead of the assassin sent to slaughter her son.

And it wrung my heart to hear her. It did. I felt as if I were swirling into the center of a vortex, a tumult of memories and associations spinning around me. I searched the mind-chaos for some moment to hold onto, some instance in my past of maternal warmth or comfort, something that would make me disbelieve what I was hearing with my own ears. But I couldn't find one. Not one.

How had I hidden this from myself so long? How had I never known what my mother was, what my youth was, my life was? How could I be so surprised at what was happening now?

I heard Slick answer her: "Where is the lad?" A smooth, self-confident voice. A voice like the look of the man.

"Upstairs, I think," my mother said. "I know he hasn't gone out. His car is still in the drive. Anyway, I would have heard him."

I stood where I was, still frozen, Hamarta still waiting for me through the veil of transition, waiting and smiling that possibly malevolent smile, while the killer stood at the kitchen door and my mother—my mother!—betrayed me to him.

"Okay, Mrs. Lively," said Slick.

"Doctor," she corrected him. "Dr. Fleischer-Lively actually."

"Doctor. Right. Maybe you ought to go someplace quiet until this is over, ma'am."

"Yes," said my mother thoughtfully. "But you won't do anything that will disturb my husband, will you? He's very distraught. Austin is our son, remember."

"Oh sure, I understand," said Slick. I could almost hear him grinning an I-understand grin. "Nothing bad's going to happen here."

"Of course. Well, if you'll excuse me, I'll just . . . "

"Yeah, you go back to what you were doing. My colleague and I will be gone before you know it."

I heard the kitchen door close. Slick was inside the house. And still I stood there, between the two worlds. Edgimond and its dangers were crowding in on my reeling consciousness now. The storm in the forest, the heavy atmosphere of evil, my sense that the wizard Curtin was rushing to the scene to destroy me, my growing suspicion that Hamarta was luring me into Curtin's trap . . . it all came back to me.

And at the same time: footsteps. Slick. His "colleague." If they found me, I would vanish without a trace, without even a mother's tears to mark my passing.

I stepped through the mudroom door.

My life had become so full of bizarre moments, I don't know where to place this one in the bizarre scheme of things, but it was bizarre all right. For a second, I was halfway through the door of the forest mansion. The savage and somehow malicious wind was making the whole tree line sway violently back and forth, like weeds in a rising sea. Forked lightning snapped across the sky like a dragon's tongue.

Then, the next second, I was in the foyer of the house and the door shut heavily behind me. With that, the raging storm outside was silent, completely silent. The tumult in the air was utterly gone. It seemed this house was so thoroughly sealed that no sound from the outside world could get into it, not even a whisper. I could see the rain streaking the windows, and I could see the wind lashing the rain, but the noise of it did not reach me. Instead, I found myself in a warm and lavish entranceway leading out past a grand staircase into a majestic front hall.

I gaped, bewildered and disoriented. Not only had I just transitioned from one world into another, I had simultaneously transitioned from being a man with a relatively normal screwed-up childhood, to a man who had grown up in the pulsing belly of homicidal darkness. *Horror Mansion*, indeed.

Blinking through my shock, I turned to face Hamarta.

There was, I saw now, nothing sinister in her smile. Nothing at all. I must have imagined it. It was the same warm, wifely, almost maternal smile that had drawn me to her in the first place. *I'll take care of you. I'll feed you. Sweetheart.* I was getting paranoid, that's all.

She beckoned me.

"Well, come on, darling," she said. "Aren't you hungry?"

I was. I hadn't eaten anything since the cheese sandwich in Berkeley the night before. Hard to keep track of these things with the times and places always shifting back and forth. But yes, as sorrowful as I was, as shattered as I was by my mother's murderous betrayal, I was hungry too.

So I walked with Hamarta down the long hall. And it was a wondrous hall now that I saw it up close. The gold and purple runner on the floor was lit by lofty candelabras standing on finely crafted brass stands. The ceiling was high, high above me, vaulted and hung with magnificent chandeliers. The walls were decorated with painted portraits: a smooth-faced knight, resting his hand on his sword hilt; an impish woman in an elfin jerkin, standing legs akimbo beneath some trees; a great black-bearded brute with a bar of iron in his hand. They watched me pass with baleful gazes, as if they were sorry to see me go.

Then Hamarta said to me, “This way, sweetheart,” and I turned and followed her around a corner.

There was another long hall with two huge, carved wooden doors standing at the end of it. Hamarta looked up at me as we walked toward them.

“Are you all right?” she said with sweet concern. “You seem upset.”

“Well, my mother just sent a killer after me and there’s a wizard riding on the wind to destroy me and I don’t know what this place is or what I’m doing here or even who I am really, who I ever was . . . so yeah, I guess I am a little upset . . . ” was what I didn’t say.

What I did say was: “Upset? No. No, I’m fine.”

She narrowed her eyes and her lips quirked, and she said, “Hm,” as if she didn’t believe me. She took my arm and pressed against me so I could feel the soft side of her breast and smell the clean incense of her hair. “Well, whatever’s bothering you, it’s going to be all right now. I promise. This is a place for you to rest and forget your troubles and grow strong again. You need someone to take care of you, Austin, that’s all.”

I did, it was true. I did need someone to take care of me. And a place to rest and sort out my thoughts and throw off this sorrow and grow steady and strong again. I needed all that, and I needed the feel of her softness against me and the smell of her hair. But how did she know my name? Had I told her? I couldn’t remember. But she really did feel soft.

We continued along the hall together.

“Isn’t it nicer in here than it was outside?” she asked me in a gently teasing tone. “Warm, not cold? Dry, not wet? Safe, not dangerous? Aren’t things a little better already. Just a little? No?” She sounded like a mother trying to coax a smile from a sulky child.

We went on walking. Which was strange. We should have reached those big double doors by now, but they were still a long way off.

"I wish you would confide in me," she said, still teasing, coaxing. "Tell me your troubles. Let me make them better."

I know I should have seen the danger. I think I did see it in one part of my brain. But I was so sad about what had happened at home. And I had been so alone these last days, without even an email or a media post or a voice on the phone. And the smell of her hair and the softness of her breast and the kindness of her voice—they lulled me.

"It's hard to explain," I told her. "I'm trying to find my way . . . "

"Across the Eleven Lands, I know. Everyone who comes to this house is on some silly quest or other. Fretting about it. Worried. Troubled. Their foreheads all like this," she said and she looked up at me and wrinkled her forehead and made a funny expression. Then she laughed.

"What do you mean 'everyone'?" I asked her.

I was glancing down at her as I asked, down at her face, and I thought I saw something, a movement, as if her skin had rippled unnaturally. But it was over in a second, less than a second. I studied her closely, but I didn't see the movement again.

"People will literally kill themselves with these quests. They really will," she went on. "They'll fret and worry themselves right into the grave. Which makes absolutely no sense when you think about it. What do you have if you don't have your life? Nothing. Nothing at all. So what on earth could be worth dying for? It makes no sense."

In the depths of my dejection, I barely understood what she was saying. I just liked the sound of her voice and the touch of her. And I was glad to be inside out of the storm.

She looked up at me again, up from under her lashes. How beautiful she was. Even in my sadness, I found her incredibly alluring.

"Now I'm sure your quest is very, very important," she said in that teasing tone. "But I think it can wait at least until the storm is over, don't you?"

I opened my mouth to answer but I didn't answer because my thoughts were all jumbled. I didn't want to go out in that storm again, that was for sure. But then, wasn't the storm bringing the wizard? Shouldn't I be out there running away from him as fast as I could?

I lifted my gaze from her and looked down the hall at the doors, still so far away. Why were they still so far? It was confusing. I glanced back down at Hamarta to ask her about it, and I caught that movement again, a ripple on one part of her face. Again, it was gone in a moment and her skin was normal. At the same time, for a second, I thought I caught a smell coming off her, or the faint suggestion of a smell—unpleasant, like food gone bad. Had I done the right thing, following her in here?

"Well, what choice did you have?" she asked me.

"What?" I said, startled. Was she reading my thoughts now? Or had I spoken the thought aloud? I wasn't sure.

"You have to rest at some point, sweetheart. You can't just keep questing forever. You have to rest. You have to. This place, this house—think of it like an inn. A warm, welcoming inn along the road. A home away from home."

The words stirred up my anguish, and I blurted out to her, "I have no home, Hamarta!"

Then, suddenly, we were at the end of the hall. The huge double doors were towering over us. Gargoyles carved into the medallions on their panels peered down at us. They looked like they were going to drool on our heads from their wide-open fangy mouths.

I stopped and Hamarta stopped with me. I glanced from the gargoyles to her. And this time, I was certain of it: the skin of her face rippled as if something was crawling underneath it. The sight made me grimace with disgust.

Hamarta only smiled, that sweet, sweet smile. She opened her mouth to speak—and a beetle crawled out over her lips, scrambled down her chin, dropped to the runner and skittered away. As I stared, my gorge rising, another bug tumbled out from beneath her hairline. It likewise fell to the floor.

"What the hell?" I whispered.

But at that, there was a resounding rush of air, and the double doors swung in and opened with a crash. Reflexively, I started and turned to look.

We were standing on the brink of a gigantic dining hall, a place alive with voices and aromas and activity. And when I say gigantic, I mean vast. So vast. I couldn't help but stand and stare at it, amazed.

There was a great wooden dining table in the center of the room. It seemed to go on forever until it faded into a shadowy distance. The fireplaces on either side of it seemed as tall as airplane hangars, and the flames in them were crackling, dancing, sparking as they devoured logs the size of trees. Enormous chandeliers hung over the table at intervals, and the flames from their candles and the flames from the hearths lit a scene of fabulous celebration.

Men and women in fanciful medieval clothing sat in heavy oaken chairs. The bright blues and reds and greens of their outfits and gowns seemed to light the room as brightly as the flames did. They were eating with gusto, dishing food from the bowls and carving boards laid out before them: fowl and beef and pork and large cooked vegetables and mashed potatoes. They were downing mugs of ale and laughing and talking, the women touching the men's arms and batting their lashes at them, the men showing off their fine white teeth in appreciative smiles.

And the smells! The smells were warm and rich and wonderful. They made my stomach growl and my mouth water. And the noise that rushed out at me like traffic was so full of jolliness that, for a second, my own dejection lifted, and I felt a powerful desire to forget my troubles and join the party. The storm-swept scene through the gigantic windows to my left and right—the trees swaying, the lightning flashing, the rain slanting in a steady downpour out of the boiling black clouds above—only made the indoor fires seem warmer, the smells more delicious, the fellowship all the more fine.

Confused, I looked back at Hamarta—but Hamarta was gone! Totally gone. Looking down at the place where she had stood beside me, I saw nothing but a large cluster of beetles and roaches and worms scrambling and squiggling off the runner to disappear under the baseboards of the wall. I felt that rise of disgust in my throat again. But the next second, the bugs too were gone as if they had never been there.

I hesitated. I didn't know what to do. That is, I did know: it seemed obvious I ought to get out of there—get out now, right away. This had to be some mental trick of Curtin's, didn't it? Yes, it had to be. But somehow . . . I don't know. I just couldn't think about leaving anymore. The storm was so strong and my life was so miserable and the smells and the sounds of gaiety coming out of the dining room were so appealing. And when I looked at the hallway behind me, it seemed like such a long way back to the front door.

I felt reckless. Indifferent to consequences. I thought: *What the hell?* and took one step across the threshold. I thought, *I can always go back. A man's got to eat, hasn't he?*

And then the great double doors slammed shut, and somehow, I understood the thing had been decided.

I drifted deeper into the room in a gormless haze. A serving girl took hold of my arm. She was wearing a simple brown dress that showed off her wonderful cleavage. With a bright smile and flashing eyes, she tossed her lavish raven hair and led me to the table.

She sat me down beside a handsome, elegant, noble-looking fellow. He looked familiar, but I couldn't imagine why. Maybe it was just that he looked like a knight from one of the stories I liked to read when I was a kid.

He slapped my back as I lowered myself into the chair. "Dig in, lad!" he said in a bold, friendly voice. He gestured toward a huge roasted bird on a platter right in front of me.

The delectable smell of the fowl filled my nose, and suddenly, I felt like I was starving. I grabbed a leg and wrestled it off the creature and started eating ravenously.

"What brings you here?" the knightly man shouted to me over the noise of laughter and conversation. "What's your quest?"

I had to swallow a great gob of dark meat before I could answer. "I have to cross the Eleven Lands. Find the emperor. Restore the queen to the throne in Galiana."

He nodded, impressed. "Sounds like a good one. 'Let wisdom reign' and all that."

I spoke around a fresh mouthful. "Exactly."

"If you can figure out what wisdom is."

He laughed. But I frowned. That was pretty much exactly what my mother had said. *What is wisdom?* I had no answer. So I just kept eating.

"Myself, I set out to slay the Rapist Troll of The Westlands," said the knightly man. "Barely a virgin left unviolated by the time I got there. The bastard needs beheading, that's for sure."

As he lifted a forkful of potatoes to his mouth, he patted the hilt of his sword with his other hand to punctuate his point. And with that, I recognized him. He was the knight from the portrait in the hall outside! Which struck me as immensely odd. I mean, if he was here, now, tonight, when had the portrait been painted?

"How long have you been here?" I asked him.

But before he could answer, a sudden deafening boom shook the entire hall. The conversation and laughter tailed off. The diners glanced nervously toward the far end of the table where it trailed out of sight in misty obscurity. The place was almost silent, except for the snapping hearth-flames.

I followed the gazes of the others. Looked off into the murky distance. There was nothing to see there—nothing except shadows—shadows and, right at the edge of the visible, a boy, a little boy, about—I don't know—eight or nine years old or so. He was dressed in a simple servant's uniform, an off-white shirt and a brown leather vest. He was standing with a napkin draped across his arm. Staring at me, very serious, very still. He reminded me of the ghosts of the unborn children in the forest. As with the knight, I had the feeling that I knew him, but I couldn't place him.

"What . . . what was that?" I said to the knightly man beside me. He was busy eating again. Everyone at the table had started eating and chatting again. The nervous moment had passed. "That noise, that bang. What was that?"

"Hm. Oh. That," he said. "You know: the time."

"The time?"

"It's almost up. Passing anyway. Night falling."

He gestured to one of the large windows that flanked the flaming hearth across from us. I looked and saw that he was right. The darkness of the storm had taken on a deeper darkness. The day was ending.

"What happens when night falls?" I asked him. But the knightly man had turned away from me. He was chatting to the woman next to him: a smiling young brunette with glittering eyes.

I looked to my other side and was amazed to see another figure from the portraits in the hall: the elfish woman who had been depicted beneath the trees. She had short, pixie-cut hair and small, pointy features. She was gnawing on a large bird's wing.

"Excuse me," I said to her.

She was less friendly than the knightly man. She barely spared me a glance. "Mm?" she said—and went on eating.

"What was that bang we just—?"

And as if to finish my sentence, another boom rocked the dining hall. This one was louder than the first. It made the cups and dinnerware rattle on the scarlet and gold tablecloth. Again, the conversation dimmed. Faces turned, glances went into the shadows as if everyone expected something to emerge from them at any moment. I peered into the obscurity. I was beginning to grow anxious. The table talk was already starting to resume, but I could've sworn I heard a strange growl rumble underneath it. Strange—and yet familiar. A sound that made my balls turn to ice.

"If you don't get out by dawn, you'll be stuck in this house forever."

The words were spoken softly right into my ear. And surprised, I realized I recognized the voice. It was the voice of the boy in the cave, the invisible ghost boy who had guided me out to the woods and then vanished. What the hell was going on here?

I swung around to speak to him.

It was the same boy I'd seen a moment ago: the boy in the servant's outfit with the napkin over his arm, the one I felt I recognized from somewhere. I couldn't imagine how he had crossed the distance between us so swiftly, but he was already moving away, back around the end of the long table, back to his position near the border of the far shadows. As he crossed in front of me, he made a subtle gesture with his head: *This way. Come with me. Quickly.*

I didn't move, not right away. I wasn't sure what I should do. True, he had led me out of the Eunuch Zombie Cave of Female Sacrifice, but was he really on my side?

On the other hand, that booming noise, that weird but familiar growl, that sense that something was coming—and it wasn't something good . . . Well, I was worried. Frightened even. I decided the boy was right: I should go.

I had just started to push out of my chair when the elfin woman next to me said, "You're not going to go with *him*, are you?" She continued gnawing on her bird wing as she spoke, as if she hardly cared what my answer was.

"He said I'd get stuck here if I didn't leave before dawn," I told her.

She snorted. Glanced at me with her tongue exploring her cheek—that sort of disdainful glance you get from girls who think they're more of a man than you are. I'd seen that glance a lot in my life.

"What was your quest?" she said, lifting her chin in challenge.

"Cross the Eleven Lands. Find the emperor. Free Galiana."

"Mm." She wagged her head, reluctantly impressed. "Not bad. I was searching for my father, me. He'd made a bargain with some demons when I was sick with fever. They cured me but then came for payment and carried him off to become one of them."

Still worried, I glanced at the darkening windows, then into the shadows at the far end of the room. I was growing more antsy by the minute. I felt I ought to get up, get out, follow the boy. But somehow, I felt compelled to ask her, "Did you find him? Your father?"

She shrugged and went on eating. "I got pretty far for a girl alone. When you're a girl, you have to be clever because you're not very strong. I tricked an ogre into a crevice, then got him to give up his gold in return for his freedom. Then I used the gold to buy a magic carriage that made me invisible as I traveled through the Children's Forest. That's the sort of thing I mean. Clever. A girl has to be."

"I guess she does," I said. "But . . . "

"But what?" She turned to stick her chin out at me aggressively, a bit of meat visible at the corner of her mouth. "You think you could've done better because you're a man?"

"No, but . . . "

"But, but, but," she echoed me, mocking. "I'll bet, bet, bet that ogre would've beat, beat, beat your butt, butt, butt until you went running home."

"How long have you been here?" I asked her.

"Oh, hell, who knows? Who counts the days anymore?"

"But what about your father?"

"My father's a big, strong man. He can take care of himself. Or if he can't, it's not on me, is it? He's the one who made the deal with the demons. Am I supposed to spend years out in the wind and rain on his account? I have my own life to live."

"So you came here to get out of the rain."

"It's more than just rain," she said.

"Yes, I know, but I mean, you came here for the warmth, for the food, the shelter."

"What if I did?"

"And then," I said, as the whole story revealed itself to me. "Then you didn't get out by dawn and so now you can't leave."

She shrugged again, eating again. "Quests!" she said, dismissively.

I studied her profile. "You look familiar to me," I said. "It's not just because of the portraits out in the hall. You. The knight. This whole place . . . the boy . . . everyone. It all looks familiar."

"Mm," she murmured, tearing off a fresh piece of gristle with her pearly teeth. "It's like that for everyone. Different for everyone. The house gets into your head. It is your head. That's what makes it so endlessly fascinating. The hallways alone go on and on. You can explore them forever."

I was about to answer, about to ask her what she meant, when a third boom sounded, much louder, much closer than the others. The entire table seemed to hop up off the floor and drop back down again. Conversation stopped cold. Everyone was silent. Everyone was glancing fretfully down the long table into the shadows. I saw the boy down there, and he was beckoning to me urgently. *Come. Come quickly.*

"This is the bad part, I admit," the elf-girl grumbled. "But it's only once a day, at sunset."

She was looking out the window across from us, a haunted look. I looked, too, and saw the night had almost fallen.

"I have to go," I said—as much to myself as to anyone.

"You're really going to follow him?" the girl repeated with a laugh. She gestured with her chin at the boy. "You can't trust him. He's the last person you should trust. He's the one who brought you here in the first place."

That made me hesitate again, but a second later: another crashing boom, really terrible this time, so loud it hurt my ears. The table rocked back and forth. The room shook. The windows rattled. I looked through the panes and saw the last light fading from the tumultuous sky.

I didn't know what to do. I only knew time was running out.

So I got up. I started moving to the head of the table. Reached it. Strode around it. Started heading down the length of it, past the fireplace, toward the far shadows, toward the edge of obscurity where the boy was standing. The boy continued to gesture at me urgently. *Come. Come.* I moved faster.

And I heard a roar from the shadows beyond.

Oh God, there was no mistaking that sound: the sound of countless women screaming in agony, all their voices blended into a single voice. Fear shot through my blood like acid.

I started running.

Too late.

The hideous dragon from the cave came charging out of the distant darkness, roaring for blood.

18

THE ROOM ERUPTED INTO PANIC. IT WAS AS IF THE appearance of the beast had taken everyone by complete surprise. The screams of pure terror from men and women both were heart-wrenching in their wild intensity. All the diners leapt from their seats. Everyone started fighting to get to the double doors behind me. A frightened mob of them rushed my way, clawing and climbing over one another, trampling the small and slow beneath their feet.

Me? I hurled myself against the wall, pressed close to it, trying to get out of the way of the fearful tide. I looked past the contorted, screaming faces of the people—people who had been dining with such pleasure and friendliness just seconds before. Beyond them, I saw the creature coming out of the nebulous distance and I realized: I had suppressed the true memory of the thing, the true image of how dreadful it was with its body made of dead bodies, a stitched-together atrocity. I had made myself forget its blood lust, its rage. How it had looked at me as it retreated from our last clash in the cave, that look that said we would meet again when the terms of battle were more to its liking. I knew that this—this bizarre house—must be the battlefield it had been waiting for. I'd walked right into it.

I glanced toward the double doors. The panicked diners had piled up against them. They were pounding on the wood, pulling at the handles. But the doors wouldn't budge. The screaming was growing louder, wilder, more pitiful. I saw the elfin girl, all her self-assurance dissolved, nothing on her face but the purest despair and dread. She reached out of the tumbling mob, fighting for breath and freedom. But the next second, she was clubbed back into the pile by the heavy fist of the knightly man. Then he, in turn, was trampled under the foot of a great black-bearded brute.

Throughout the riot, it was all like that. The women were being crushed beneath the men, the smaller men beneath the larger men, and even the largest men were weeping like babies as they scratched uselessly at the doors or stood paralyzed with their fingers to their lips and blubbered in fear of the onrushing monster.

Well, I could see there was no point in joining the mob. There was nowhere to run, no way out of here. The panicked crowd had rushed past me, but I was still pressed where I had been against the wall. From there, I turned to face the creature.

It came toward me at a gallop. The thunder of its footsteps made the great dining hall shake as if an earthquake had hit it. Its furious, ravening roar—the roar composed somehow of the cries of its victims—seemed to make the very air vibrate. I thought I could smell its breath, stinking of death. It was barreling toward the edge of the shadows with such ferocity, I doubted anything could stand in its way.

But I had to try. I reached for my sword.

My hand closed—on nothing. A fresh gout of liquid fear shot through my veins. I looked down. No sword. No armor coating my body. Somehow, the magic of Shadow Wood, the magic of Queen Elinda's gifts, was not working here.

The house gets into your head. It is your head.

Yes, that was it. I couldn't mentally connect with the magic. I couldn't complete the circuit that made the sword appear. I looked at the onrushing monster, helpless and unarmed. I felt my bowels turn to water. The thing was going to tear me to pieces.

The dragon burst from the shadows into the fiery light of the hall. It would have been on me in the next second, but there were still a few bodies between us, blocking its way. It stopped to devour them. It seized a woman who'd been struck to the ground, lifted her in its forepaws and ripped her in half with its teeth like she was a sheet of paper. I won't try to describe the scream the upper half of her gave as the beast consumed it or the scream of the small man on his knees nearby, gibbering insanely as he begged for life until the beast took him, too, and swallowed him in three great bites. Most awful of all was the way their wild-eyed, shrieking faces reappeared moments after their deaths, became part of the creature's body after it had eaten them, one face on a thigh, one face and torso on a shoulder.

Horrible. It was horrible.

Only a few more diners, crippled by the riot, remained between the creature and me. They howled in helpless terror as the thing steadily thumped toward them.

And as it did, a familiar hand slipped into mine. I looked down.

The boy!

"This way," he said.

He drew me along the wall, closer to where the ravenous creature was dismembering another of the hobbled diners. I could barely move my legs to follow him. I could barely turn my eyes away from the blood-soaked spectacle. The whole room was a cacophony of screaming, a jumble of bodies cowering, waiting helplessly for their turn to die in slow, violent agony.

Holding my hand in one of his, the little boy pressed a panel in the wall and a narrow passage opened. He pulled me into it and shut the panel behind him.

Suddenly, it was quiet. The screaming continued, but it was dim, as if far away. The boy began to sidle down the narrow corridor, clutching my hand. For a moment, I held him back.

"What about the others?" I asked him breathlessly. "We might save a few."

"We can't," the boy said. "They can't come with us. This is what happens to them. Every night at sunset."

He kept tugging my hand, so I followed after. Down the corridor to another swinging panel where we pushed out through another secret doorway into a grander hall.

As I tumbled out, my legs gave way. I fell to my knees and retched painfully, vomiting onto the scarlet runner. I was all nausea, no thought. It was long moments before I recovered my senses.

Then, trembling on my hands and knees, I looked up from my own mess to where the boy stood over me, gazing down at me with his round, serious face.

"Will it come after us?" I asked him in a small voice.

He nodded solemnly. He looked as frightened as I felt. "First it will kill them all. Then it will come for you."

I stared at him, remembering the chaos and the screaming and the fear on the diners' faces. "It'll kill all of them?" I said.

He nodded again. "Every night. That's what it's here for."

"Every . . . " I gagged again and choked back vomit. I rose onto my knees and wiped my mouth with the back of my hand. Then I stood up slowly, unsteadily. I remembered what the elfin girl had said: *This is the bad part.* "They must know," I murmured, amazed. "They must know it's coming. They sit there eating like that, but they know."

Once again, the boy nodded. "I don't think they let themselves remember how bad it is. But yes, they know."

"How bad it is," I whispered, my voice breaking. "It's hell. We're in hell. This house: it's hell. Can't they ever get out of here? Ever?"

"Not once they've stayed here through the night. If you can't escape before morning comes, you can never leave. That's Curtin's curse."

I was beginning to recover a little—a little. My mind was beginning to work again—a little. Whatever happened, I mustn't get stuck in here past dawn. Even if I went through a door that only took me back to California, I would have to find some way to stay there forever.

My eyes must have been the size of saucers when I faced the boy again. "Which way is the exit?" I asked him.

He shook his head. "I don't know. You'll have to find it."

"It's a house. How big can it be? Where's the nearest door?"

"I don't know."

"Damn it, boy!"

"Only you can find it. That's the magic, Curtin's magic," he said.

"I thought his magic only worked in a person's mind," I snarled at him.

"This is your mind," said the boy quietly—and he faded away into nothingness.

Open-mouthed, I watched him vanish. I saw him grow transparent, then grow dim.

"No, wait! Wait!" I cried out. "You can't just leave me here!"

But he was gone. I was alone. Lost. With the time till morning ticking away. I wanted to weep. I wanted to fall to my knees, clutching my hair in panic.

But I couldn't. Not now. Not here. Not in this house. I had to get out before dawn. I looked around me. Like I said: how big could the place be?

Big. It was big. It was big and crazy; the layout made no sense.

The first thing I did was move down the large hall to the nearest window. I passed by candelabras and more portraits. I saw the sad painted faces looking down at me and realized I recognized many of them. They had been around the table in the great dining hall. But even before that, I had known them. From stories I had read. From stories I had written. From memories and daydreams . . .

It made my stomach churn to think what was happening to them now, what would happen to them every nightfall, the fate that would hang over them through every day they were stuck inside this house—every day, forever.

And me, too, if I didn't get out.

I reached the window and looked through. It was full dark now. I couldn't see a thing but my reflection on the glass. I pressed my nose against the image of my own face on the chilly pane, trying to see. Then, a long flickering streak of lightning shot east to west across the sky. I saw a courtyard, walled all the way around. Grass and walkways and a stone statue of the wizard on a pedestal at the center. But no way out.

I backed away, licking my lips, breathing hard, thinking. I didn't want to just run around the square of the closed courtyard forever. But if I went to the end of the hall and turned left, maybe I could find another way.

I ran. Down to the end of the hall. Around the corner.

I came into another hall, exactly like the last. Candelabras, portraits, windows looking out into the night. I stepped to one of the windows, pressed my nose against it. Lightning flashed.

"Shit," I whispered.

Another closed courtyard out there. Another statue of Curtin at the center. No exit.

The hallways alone go on and on, the elfin girl had said. *You can explore them forever.*

I started running. Down the hall, around the corner. Stopped at the window. Looked out. Cursed. Ran. It didn't matter which way I turned, how far I went. Every corner I came around, it was the same. Another hall. Another window. Another flash of lightning showing another courtyard with another statue of Curtin and no way out.

I don't know how long I ran like that in a growing panic of desperation. Ten minutes? Twenty? An hour? Two? My already queasy stomach was cramping painfully. I was gasping for breath.

Finally, exhausted, I came to a stop, bent over, panting, my hands on my knees. Somewhere, I heard a clock chime the hour. Eight chimes. The sickening realization rose inside me like a green cloud: This—this running, this searching, this maze of sameness—this could go on until morning. After that, I would be stuck here forever, cursed forever like the other diners, to be devoured by that creature night after night after night.

And just then, the floor trembled underneath me. I let out a little cry of fear and stood up straight, trembling. I listened. I heard a distant reverberation.

Boom.

It was the beast. Its heavy footsteps. Distant now but getting louder, getting closer.

It was coming for me.

19

DESPAIR WASHED OVER ME. I STOOD THERE HELPLESS and pressed my head between the heels of my hands. What was I going to do? I could hear the monster's booming footsteps growing slowly, steadily, louder, closer every second. Every instinct of my body told me to run, but where? If I just continued to go down corridor after corridor, around corner after corner, lost in this impossible labyrinth, eventually either the beast would run me down or dawn—and Curtin's curse—would catch up with me.

I needed to try something different. But what? With the booming footsteps filling my brain, I could hardly think. But really, there wasn't that much to think about. There was only one option.

I went to the window. Unlatched it. Opened it. Climbed out.

I fell onto wet grass and scrambled to my feet again. The rain lashed me, icy cold, stinging my face. The storm had not subsided, not even a little. It was still at its raging, furious height. Without the weird muffling effect of the house, the thunder was deafening, and within the thunder, I thought I could hear laughter now, the wizard's rasping laughter, as he came after me, as he closed in. When a broad bolt of lightning split the sky in two, I half-expected to see him bearing down on me on a winged black horse, his starry robe flung out behind him. Then darkness closed over the scene again, and I was lost in the storm, alone.

I scanned the courtyard, holding up my hand to shield my eyes from the whipping wind and rain. I was looking for a way out but there was none. I peered through the windows across the way. At first, all I saw were the corridors inside, one after another, each the same. But then, I stopped. I noticed something. At one corner of one wall, one room seemed slightly different. There were French doors, a higher roof, a subtle change in the quality of the light within.

I started across the court, slipping and skidding, falling to one knee on the wet grass, the rain driving down on me, the wind blowing, the thunder crashing. The statue of Curtin watched me from its pedestal, its red eyes blank and staring. I gave the creepy thing a wide berth as I went around it. But when I looked back over my shoulder, it was—impossibly—still facing me, still watching me go.

I made it to the French doors. Pulled them open. Stepped though. There was a great gust of wind and the doors slammed shut behind me.

I had come into a ballroom. It made no sense that it was here, but here it was. It was big and hollow. Quiet. Lit by an uncanny multicolored light that streamed in through an enormous stained glass rose window on one wall.

Dripping rainwater, I moved across the checkered marble floor to its center. I turned this way and that, looking for an exit. I didn't see one.

Then, I seemed to sense someone looking at me from above. I lifted my eyes. There was an enormous mural painted on the vast ceiling.

I clutched my throat. I heard myself make an awful gurgling noise.

My God, I thought. *My God.*

I will never, ever tell what I saw up there, not to anyone. The painting, quavering and alive in the colored light, was obscene and disgusting, beyond the power of language to describe. Even the lowest filmmakers of Hollywood had never debased the human imagination with images like these. The worst, most violent, most sick and perverted film would have been only a suggestion, a polite symbol, of what was painted up there.

As I stared up in horror, the elfin girl's words returned to me again: *The house gets into your head. It* is *your head.*

No, I thought, frozen where I stood. *Not my head. Not my mind. Not mine.*

And then—the dragon's footstep: *boom.* Not far away. Close. He was suddenly right outside the ballroom.

The colored light from the rose window dimmed. The beast's shadow rose up behind the stained glass.

The creature had found me.

"This way."

The boy—the boy's voice. I spun toward the sound, trying to find him. All I saw was an empty corner of the room. The boy himself was nowhere to be seen.

There was another booming footstep. The ballroom quaked.

Then: one terrifying roar that contained a thousand dying screams—and the rose window shattered and the beast came plunging through.

Which way to run? The French doors just led out into the courtyard, back into the labyrinth. But in the corner from which the boy had spoken, I could see no exit at all.

There was no time to think it through. The boy had saved me twice. I ran toward the empty corner. The dragon thundered after me with unimaginable speed. The vast room shook with its footsteps, filled with the shrieking chorus of its roar. I looked over my shoulder and saw its huge body bearing down on me—its patchwork body made of all the bodies of the diners it had devoured, their shredded flesh still dripping gore. I looked ahead and saw—nothing—an empty corner. No way out.

I reached the wall. Only then did I see the iron handle anchored in the floor. A trap door! I had about three seconds before the beast was on top of me.

I grabbed the handle. Hauled up on it. The heavy trap lifted, revealing a stairway underneath. The dragon loomed above me, immense and terrible. Its shadow covered me. Its screaming voices and its hot and rotten breath washed over me.

I hurled myself into the open trap.

The door of my parents' house clicked quietly shut behind me, and I was in the backyard, my childhood yard.

I EXPERIENCED ONE split second of unutterable relief. To be in the light of day, to be out of that mansion, away from that monster, to be in the real world of grass and trees and blue California sky—it felt for that single instant like pure salvation.

Then I remembered: Slick, the assassin. He was right behind me. My mother had betrayed me to him. My whole life was a miserable, twisted lie. Even worse, it was a miserable, twisted lie that would be cut short if I didn't manage to escape. The relief drained out of me and the fear came rushing back.

What the hell had I been planning to do here? Oh yes, I remembered. I ducked my head so that Slick wouldn't see me pass by the windows. Keeping low like that, I ran around the side of my parents' strange, storybook house, hoping to make my way back to my car.

I reached the house's corner. Knelt in the grass to keep below the window, out of Slick's line of sight. I peeked around to the front yard. There was Slick's car—the dark blue Escalade—parked at the curb. And there, beyond it, in the driveway, was my car, Riley's Volks.

And there—*crap!*—there was Slick's partner, too, the big football player type, the muscle man. He was standing at the kitchen door, slowly scanning the front yard, looking for me in case I slipped out of Slick's grasp.

My mind was still reeling, still filled with images of the dragon about to lunge down at me in the ballroom. Somehow that made Slick and the muscle man seem less terrible than they were. They would kill me just as dead if they caught me, but they were only men, not monsters. I could fight men. At least, I felt like I could.

I took courage. I got ready to make my move.

It was like one of those prison escape scenes in a video game—you know, where the searchlights are passing over the yard and you have to time your run so you don't get caught in the beam. Except in this case, the searchlight was the muscle man's gaze passing back and forth over the front lawn—and I only had one turn to get it right with no extra lives.

I waited. I drew back as the muscle man's eyes went over the place where I was crouched behind the corner of the house. When I peeked out again, he was turning away to look up the street.

I took off, crouched low, running.

The muscle man was just turning back my way when I reached the Escalade and hid behind it. Now I could creep the length of the car unseen. When I peeked out from behind the front fender, I saw the Passat in the driveway, close now, only about five steps away. Yes, but how could I open the door and get in and start the engine without the muscle man hearing me? I thought maybe I would have to escape on foot.

But then I got a break, a lucky break. Look, it had to happen sometime.

Slick called from inside the house: "Hey! Moses!"

The muscle man answered him in a deep booming voice: "Yo!" He turned his back on me, opened the kitchen door and stepped inside my parents' house. I heard him shout again, "Yo!"

I didn't hesitate. I ran to the Passat, pressing the button on the key to unlock it as I went. I yanked the car door open and dropped behind the wheel and started the engine.

The Volks was already out of the driveway, already swinging around, tires screeching, when Moses the Muscle Man heard it and came running back outside, shouting, "Hey! Hey!"

I hit the gas and shot off down the road.

20

DID OROSGO'S GOONS CHASE ME? I DIDN'T KNOW. IT didn't matter. This was my home turf, my childhood neighborhood. A map of every turn and side street was etched on my nerve endings. In seconds, I had lost myself in the spaghetti tangle of winding roads—and I didn't stop until I was on the far side of the hills, deep into Cragmont.

There, on a broad stretch of Arlington Road, I found a mini-mall I remembered from my youth: a little line of quaint-looking stores and a gas station. I pulled into the station. Stopped at the pumps.

I knew I was about to crash—emotionally crash, I mean. So I just kept moving, moving like a bot, like a zombie, not thinking, just moving, moving. I went into the gas station market. Paid cash for gas. Bought myself a burner, one of those anonymous prepaid phones that can't be traced. After I gassed up, I drove away to an obscure cul-de-sac, where the few houses were set far back on broad lawns. I parked there, out of sight of the main road. I killed the engine. I fell back against the seat.

Only then did I allow the full trauma of the day to drop down on top of me like an anvil hurled from the sky. My whole body trembled. I felt shattered inside, my identity in shards and splinters. Who the hell was I now? What was my life? Just days ago, I was a perfectly happy miserable Hollywood failure going nowhere in comfortable despair. And now? Death around every corner. My own mother sending assassins after me. My whole childhood a lie. Even the cops hunting me. And at any moment, I might step through a door and find myself back in that dreadful house with a monster horrible beyond imagination poised to rip my head off.

After a while—a long while spent trembling in the driver's seat—I noticed a sensation of pulsing heat on my chest. *Oh good,* I thought. *Maybe I'm having a heart attack. That would be a relief at this point.*

But no such luck. It was Betheray's locket. I drew it out of my sweatshirt and gripped it in my fist.

For one second—like a flashback in a movie—I was in the past again. On Riley's bed again, propped up against the headboard. Reading to her—*Nobody Listens*—while she peered up at me with her worried, frightened face. My child self lifted his solemn eyes from the book, looked across the room and saw . . . something . . . something that startled him.

But before I could see what it was myself, the moment was over. The locket went cool in my fist. The flashback ended.

I opened my hand and looked at the locket. Pressed the latch and raised the cover. There was the portrait of Queen Elinda—Queen Elinda who was also Ellen Evermore, the author of *Another Kingdom.* She seemed to be looking directly out at me. Strange to say, but her expression of serene majesty calmed me somehow. I read the inscription for the hundredth time:

Let Wisdom Reign and Each Man Go His Way.

Yes, I thought—my mother's answer automatic in my head now. *But what is wisdom?*

I snapped the locket shut and stuffed it back inside my sweatshirt. Then I lifted the shirt's hem and drew out the DVD case I had found in the air duct at home. *Horror Mansion.* I opened the case. There was the phone number scrawled in marker ink on the shiny disc. Surely, it was my crazy kid sister who had scrawled it there. I tore the packaging off the burner phone and turned the phone on.

I was about to dial the number on the DVD, but I didn't. On an impulse, I dialed another number instead, the only number I knew by heart. I don't know why I did it. I shouldn't have. It was the loneliness, I guess. The days without internet or social media or a phone or any friendly face. I listened to the ringing on the line. Then the click.

Then Jane Janeway's recording—her soft, her tender, her sweet, her gentle voice: "Hi. This is Jane. Leave a message."

Then a tone. I opened my mouth to speak but didn't speak; couldn't. My throat closed. My eyes filled.

I cut the connection and dialed the number written on the DVD.

I fought to get control of myself while the phone was ringing. It rang three times. Then a man answered. Sounded like a youngish man. He had a sure, strong voice.

"Jason Broadstreet," he said.

I hesitated before I spoke. Jason Broadstreet. I knew that name. Some big tech guy. Some Silicon Valley muckamuck. A billionaire who'd made a fortune in some startup or other, I couldn't remember which. I had an image of him in my mind, a picture I'd seen in a news story: a small, square-shouldered, dynamic guy. Determined expression. Swept-back hair. Jutting, rock-like features. How on earth would Riley know a guy like that?

"Mr. Broadstreet," I said—I spoke slowly, uncertain of what I would say next. Then I said the only thing I could think of: "My name is Austin Lively."

"Oh. Right," said Broadstreet—simple as that. "Your sister told me to expect your call."

I let out a startled laugh. "She did? You know Riley?"

"Yeah, sure, of course. How do you think she got my number?"

I could not imagine. "Well . . . " I said. It seemed worth asking: "Do you happen to know where she is now?"

He made a whiffling snort. "Hell no. I told her to come here, to Wonderly. I told her I could protect her. Hell, I've got all the security in the world but . . . she was too paranoid. Too scared. She said she didn't want anyone to know where she was, not even me. Not even you. She said she'd find a way to get my number to you, a way they couldn't trace. She's a bit of a kook, your sister."

I smiled in spite of myself. "A bit, yeah," I said. "But she did get me the number. How do you know her?" I asked. Meaning: how did a billionaire get friendly with the looney girl who played the goblin at the Halloween Horror Walk at Happy Town Theme Park?

"Look, we shouldn't be talking about this," Broadstreet said. "Not on a cell phone."

"I just bought it in a gas station. It's a burner, prepaid, anonymous."

"Oh yeah? Is this the first time you've used it?"

My lips parted, then shut. I swallowed. Only now did it occur to me what a mistake I'd made. If Orosgo was monitoring Jane's line, looking for me, he might have heard my call to her. He might know my number now. He might be tracing me right this second. He might even be listening in.

"You know who you're dealing with, right?" Broadstreet said. "You know what he can do."

I nodded numbly at the windshield. "I know."

There was another long pause. Then Broadstreet spoke again. I got the feeling he had to. He had something to tell me, and he felt compelled to tell me even if he risked being overheard.

"I was her source on Seven Thirty," he said.

"Whose source? Riley's?"

"Yeah."

"And Seven Thirty. What's that?"

"She didn't tell you anything."

"No."

"The 730 Club," he said. "I saw her *Ouroboros* videos online. That's why I called her. That's how we met. She was the only outsider who knew the truth."

I was silent, startled. The truth? My sister? My nutso sister knew the truth? "You mean, there really are aliens trying to take over the world?" I said.

"No!" He snorted again. "What are you, some kind of idiot? There are no aliens. There are just people." I heard him sigh. "The old man. You do know who I mean, right?"

"Yeah, yeah. I know."

"He bought me when I was young. Just a kid really."

"Bought you."

"You know: made me what I am. Helped me make my first billion. Drew me in. Made me one of them. Seven Thirty."

I shook my head. I was worried now, worried about the phone, worried Orosgo's men were tracing me. I scanned the outdoors through the windshield, watching for the Escalade. "Look, I still don't get this," I told him. "The Seventy Thirty Club. I still don't know what it is."

Another sigh. "All right. Listen. We really can't do this on the phone. Come to Wonderly. It's safe here. Like I told your sister: I'm surrounded by enough security to hold off an army."

He gave me the address and cut the connection.

I put the car in gear and drove to the corner. There was a wastebasket there. I pulled up beside it, buzzed down the window. I tossed the phone into the trash. Then I drove away.

IT TOOK ME hours to get to him. I had to buy more maps first—just finding maps took me an hour. Then I had to cross the Bay and head for the valley. I kept to the smallest roads I could find. It was late afternoon by the time I got close. By then, I was cruising through a dramatic green wilderness. Crags of gray rock rose from rolling green hills, hills fringed on their crests with windswept trees. I drove deeper and deeper into the empty land until I came to Wonderly. That was the name of his estate. It was written in iron script on the ornate gate that stood at the entrance, an ornate gate with a guard house beside it.

The gate was open. The guard house was empty.

I slowed the car as I approached. My gut went sour. I did not like the look of this.

It's safe here, Broadstreet had told me. *I'm surrounded by enough security to hold off an army.*

Right. But where were they?

I drove slowly through the gate. Slowly up a narrow dirt road. Through a dense orchard of trees with flaming orange leaves. There was no one in sight here either. No workers, no gardeners, no guards. What the hell was going on?

I came out of the flaming trees, came around a wide curve and saw the house. It was a stalwart mansion. A modern version of an old plantation house, stately brick and white trim. It had a louring, heavy, haunted look. It seemed very still. Empty.

Where was all the security?

The dirt road ended in a paved circular driveway. I parked. Stepped out. A cool wind stirred the orange leaves in the orchard. I could hear them *whish* and rattle behind me. Otherwise, it was quiet. Very quiet.

I walked up the stone front steps to a grandiose portico. My footfalls on the stone sounded loud to me. I reached a large, forbidding green door framed between white columns.

I was reaching out to ring the bell when I noticed the door was ajar.

Not good. This was not good.

I pushed the door open. I stepped inside. Into a large entrance hall, modern, with white walls and columns and wood floors and a blonde wood balcony up on the landing atop a sweeping flight of stairs. A chandelier of brass and glass hung above it all, the bulbs on, shining.

I stood in the center of the foyer and listened to the eerie quiet.

Then: a sound. A creaking sound. A footstep? No. Too slow, too long, too steady. More like a door with rusty hinges blowing back and forth in a wind.

The source of the noise was on the second floor. I went to the stairs. Climbed them slowly, listening. The creaking sound grew louder with every step, even louder when I reached the landing. It was coming from the end of the hall.

I should have run then, gotten out of there. But my sister was missing. Hiding. In danger. She had wanted me to find Broadstreet. Broadstreet was the only lead I had. To hell with running.

I followed the creaking noise. I went down the hall. There was a door at the end, half open. I heard Broadstreet's words again:

It's safe here. I'm surrounded by enough security to hold off an army.

Yeah, I thought. Maybe. Or maybe not. Maybe nothing could protect you from Orosgo in the end.

I reached the door. Pushed it open the rest of the way.

I looked inside and saw him.

The magnificent windows of his large home office stood open onto a balcony. The sweet, cool air was streaming in from the distant hills. It blew across the figure of Jason Broadstreet, where he was hanging from the rafter above his desk.

His gorged and strangled figure swung slowly back and forth and set the rope creaking.

21

I CUT HIM DOWN. IT WAS AN AWFUL BUSINESS. I PROBABLY should have left him for the police, but I couldn't stay in that room another second with him hanging there. Anyway, what if he was still alive somehow?

He wasn't. If I wasn't sure before, I was once I got up close. I found scissors in his desk drawer. Climbed up onto the desk and went to work on the rope. The whole time I was sawing through, Broadstreet was swinging against me, twisting around to look at me with his purple face and his bulging eyes and his tongue all stuck out. Yeah, he was dead all right. If I hadn't just finished watching a creature made of body parts devour an entire dinner party, he might have been the worst thing I'd seen all day. As things were, he hardly made the list.

Swallowing my disgust, I held the body around the waist with one hand while I cut through the final strands of the rope with the other. Then I lowered Jason Broadstreet to the desk at my feet. Breathless and queasy, I climbed down to the floor.

That was the first time I really looked around the place. It had been searched, just like Riley's room, but not as thoroughly. The leather cushions were askew on the sofa, but they hadn't been tossed off and gutted like Riley's had. The papers in the desk drawers had been rifled, but the drawers had been closed up again, though some were still open partway. There was a painting of a garden on the wall, and it was slightly tilted. When I looked behind it, I found a wall safe with the door unlocked. The papers and jewelry and cash were still inside, though they'd clearly been tampered with. Whoever had done this, they weren't looking for valuables. But then I already knew that. They were looking for the manuscript, *Another Kingdom*.

I grabbed a handful of cash for myself and shut the safe door.

I glanced over at Jason Broadstreet's body where it lay splayed across the desktop, his arms flung out, his distorted face gaping up at the ceiling. I wondered if there was any chance he had left a message for me the way Riley had. It didn't seem likely. Unlike Riley, he didn't know me well enough to leave me a message in code, something Orosgo and his goons wouldn't understand but I would. Anything else would've tipped his hand. The searchers would have removed it. I took a quick look around the place, then decided to let it go.

I went to the desk and picked up the phone. I figured I ought to call the police then get out of there before they showed up. That way, I could report the death just as I would have if the whole universe weren't in a conspiracy against me—then run for cover, because it was.

I had the handset to my ear and my fingers on the buttons when I paused. Picking up the phone gave me an idea. There actually was one possible way Broadstreet might have left a message for me that the goons couldn't find.

I closed my eyes and tried to remember the number written on the *Horror Mansion* DVD. It came back to me. I pressed the phone buttons.

Clever me. I heard a faint buzzing. Broadstreet's cell. The sound was coming from right below me. I lowered myself to the floor and looked. Yes, there it was. Broadstreet had secured his cell phone under the desk, sealing it there, way in the back, with a whole bunch of scotch tape. I crawled under and worked the phone free and slipped it into my pants pocket.

Then I climbed out and called 911 from the desk phone.

"I'm at Jason Broadstreet's estate: Wonderly," I said to the woman who answered. "He's here. He's dead. I found his body."

"You found a body? Could you tell me your name, sir?"

That's what she was saying when I hung up on her.

THE COPS SHOWED up fast, really fast, as if they were already on the way before I called. By the time I slipped behind the wheel of the Passat, I could hear the sirens closing in. I didn't think I'd have time to get off the property before they arrived, so I drove back around the bend of the dirt road to the orchard. Then I turned off the road and rolled the Volks into the lines of flame-colored trees. I pulled up close to where two of the trees were bent low and pressed together, like two red-haired girls sharing a secret. Now my car was hidden by their hanging branches. I switched off the engine and sat there, waiting for the cops, trying to think the situation through.

My earlier emotional reaction had faded now. I felt strangely calm. Not sure why exactly. Maybe anything was better than being in Curtin's mansion in Edgimond with the monster after me. Or maybe I was just so depressed about my mother and father, I didn't care what happened next. I don't know. Anyway, I was calm, and I sat there, waiting, thinking about what had just happened.

Here's how I had things figured out so far.

Jason Broadstreet had been part of Serge Orosgo's worldwide Orosgo Age conspiracy, whatever it was. He had been drawn in as a young man after Orosgo helped him get rich. But then he started to have doubts about the enterprise. Somehow he saw one of Riley's loony videos online. He saw past all her craziness—the crap about the aliens and the Illuminati and so forth—and he recognized that Riley was onto something, that she knew about the real conspiracy. How did she know? It must've been because she'd heard my parents and my brother discussing it when she was climbing around inside the walls of the house, when she was sitting at that juncture where all the house's voices came together. The truth about my parents—the truth that I had denied to myself as I escaped into movie-making fantasy—had driven Riley half-insane. But deep down inside her insanity, she still knew the truth.

Broadstreet wanted out of the conspiracy, but he was afraid if he turned against Orosgo, Orosgo would have him killed. So he began feeding Riley information for her videos, hoping someone would see them and catch on. He knew he was taking a big risk. He surrounded himself with security men to keep himself safe. But surprise, surprise, Orosgo got suspicious. He bought off the security men. Now, instead of standing guard over Broadstreet, they were watching him on Orosgo's behalf.

I didn't know how it ended. Maybe they'd overheard him talking to me on the phone or maybe Orosgo just got worried I was getting too close to the truth. In any case, Orosgo gave the command and the security men transformed into assassins. They strung Broadstreet up and searched the place—although they didn't have to search much, since they'd been in the house for a while and knew what was there. Then they took off.

I guess Broadstreet saw his murder coming. He had left his phone for me under the desk. I wondered what was on it. What did he want me to know?

Well, there was no time to find out now. Here came the cops, sirens blaring. Through the hanging flame-orange leaves, I could just make out the flashing red lights of three cars racing up the dirt road into the orchard. There was a gap through the trees right in front of me, and I could see the cars go past, each one moving into view for a second then passing by, obscured behind the leaves again. The first car was a local patrol car. The second was a state police cruiser.

The third car, with a whirling red light on top, was a dark blue Cadillac Escalade.

Slick was driving.

22

MY JAWS CLAMPED TIGHT WHEN I SAW HIM. *DAMN*, I thought. So Slick wasn't just a killer. He was a cop too. Well, sure. Orosgo bought people, didn't he? If you're going to buy people, you might as well start with the police.

I waited until the three cars went by me, until they disappeared around the long curve that led up to the house. Then, quickly, while the sirens were still blaring loud enough to drown out the noise of my engine, I started the Passat. I pulled out of the orchard and took off down the road, out of Wonderly.

I DROVE A long way, a long time, on snaking forest lanes off the main freeway. I headed for the coast, just because, just to keep things random. The sun went down into the trees, then behind the hills. Through gaps in the hills, I saw it sink into the distant water. It was dark by the time I found a three-story box of a motel not far from Half Moon Bay.

The clerk in the rustic front office was an old man. He looked like a worn-out hippie from the 1960's. He had a high forehead and a silver-red pony tail and anesthetized eyes with great big black pupils. He gave me a little trouble about checking in without a credit card, but I finally talked him into it with some charm and a bit of Broadstreet's cash.

I went up to the second floor, to a soulless room with a view of a weedy back lot. I sat down on the edge of the knobbly bedspread and went through Broadstreet's phone.

There was no password to get into the thing. Of course not. Broadstreet had wanted me to get in. He'd left it wide open. But once I was going through the files, there wasn't much to see. No recordings. No notes. No messages. Nothing.

And then—something. One thing. I found it in the address book. One number. One name.

Ourobouros.

I straightened where I sat. My mouth opened. My eyebrows lifted right into my hairline. I understood. This—this phone in my hand, the phone Broadstreet had left for me—this was the phone he'd used to communicate with Riley. Only with Riley.

I called the Ourobouros number. It rang three times, then a fourth. Then I held my breath as the ringing stopped. There was a click, followed by silence. I waited. A moment passed.

"Riley?" I said.

"Your phone is being answered by an automatic voicemail system," said the recorded voice on the other end. "Please leave a message after the tone."

I hung up. I was afraid to say anything, afraid Orosgo might be listening. Maybe I was getting paranoid now, but then that'll happen to you when people keep trying to kill you.

I dropped back onto the bed, heavy with weariness. I closed my eyes. I just wanted to rest a little, think a little, but sure enough, I fell asleep almost right away.

I had a dream—a nightmare. I dreamed I was driving through a small New England village hung with heavy fog. The shadowy figures of men and women watched as I passed. A building loomed in the distance, just a dim outline in the mist. Then, as I got close, as the mist parted, the building showed itself to be a looming haunted house. The house looked familiar. Finally, with a jarring chord of scary music, the mist blew around in spirals and took the shape of ghostly words: *Horror Mansion.*

My eyes came open. I was suddenly fully awake, my heart pounding. I sat up on the edge of the bed and rubbed my eyes.

The DVD, I thought. I have to see what's on the DVD.

I checked my watch. It was still early. Not yet nine. I needed to find a DVD player. Not easy to do in the dead of night in the middle of nowhere. Who even watched DVDs anymore?

I got up. I picked up the DVD case from where I'd left it on the bedside table. I studied the cover of the box. Sure enough, there was the picture of the mansion in the fog. The ghostly words. Just like in my dream.

I headed to the door. I was still looking down at the picture as I pulled the door open. I almost walked right through without looking.

But then I caught myself. I stopped on the threshold, wide-eyed. With a spiraling sensation of fear, I realized I could easily have walked through that portal and suddenly found myself back in Curtin's mansion, jumping through the trapdoor with the monster on my heels.

Luckily—no—there was nothing through the door but the second-floor hallway. I went out. I took the stairs back down to the lobby. The hippie clerk was sitting behind the front desk, tilted back in his swivel chair, feet up on the counter. He was reading a magazine, a real magazine made of paper and everything. The glossy cover had pictures of some kind of bacteria. There was a scary headline about how the bacteria had been manufactured and released by a secret government cabal. Classic. People from his generation believed in every conspiracy except the real ones.

I asked the guy if there was a computer for guest use. He gestured with his stubbly gray chin. I found the machine down a short hall off the far end of the lobby. It was a dusty old white box set in a cranny just outside the motel coffee shop. The coffee shop looked like it had been closed since the clerk was a juvenile delinquent. The computer didn't look too fresh either. But at least it was hooked up to the internet, so there was some chance I might make contact with the current century.

The computer didn't have a DVD player so I couldn't watch *Horror Mansion.* I searched the title instead. There were no clips online, just a Wikipedia entry:

> **Horror Mansion**
> **(British Title, "The Devil")**
> A professor who made a pact with Satan must offer the devil a yearly human sacrifice or surrender his soul in payment.

The description didn't sound familiar. Had I really seen the film at some point? I tried to remember. I pictured that scene again. The scene in the small bedroom. A lantern on a shelf. A woman? Yes, a woman in a white blouse and a black dress. She was holding a dead bird in her hand.

That was all I could come up with. I would have to wait until I found a DVD player and could watch the whole movie.

So I moved on. I searched for the 730 Club. I wasn't expecting to find anything. The name sounded so super-secret and conspiratorial. But not at all. There were pages of entries on it. I even found a feature in *The New York Times* from a few years back. It was an enthusiastic puff piece written by one of the paper's op-ed columnists, Charles Head.

730 Club Billionaires Try to Imagine a Better World.

According to the article, the 730 Club was a collection of "forward-looking" billionaires who got together once a year for a week around July 30 to discuss how to "make the world a better place." I smiled at that—smiled ruefully. It reminded me of my brother Richard. He worked for Orosgo's think tank, the Orosgo Foundation. He was always writing books about making the world a better place. I was beginning to think "make the world a better place" was the most dangerous phrase in the English language.

Anyway, the club was made up mostly of techie types, all men. Every July, they gathered at a secret, faux-macho woodland retreat outside of Bend, Oregon. They hiked and made campfires and did trust and bonding exercises like jumping off rocks backward and catching one another, stuff like that. Then at night, according to the article, they gathered in a rustic dining hall with a moose head mounted on the wall and listened to speeches from various experts while they drank good whiskey and ate good steak.

Who owned the Oregon retreat? Who else? Serge Orosgo. A large section of the article was Charles Head's interview with the great man himself. In fact, Charles Head seemed to think Orosgo was a helluva guy. "Elegant," he called him. "Sophisticated," with a "searching, sensitive intelligence" that "practically beamed from his gentle features." Well, maybe Head had never seen one of Orosgo's killers shoot someone to death without a second thought. Or maybe he had seen it and he just didn't care.

"What is holding us back?" said Orosgo in the interview. "What besides superstition, tribalism, religion, and the fiction of human rights?"

I could practically hear the old man speaking in that faintly romantic Russian accent of his. I could see his ancient-yet-lively face with the wrinkles surgically smoothed away. I remembered his pale blue eyes, perpetually jacked wide so that, for all he was in his eighties, he bore some resemblance to a startled baby.

"Where are these human rights?" Orosgo went on. "Show them to me. Are we endowed with them by our Creator? Then show me. Open up our bodies. Do you see human rights in there? Of course not. You see blood and viscera and DNA, that's all. Our rights are as imaginary as the Creator who endowed us with them. They're a story we tell ourselves. If the story is useful to us, if it makes the world a better place, fine, I say. But if it gives small-minded troglodytes and bigots the power to vote against humanity's best interests, to vote down the plans and treaties of experts and global statesmen with a hundred times the wisdom of the so-called common man—no, of course not. Then the story of human rights has become obsolete, an outdated fairy tale. It's madness to go on believing in such a thing. Get rid of it, I say."

Orosgo acknowledges that such talk is guaranteed to raise the hackles of constitutional and religious fundamentalists as well as other extremists who seem ever-ready to defend their eighteenth century philosophies with twenty-first century weapons. So wrote Charles Head. *He chuckles at their increasingly desperate attempts to protect such outmoded superstitions as free will and its corollary self-determination.*

"Self-determination," Orosgo exclaimed with a dismissive gesture of his diet soda glass. "Another fiction, isn't it? Free will? The science simply doesn't support the notion of its existence. What we call 'decisions,' are made at the quantum level and only then recognized by consciousness. That means the human body is a complex machine that manufactures the hallucination of self and free will as a survival mechanism. There's nothing sacred about hallucinations, especially if they become impediments to making the world a better place. When the so-called individual's so-called choices cause our society to veer into increasing inequality and injustice—when they threaten to compromise or even destroy the very environment that sustains us—well, then, the hallucinations must yield to reality."

A listener finds himself swept up in the sheer prophetic scope of Orosgo's vision, Charles Head wrote. When he speaks, it is as if some fog of tradition were finally parting to reveal the gleaming magic city of peace and equality that has lain hidden in that fog for centuries.

"Again I ask: what is holding us back?" Orosgo again asked, gazing into the middle distance, wrote Charles Head, as if into the future itself. "America? The West? Christianity? All stories. All ideas left over from pre-scientific horse-and-buggy days. Are we going to allow centuries-old notions to stop us in our tracks? I say, push them aside like the rotten timber they are. Push them aside and march on into a new tomorrow."

In spite of everything—everything I'd been through, everything that might happen yet—I laughed at that, a single laugh out loud. "A new tomorrow." "A better place." "The sheer prophetic scope of Orosgo's vision." Orosgo. A smarmy ex-Communist oligarch, a man who'd made his billions pillaging the confiscated wealth of his mother Russia, a man who trained a boy from youth to be his catamite assassin so he could erase anyone who got in his way. And what was this prophetic vision of his? No God. No human rights. No individuals. No free will. No freedom. Just Orosgo. Orosgo and his billionaires and his experts making the decisions for all of us. A prophetic vision of a new tomorrow of equality and peace—a new tomorrow as old as the tyranny of the pharaohs.

No wonder the 730 Club was no secret. Orosgo's whole conspiracy was right out in the open. He could explain the whole thing to Charles Head of *The New York Times* and Head would nod and murmur admiring exclamations like some teenage girl being seduced by a slick college professor.

So I laughed.

Then I stopped laughing. Because who was going to stop this madman? Who was going to stave off his vision of a new tomorrow? Me? A failed Hollywood nobody trapped in a brain tumor phantasmagoria? My sister? A crazy, child-like videomaker? Jason Broadstreet was a big-shot tech billionaire and look what happened to him. Did I think I could do any better?

Oh well, I told my seething stomach. *Don't let it get to you.* It was just the world, after all. Who cared who ran it? If they took my freedom away, would I even notice, day by day? Wouldn't I still be able to watch the movies I wanted to watch? And sleep with whomever I could? And take whatever drugs I wanted? And speak my mind—as long as it didn't offend anybody or upset the powers that be? Why was I responsible for fighting these bastards? What did any of it even have to do with me, when you really thought about it? Bad enough I was supposed to restore Galiana. Did I have to save Western civilization too?

I scrolled through the rest of the interview quickly. It just seemed to be more of the same. But as I was scrolling, I came upon a full-page photograph. I took one look at it—and then another look.

And then, for a moment, my little motel nook grew very dim and far away. I felt the blood drain out of my face. My head went woozy. I swayed where I sat.

The photograph was taken with a wide-angle lens. It showed the 730 Club gathered at their retreat: a group of men in jeans and button-down shirts and sports jackets. Maybe fifty of them, old and young, mostly white, some Asian, a couple of blacks. They were standing together but each alone, no one touching, all gazing at the camera. Orosgo was there, front and center, leading the pack. His pale, weirdly unwrinkled baby face was fixed in a thin-lipped smile as if he'd just swallowed one of his enemies whole.

But none of that is what shocked me. What shocked me was their surroundings, the scene. A forest typical of the Pacific Northwest, lots of stately evergreens, the sun streaming through their branches in hazy columns, tidy cabins hidden amid the foliage to the left and right.

And, in the middle distance, directly behind them: a large house, the main house where, according to the caption, the club held its nightly gatherings. I call it a house, but it was more than that. It was a mansion, brown and white like the brown-and-white of the tree trunks around it, wide and broad with peaked roofs and plenty of gables and bay windows.

So help me God, it was the mansion in the Edgimond woods. The same mansion, or a close copy of it anyway. Close enough to make the hairs on my arm stand up straight.

How was it even possible? What did it even mean?

I stared at the photograph, unblinking, open-mouthed. Looked down at the group of men again, at Orosgo again, smiling blandly as he conspired in plain sight. Then my eyes were drawn back to the house.

And I saw the figure at the upstairs window. A man, standing there, just standing, just looking out. The shape of him was so dim behind the glass that I had to enlarge the picture on the monitor, then lean in close, squinting, in order to see it clearly.

But then I did see it. I saw *him*. His outline, his shape.

It was the shape of a man in a flowing robe. His head was covered by a hood of some kind, but I could see his features underneath, wizened features crowned with a tuft of hair, decked with a wisp of beard.

Orosgo had told me about a man in a cowl. The man who had come to his dacha back in Russia after the Soviet Union's fall, the man who had offered him the chance to remake the world in his own image, to use his riches to create an ideal future of equality for all, the Orosgo Age.

But the cowled man had wanted a payment, and now that payment had come due, and the only way to defer the payment was to deliver instead the manuscript the man wanted, the novel, *Another Kingdom.*

And that had to be him, I thought. The man in the window had to be the man in the cowl from the dacha of Orosgo's youth.

And it was Curtin, the wizard. So help me. I could only see his shape, not his face, not clearly, but I was sure of it.

It was Curtin. He was here. In the real world.

YOU WANT TO HEAR SOMETHING HILARIOUS? HILARious, I mean, if you're a sadistic psychopath who glories in the suffering of others. If you're one of those guys who spent your formative years vivisecting living squirrels with a dull pocket knife, this'll give you your big laugh of the day.

I was so unnerved by the photograph of the mansion that looked like the mansion in Edgimond that I stumbled back into the mansion in Edgimond, the real deal.

Here's how it happened. The photograph of the house—and the image of Curtin faintly visible in the upstairs window—made my brain short-circuit. I should have been used to impossibilities by now, but the fact is you don't get used to them. They always take you by surprise. And when I saw the photograph, when I realized what it was, my thinking went all haywire, notions and images started frizzing and flashing behind my eyes. Was Curtin here in the Real World? Was that house his house? Did that mean the dragon was here too? Was that the dragon's breath I felt on the back of my neck? Were those the dragon's footsteps I heard coming up behind me?

I only just managed to close the page on the computer before I stumbled back from the cranny, then stumbled down the hall to the motel lobby. The moribund hippie behind the reception desk glanced up from his magazine and blinked in dull puzzlement as he watched me stagger to the motel's front door.

Air, that's what I needed. A breath of fresh, cold evening air.

I threw the door open and rushed outside without thinking. And, yes, at the very last second, I saw where I was going, saw through the wavery veil of transition that I was about to reenter the mansion ballroom, about to plunge from the ballroom into the stairwell beneath the trapdoor. I gave a wail of anguish and tried to pull back, tried to stop myself.

But it was too late. I was through.

The monster in the ballroom roared—that hideous screechy roar that was a chorus of murdered voices. It roared and lunged down at me from above. But as I dropped through the opening into the stairwell, I snagged the under-handle of the trap door with my fingertips and yanked it down after me. The door slammed shut above me and the whole stairwell rumbled and shook as the beast smacked against it.

For a second, I was balanced precariously, one foot on the edge of a step and one in midair. Then I slipped off the end and tumbled down. The stairwell was dark but not pitch black. I caught a glimpse of a bannister and grabbed at it wildly. I held on as the force of my fall swung me around until my butt hit the stairs and my back slammed into the wall.

"Oof!" I said, as the air was knocked out of me.

I sat where I was, clinging to the bannister above me. The stairwell shuddered again as the beast stomped in a tantrum overhead. His screaming multivoiced roar was muffled and seemed far away, but not half far enough. The sound of it still made the air vibrate and turned my guts to water.

I sat there, gripping the bannister, my eyes squeezed tight, as I mentally babbled prayers to God. After a moment or two, I heard the creature's footsteps retreating. *Boom, boom, boom.* The stairwell shook with every step until the sound grew dimmer and finally faded away. Then the place was still.

I sagged where I sat. I was gasping for breath. I tried to collect my thoughts. The mansion in the woods. The wizard at the window. The dragon. The maze of corridors. The deadline at dawn. Time was running out. I had to clear my mind. I had to figure out what to do next.

My attention was drawn to something below me, down the stairs. A glow. A tremulous glow. Torchlight. It danced on the surface of a spider-webbed wall.

I labored to my feet. At least I was in a new place, I thought, away from the endless labyrinth of hallways and courtyards. Maybe there was some hope now, some chance I could find an exit out of the mansion before morning came and I was trapped here forever.

Gripping the bannister, I went cautiously down the stairs.

It was a long descent. The stairs went down and down and down some more. The light below never seemed to grow closer. I lost track of time. I don't know how long it took me to reach the bottom. Long enough. Too long. At last, the bannister ended. My foot landed on cobblestones. I saw the torch in a sconce on a stone wall just over my head. I reached up and lifted the torch free. I held it in front of me, peering into the surrounding gloom.

For a moment, my heart lifted. I was outside! I had done it—so I thought. I had gotten out of the house before morning came. Hooray—right?

Well, maybe.

I waved the torch back and forth, trying to get a better look at where I was.

I saw a square in a small village. Torches lit the foggy night. I could make out the lines of old buildings: attached dwellings in a long row, a tavern with a hanging sign, a church in the distance, its steeple rising against the moon, its graveyard spread beneath the naked branches of an old tree. I heard a noise and turned. A horse and buggy emerged from the mist a few yards off to my right. I heard the animal snort, its hooves clopping on the cobbles. Then the carriage passed before me and disappeared into the fog again, off to my left. I noticed other figures moving now. A woman wearing a bonnet and a long cape, carrying a basket. A man in a jacket and a strange, squarish hat, swinging a cane. A witchy crone gliding through the mist. Slow, stately silhouettes, all of them, drifting past like ghosts or dreams. The fog eddied and rolled around them.

I felt my hopes begin to dim. I had a bad taste in my mouth. Something was wrong here. Another second or two, and I realized what it was.

No wind. There was no wind at all, not a breath of it. The fog was moving, swirling, dissipating, gathering, reaching with finger-like tendrils into the branches of trees—but there was no wind to make it move, not even the sound of wind. Somehow, it did not feel as if I were really outdoors.

And there was something else. The time. The era, I mean. It wasn't right. The dress, the buildings, the horse and buggy: they didn't have the same medieval feel as the rest of Edgimond and Galiana. This looked more like a village in Puritan America. What's more, it was a village I had somehow seen before. How was that possible?

Before I could answer my own question, I heard a sound off to my right and turned. Another horse and buggy emerged from the fog there. I felt my throat close when I saw it. I tried to swallow but couldn't. My mouth felt as if it were full of dust.

Because it wasn't another horse and buggy. It was the *same* horse and buggy, the same one as before. It made the same sounds. It traced exactly the same path, out of the fog to my right and into the fog on my left. And there were the same figures moving over the same ground on the streets, the woman in the bonnet, the man with the cane, the witchy crone and so on.

The house gets into your head. It is your head.

Maybe I had not escaped Curtin's mansion after all. Maybe this was just the wizard playing with my mind again, bringing images out of my mind, keeping me lost in the maze of my mind until he trapped me there forever.

I felt a touch of blackness inside me: the black touch of despair. If the house was my own brain, how could I ever escape it?

Holding the torch up in front of me, I shuffled forward slowly into the center of the square. The horse and buggy passed by me again. The same figures drifted in and out of the same places in the fog. Bonnet Woman. Cane Man. Witch. The fog grew thicker in front of me. It congealed into a white morass. I felt the cold damp of it clinging to my skin as it surrounded me. I could see nothing in front of me now, nothing at all anywhere. I pushed on through the miasma, step by step. Finally, I emerged on the other side.

And I was back in the same place! On the edge of the village again, the same edge. Watching the same horse and buggy pass, right to left again. Watching the same people pass through the fog—the fog that stirred and swirled even though there was no wind.

I had become part of the loop. Of course I had. I was the maker of the maze. Everyplace I went was just another dead end of my own design, another dead end that would keep me here until morning.

That black despair inside me—it started to spread. But no, I thought, despair was death. I knew that. I *knew* that. I fought against it. I thought to myself: *Come on! Come on!* If the prison was in my own mind, then the key must be in there too, right? If this was a story out of my imagination, then I could write the ending. Couldn't I?

Just then, something happened—something moved—something new, not part of the loop. I looked. Someone was ducking through the door of the tavern across the square. A boy. Was it the same boy I had met in the cave and in the dining hall and in the ballroom too? Maybe. He had shown me the way before. Maybe he would help me now.

I went after him. Crossed the square again, heading for the tavern this time. The fog began to gather around me as it had before. I tried to clear it, to think it away. *This is my mind. My story,* I thought. I thought: *Fight it. Think of something to fight for, something you love.* I thought of working at my desk, back in the old days, before I became desperate to end the rejections. I thought of my sister, Riley, gazing up at me as I told her stories. I thought of Jane, sweet Jane, soft, ever-so-womanly Jane. *Dear God, let me live to see her again.*

And yes, the mist began to grow thin, then thinner. I broke through it. I reached the tavern. I tossed the torch down onto the cobblestones. I pushed inside.

The tavern door creaked as it swung shut behind me. It was gloomy in here, as gloomy as the square. Instead of fog, it was the darkness itself that swirled and gathered all around me. Unnatural shadows pooled and separated and seemed to drift and spiral, obscuring the shape of things. Through that strange and moving darkness, I caught glimpses of the place in patches of dim light from hanging lanterns. Not a tavern but an old house. Rickety stairs leading up into cobwebbed nothingness. Portraits staring from the wall with living eyes. Hallways running into crawling black shadow. All empty. No people anywhere. No one at all. I was alone.

My eyes panned across the space. And I gasped, startled.

Suddenly, there was a man.

He was standing stock still in the center of the room. Tall and thin and stately, dressed in black. He had a long face with solemn features, a widow's peak of dark hair. Spooky: the way he just appeared there suddenly—the way he didn't move or speak at all—the way the shadows seemed not just to wander over him but to meld with him, their darkness blending with his darkness, so that his appearance shifted and morphed and then came clear again, a little different than before. Was he a servant? Was he a priest? He had a morbid presence that sent a chill through me.

"Welcome," he said. His tone was low and hollow, eerie to the point of cliché. He sounded like the guy in the horror movie who whispers something like, "*No one can hear you scream.*"

I gave a snort, trying not to show how freaked I was. "Who are you? Are you even real?" I asked him.

That got a small smile out of him. Or maybe it was just the shadows moving around his mouth. "Everything is real, one way or another."

I made a face. "Deep," I said. "Real deep."

A bell chimed to my left. I glanced toward the sound. The shadows shifted and revealed an old grandfather clock against the wall. The clock was just like the man, tall and thin and very still. It chimed again. And then again and then once more.

"Four a.m.," the man said. "Just a little more than two hours until the sun comes up." He smiled again. "Twelve hours after that, dinner is served."

"Right. Dinner. You're trying to frighten me."

"Is it working?"

"Oh yeah."

I could just imagine myself sitting in the grand dining hall with the others. Trying to focus on the food, trying not to think about what would happen next. Waiting for the dragon. Sundown after sundown, forever.

I think the dark servant-priest man sensed my fear. He smiled quickly with lots of teeth. And, as if the smile had sent a wind passing through the weird and gloomy room, the shadows swirled and coiled around him and obscured him. I squinted hard into the darkness and thought I saw him in there, the same man, only changed, smaller, more wizened, red-eyed.

"Curtin?" I whispered. "Are you Curtin?"

As if in answer, thoughts came into my mind unbidden, like words spoken, the sort of words no one ever wants to hear. *I don't love you anymore. You aren't forgiven. You too will die.* Thoughts like those. My mind was loud with them, and at the same time, images filled me. The unspeakable images from the mural on the ballroom ceiling—they filled all of me, as if they were painted now on the nether-surface of my skin. The words were spoken, and the images crawled over my interior until I felt like a sack full of demon tarantulas, all whispers and legs and eyes. He was some wizard, this Curtin. Some bad, bad guy.

I felt him smiling in the deeper darkness. I shuddered. But I told myself: *Wait. Don't give into him.* After all, if he was here in front of me, if he was working on me as hard as this, I must be near the heart of the house. Sure. If this were my story, the villain wouldn't show himself until the climax, would he? I looked around at the room, what I could see of it.

"I'm close, aren't I?" I said aloud. "That's why you're here. I'm close to the exit."

"You've done well, I must admit," said the dark horror movie servant-priest. "Most of my visitors never get this far. They get lost in the corridors. They run around the courtyards again and again, tracing the same path until the sun comes up. And then they're mine."

I bit my lip. *Well, good,* I thought. I'd broken the pattern at least. And if I'd gotten this far, I could get the rest of the way. I felt so close to escaping.

"Oh, you are," said the dark man, answering my thought. "You're very close indeed. So close that it would really be a shame if the dawn should find you here."

I felt a flash of anger. He felt what I was feeling. He smiled again, more thinly this time, fewer molars. His eyes seemed to catch flamelight from somewhere. Or maybe they just glowed red: the wizard's eyes.

"Are you offering to show me the way out?" I asked him.

He made the slightest gesture. A little tilt of the head. "It's possible. An arrangement might be made."

I took a step toward him, hoping to see him more clearly, hoping to confront him face-to-face. But I stopped short, my brain filled with words, my heart filled with images. I couldn't bring myself to get any closer. I was afraid.

"Go on," I said, my voice strained. "What kind of arrangement are we talking about?"

"You'd have your freedom."

Just the word—*freedom*—made my pulse quicken. "My freedom." I rolled it around on my tongue. "From this house, you mean?"

"This house. Edgimond. Galiana. From all of it, Austin. I can make it so you never have to return here ever again."

"You can do that?"

"Oh yes."

One corner of my mouth lifted. It's amazing how tempting temptation is. Not when you imagine it, but when it's really real, right there in front of you. What wouldn't I have done to have this nightmare life be over? This passing in and out of doors, one world into the next. And what difference would it make? If I never found Anastasius? If Queen Elinda never reclaimed her throne? If Maud was never made whole and never found her lover again? What difference would it make to anything? They weren't even real. They couldn't be real.

"You wouldn't even remember," said the dark man, still speaking into my thoughts.

"You could do that?" I said again.

And he said again: "Oh yes."

I met his eyes and he met mine. I tried to gauge the truth of his words. I remembered the photo in *The New York Times*. The mansion in the Oregon woods. The shape of him, Curtin, at the upstairs window. Not for the first time, it occurred to me: Galiana, Edgimond, California, the real world—it was all one story somehow.

"What about . . . you know . . . Orosgo?" I asked him. "What about my real life? Could you fix that too?"

"Of course I can. As I say, Austin, everything's real life, one way or another."

I nodded. He didn't move, but the shadows passed over him and they changed the look of him. I could still feel the mural images crawling inside me like spiders. Still hear the voices whispering. It was awful. I would have done anything to make it stop.

"What do you want?" I asked him.

"What does it matter?"

"What do you want?" I said, my voice rising.

"You already know."

"The book. *Another Kingdom.*"

He didn't answer.

"And the Eleven Lands," I said.

"You won't even remember them. You won't even know they're gone."

Yes, I thought. *What difference would it make?*

"This is some old quarrel, isn't it?" I said impatiently. "Some old business between you and Anastasius. Isn't that it?"

"It's an old conflict, yes," the dark man said. The shadows pooled around him. He changed into Curtin and changed back again. "I was to Anastasius once what I am to Lord Iron now. His advisor. His friend. The power behind his throne. Galiana was supposed to be my reward for my labors on his behalf, but he gave it to Elinda instead. His bride-to-be. He always was a fool for a pretty face."

"Right. So you waited for him to go off to war," I said. "Then you found an opening and set up your base here in Edgimond. Then what?"

"When Elinda heard reports of what was happening here, she sent Lord Iron to me as her ambassador."

"And you turned him against her."

"He wanted power. I gave it to him."

"And Orosgo—he wanted to write his name on a generation. Was that you too? The cowled man at the dacha?"

He didn't answer. He only said, "You're running out of time, Austin. Dawn is near. Do you want your life back or not? I can give you that. I can give you your life—and more than your life. A better life. The life you've always wanted."

"You could do that," I said. It wasn't a question this time.

And he said once more: "Oh yes."

The darkness kept swirling, whirling, not just around him but around me too. It was creeping in from every corner of the room, drifting toward me in tendrils, spreading in black pools. It was growing thick and close around me, thick as the fog in the square outside, close as my own skin. It threatened to swallow me. It *would* swallow me if I stayed here, mesmerized like this, another second.

I had to fight it. I had to move. *Think of what you love,* I reminded myself. And I tried. I thought of working at my computer again, back in the old days, back when I dreamed of success, dreamed of cameras flashing at me on the red carpet, of giving interviews and making millions and having too many women to count. I shook my mind clear. The darkness thickened. I clenched my teeth. I forced myself to push into it, push through, confront the dark man face-to-face. He sank back from me, even deeper into shadow.

"Damn you!" I shouted.

And I lunged in after him, plunged into the shadows after him. Deeper and deeper into the darker and darker dark. I reached the lightless center of the obscurity.

And there was nothing there. The man was gone. I forced myself to keep moving, pushing shadows aside with my hands, wading through them. They were so thick now I was suffocating in them. I was blind. Claustrophobia clutched me, squeezed me. But I kept moving, kept moving, and then—then I broke through. I came out on the far side of the darkness.

And I saw a door. It was right there on the wooden wall in front of me. I grew breathless with fresh hope. Was this the way out? Out of the maze? Out of the mansion? It had to be. It had to.

I stepped toward it, my arm rising, my hand reaching for the iron ring that would pull it open.

The grandfather clock on the wall chimed once. Four-thirty. Time was passing so fast, too fast. It was almost morning.

My hand closed on the cold metal of the iron ring. I marshaled my will. I drew the heavy door open.

More darkness. More shadows. I couldn't see beyond the threshold. But if there was a chance, any chance, that this was the way out, I had to take that chance on faith.

I stepped forward into the dark.

I caught a glimpse—a single glimpse through the shadows—of a small rustic bedroom. Then I heard the door slam shut behind me.

I spun around at the noise. I stared at the wall.

The door was gone. It had vanished. There was no exit. I was trapped.

24

FOR A MOMENT, I JUST STOOD THERE, STARING AT THE place where the door had been. My pulse was hammering so hard inside my head that it drowned out my thoughts. I felt it like the ticking of a watch, every heartbeat a second lost, morning coming, tick by tock.

I turned back to the room. My heart sank. I knew this place. It was familiar—like everything in Curtin's maze. It was a small space, narrow. The walls were wood. The floor was wood with an oval braided rug covering part of it. There was a small bed against one wall, a small window above the bed. A shelf, set just above eye level. A lantern on the shelf . . .

The shelf. The lantern. Yes, it came back to me.

It was the scene from the movie, from *Horror Mansion.* The one scene I half-remembered. I moved to the little bed. I knelt on the mattress and looked out the window. I saw the square down there. I saw the horse and buggy come out of the fog. I saw the woman in the bonnet. The man with the stick. The witchy crone. It was the same scene, the same loop as before, except now I was watching it from the other direction.

Of course. I remembered. The square—that was from the movie too. That's why it never changed. That's why it kept on repeating. I was trapped in a scene from the movie. How would I ever get out?

I panicked then. I lost control. I tried frantically to open the window. It wouldn't budge. I lay down on the bed and tried to kick through the pane. Once, twice, again. The glass wouldn't break. Down deep, I knew it never would.

Fighting pure hysteria, I stood up off the bed. I looked up at the lantern. I knew I had to take it down. That was the next part of the scene. I had to play the scene out. I didn't want to. I would be part of it then. Caught in the loop. But I couldn't think of anything else to do.

I reached up to the shelf. I thought: *The bird. The dead bird. That's where it is. It's up there.* The image came into my mind clearly now: a dead sparrow with some kind of ceremonial knife stuck through the heart of it. Only it was not a knife. That was the twist in the plot.

I took hold of the lantern. I drew it toward me. As I did, it bumped into something. The corpse of the sparrow. The dead bird fell off the shelf and landed on the floor at my feet. I knelt down beside it to get a better look.

The bird was stiff and staring. The narrow knife was stuck into its breast. The handle was etched with mysterious runes.

I gazed down at the creature. I remembered the scene from *Horror Mansion.* There was a woman in this room, a woman doing what I was doing now. A blonde in a black skirt and a white blouse. When did I watch the film? Why did I watch it? I couldn't remember. I didn't want to remember.

Almost without willing it, I knelt down and set the lantern on the floor beside me. I took the bird into my hand. I remembered the woman in the movie holding the bird as I was doing. I remembered how it had dripped blood.

It dripped blood. As I watched, I saw the warm fluid run out of the bird's body and dribble along the length of the small blade. It fell onto my fingers and leaked through, pattering on the floor.

The woman in the movie had pulled the blade out next.

I pulled the blade out. It stuck just at the very last and I had to turn it to work it free. That was when the plot twist revealed itself. The knife wasn't a knife. It was a key. And the moment I turned it and pulled it out of the bird, there was a click. I looked up: a rectangular portion of the wall swung open.

A secret door.

More of Curtin's maze.

I held my breath, staring through the doorway into the darkness beyond, more darkness. A sound came to me. People chanting, murmuring some cultic plainsong in low voices far away. The song was rhythmic, ritualistic, solemn. It sent a chill all through me. Something terrible was in there. I could not remember what, but in the movie, something terrible happened next. I did not want to remember.

But what could I do? There was no way out but in. I heard the bell tolling in the church tower: Five a.m. Time was passing faster, speeding up. At this rate, the sun would rise in mere minutes.

I set the bird aside. Picked up the lantern. Rose from my knee. I wiped my bloody hand on my leggings. I stepped to the door. I stepped through.

Suddenly, light-headed, I saw the stars spinning around me. I dropped onto one knee again, feeling not wood now but the rough asphalt through my jeans.

I was back in the real world, back in the parking lot of the motel near Half Moon Bay. I could hear the bay water plashing and the traffic whooshing and the wind whispering through the branches of a nearby tree.

Reality! Blessed reality! Reality had never seemed so sweet! And yet, still haunted by that ghostly room, by the knowledge that any moment I might be flung back there, imprisoned in that movie scene again, I felt I couldn't bear it. I felt I might lose my mind.

Something fluttered then against my thigh. I was so disoriented, it was a moment before I realized what it was: the phone in my pocket was buzzing. Jason Broadstreet's phone. The phone I had used to call Riley. Was she calling me back?

I dug into my pocket quickly. I worked the phone out, rising to my feet. I answered eagerly. "Hello? Hello?"

No response. Silence. I stood in the chill of night, listening. I was afraid to speak, afraid of who might be on the other end of the line.

Then came the broken whisper: "Jason?"

"Riley!" I breathed.

She gasped. "Aus?"

"Yeah. It's me."

She began to whimper like a child. "Where's Jason?"

There was no hiding it from her. It would make the news soon, if it hadn't already. "They got him, baby."

"Oh God!"

"It's gonna be all right."

"Oh God."

"Hang on to yourself. Hang on."

"Oh, Aus! Austin, I'm in so much trouble!"

"I know. I know it, kid. You and me both." I began to pace around the lot as I spoke. "Just hang on, okay? Hold it together. I'm going to help you."

"How?" she wailed. "How can you help me? They got Jason! Oh God."

"I know. But I'm still here. I'm coming for you."

Her voice rose to a high, crazy note. "Don't let them get me, Aus! Don't let them."

"I won't."

"I'm so, so scared! Oh God. Jason!"

"I know." I could hear her crying over the line. It hurt me inside, just like it used to hurt me when we were little. "Where are you, Riley?"

It was a moment before she could speak. "I can't tell you. I can't say it over the phone. They might hear me."

She was probably right. Look what had happened to Broadstreet. "What about your phone?" I asked her. "Is it safe? Can they trace it?"

She came out of her hysteria just long enough to get petulant with her annoying big brother. "I know how to hide the phone from them, Austin. I'm not a baby."

I smiled. It was good to hear there was still some spirit in her. But she broke down again at once.

"They're all around me, Aus. They can't see me, but they're everywhere. They've been all around me for days."

I could feel her terror. I could feel it inside me. It was incredibly frustrating. Here she was on the line and there was no way to reach her. No way to help her. I ran my free hand up through my hair. I had to stay calm. Stay focused. Do what I could do. One step, then another. If I kept moving, maybe the path to her would open up.

"The movie, Ri," I said now.

"What?"

"Tell me about the movie. The one you left for me at the house."

"The movie?" she cried. "You know the movie. You watched the movie. Don't you remember?"

I stopped pacing. I tried to think. Did I remember? I wasn't sure. I reached into my shirt to touch the locket there. There was no warmth coming off it, no magic power. But it didn't matter. The memory came back to me anyway. I saw myself lying on my bed as a kid, my laptop on my belly, the headphones in my ears. I was glancing from the monitor to my bedroom door, afraid someone might come in and catch me.

"Sure," I told her. "I watched the movie. I remember. But I don't remember why."

"Because Daddy made *me* watch it," Riley cried out, sobbing harder. "He made me watch that scene again and again and again. I screamed and screamed, Aus, but he made me."

No, Daddy, no! I don't want to see it again! I won't tell! I promise!

"I remember," I said softly. I remembered that high-pitched little girl shriek of hers. I remembered creeping down the hall to see what was happening. How had I forgotten? What my father had done to her. What I had let him do.

You were just a child, I told myself. *You were a little boy. There was nothing you could've done to help her.*

But it didn't make me feel any better. I was choking on guilt and pity. Poor Riley. Poor little girl. Poor me. Poor boy. Poor everyone.

Riley was flat out sobbing now. "Oh, Aus," she just managed to say. "I'm next. They're going to kill me next."

"I won't let it happen, Riley," I told her. My voice was trembling.

"I won't tell. I swear I won't tell. I won't make any more videos, I swear. Tell them, Aus. Tell Mom and Dad."

My breath came out of me in a long angry hiss. Mom and Dad. Dear old Mom and Dad.

I stood in the parking lot, my head tilted back, the phone lifted to my ear, my eyes lifted to the stars. The stars were only dimly visible above the light of the motel sign. I stared up at them and listened to my little sister crying. All my life, her tears had fallen on my heart like acid. All my life, they'd scalded me inside so that I could hardly stand it. Her tears. Her shrieks of terror. I had made myself forget them because I couldn't stand the pain.

My eyes filled. The dim stars blurred. I clenched my free hand in a fist and raised it to the sky.

"Tell them, Aus." Riley went on sobbing. "Tell Mom and Dad I won't make any more videos. I swear. I'll never tell."

"You'll tell," I said. I had to force the words out through my tight throat. "We're both gonna tell. We're gonna tell everyone."

"No, no, no, no," she cried. She sniffled. She sobbed. "You don't understand. They're too powerful. They control everything. They are everything."

"Come on, Riley. Don't get crazy on me. There's got to be a way to stop them. We just have to figure it out, that's all. We'll expose them to the news sites. On social media. To the police."

"They write the news sites! They run social media! They are the police!"

Still looking at the sky, I brought my hand down on top of my head. "Well, they can't be everybody," I told her. "There has to be a way. Broadstreet thought there was. He was one of them, and he thought they could be stopped. He thought there was a chance at least or he wouldn't have called you in the first place."

Broadstreet's name seemed to have an effect on her. I heard her ragged breathing get steadier. "He said . . . Jason told me . . . he told me everything was at the 730 House. He said it was right there, in plain sight on the wall. All he had to do was take a picture and bring it to me. He said I was the only one he could trust."

I rolled my eyes. Terrific, I thought. If crazy Riley with her banned videos was the only trustworthy news source in America, we were all in big, big trouble.

"All right," I said. "Do you know where the house is?"

"Jason told me. In the woods somewhere. Near some town."

"Bend, Oregon," I told her.

"That's right. Bend. A hundred and thirty miles northeast of Bend. On some road. Route 27, I think. That's it. The trail at the top of the mountain."

"All right," I told her. "I'll find it. Just stay by the—"

I heard her gasp.

"What?" I said. "What is it?"

But the line was silent for a long moment—a long, long moment. She didn't say a word. Then came her squeaky whisper: "They're close."

"Who? Who's close, Ri?"

"I have to go."

"Riley . . . " I said.

But there was a click and the sound of the line changed. I knew she was gone.

I cursed. I lowered my hand, slowly, slowly. I shut off the phone. I stood there in the parking lot and drew in breath and smelled the distant bay on the night air.

I felt my sister's terror in my heart.

LONG NIGHT. NOT much sleep. In the first dull light of a gray morning, I drove away from the motel. I went into the little city. I drew out a long breakfast at a quaint diner on a corner of Main Street. As I ate, I watched the electronics store across the street. Waited for it to open.

I had made my plan. I had to find the 730 House, the mansion in the Oregon woods. I had to get into the house and find the information Broadstreet was hoping to pass on to Riley. It was in plain sight, he'd told her, right on the wall. With that information I would expose Orosgo and whatever he was up to. He'd be arrested or at least disgraced—and that would take the heat off Riley so she could come out of hiding.

I know. It was a crap idea, virtually guaranteed to accomplish nothing and get me killed. But hey, every plan has its flaws, right? It was the only thing I could think of.

Before I did anything else, though, I had to watch the DVD. *Horror Mansion.* Why? Because any minute I could walk through a door and find myself back in the movie, stuck in the loop in the horror mansion of Edgimond with time careening toward dawn. If I could just see what was in that scene, maybe I could figure a way out of it. Maybe.

The electronics store didn't open until ten. As soon as I saw the store clerk unlock the door, I crossed the street, went in, and bought an external DVD drive and a headset.

"Last one I've got," the store clerk mused aloud. He was a tall, overweight red-haired nerd with wireless glasses. "No one uses DVDs much anymore."

"Well, I'm stuck in a horror movie in an alternate universe in danger of being devoured by a dragon every night for the rest of eternity, so I've got to watch the DVD to find a way out."

I actually said that—out loud—and the nerd, so help me, nodded thoughtfully, as if it made perfect sense to him. Hard to know who was crazier: me or the rest of the world.

I carried the DVD drive down the street to the library. I spoke with the librarian there, a short squat lady who looked like the Old Maid on a kid's playing card. I told her I was a film student who had to watch a movie for class. She set me up at a computer in one of the carrels against the windows.

I sat at the carrel, a desk surrounded by three walls made out of something meant to look like wood. Beyond the not-wood walls, the floor-to-ceiling windows looked out on the bay. If I tilted back in my chair, I could see it, the water appearing metallic under the low clouds.

I plugged the DVD player into the computer. I slid Riley's disc into the player. I started the movie.

The credits were like my dream. Swirling mist condensed to spell out the title words. *Frang,* went the music. *Horror Mansion,* spelled the mist.

The story begins with a creepy little scene that takes place in the Puritan past. A mob is burning three witches at the stake in a square of the small New England town of Wildwood. The mob is screaming. The witches are writhing in their bonds. One witch offers to expose the witch leader in exchange for her life. It's the judge, she says. The most respected man in town! The mob only mocks her. The witches shriek in agony as they set them ablaze.

We pan away from the field to Horror Mansion, a spooky old house that overlooks the scene. Lots of gables and peaked roofs, like the mansion in Edgimond. There's a light on in the window of an upstairs room. We zoom in and enter a study decorated with a desk, a globe, a leather wing chair, and shelves of books. There's a shadow on the wall, the shadow of a man. We never see his face, but we hear his voice. It's the judge. His daughter comes in, a sweet, virginal girl in her twenties. The judge thanks her when she serves him tea. She leaves and locks the door.

The judge rises to his feet. And yes, it turns out, he is a witch, the last witch, the Chief Witch, whom no one suspects. He's desperate to avoid the fate of his followers. So he conjures the devil. The devil arrives: another shadow, darker but shapeless. The Chief Witch makes a deal with him. The deal is this: the Chief Witch promises he will sacrifice an innocent victim to the devil once every year. As long as he supplies the victim, the devil will let him live.

Shortly after, the mob, carried away with bloodlust, storms the judge's house, calling for him to come out. The judge does come out. He is dragging his daughter with him by the arm. He denounces her to the mob. She's the witch, he says. As the daughter screams piteously for her father, the mob carries her away to be burned at the stake.

She's the first sacrifice.

I sat in the carrel, watching. I felt a tightness at the pit of my stomach. The movie's production values were garbage, and the acting was hilariously second rate. But all the same, it was a scary scene. Convincing. Disturbing.

Now we cut to modern-day Boston. A college classroom. The whole opening flashback turns out to be part of a lecture that's being given. We see the professor standing before a blackboard, talking about witches and superstition and the paranormal and so on. The professor is a tall, lean man with a widow's peak.

The scene blindsided me. It was a real shock. My stomach lurched. I felt my breakfast surge up into my throat. The professor was the guy from the house in Edgimond, the servant-slash-priest, the dark man who was really Curtin. The wizard must have found the repressed image of this character in my mind and used it as a disguise.

I swallowed my bacon and eggs for the second time that morning. I forced myself to focus on the movie again.

The professor finishes his lecture. A pretty young co-ed approaches him. She's the woman I remembered, the blonde in the black skirt and white blouse. She's the professor's protege. Inspired by his lectures, she plans to go to Wildwood to do research into witchcraft. She will write her thesis on what she finds. The professor is pleased with her decision.

So off she goes. She drives to Wildwood in a gigantic old American car. It's the size of a dirigible; must get half a mile to the gallon. She reaches the town. At night, of course—because it's a horror movie.

The blonde parks her car. Steps out. It's dark. It's foggy. And weirdly, Wildwood looks unchanged since Puritan days. It's lit by torches instead of street lights. There's a line of old buildings across the street, including a tavern. There's a church in the distance and gravestones under a silhouetted tree. There's even a horse and buggy that passes in and out of sight in the fog. There's a woman in a bonnet. A man with a cane. A witchy crone . . .

As I stared at the computer monitor, I felt sweat break out on my forehead. It was the same scene—the scene I'd been trapped in in

Edgimond. I had to lean back in my chair and look out the window to assure myself I wasn't trapped there now.

I leaned forward to watch the movie again. The sweat on my forehead beaded. The bead ran down my temple. My breath grew shallow and quick.

The girl turns around and there behind her is Horror Mansion: the spooky old house from the opening sequence. It's the Wildwood Inn now. She goes inside.

I watched, sweating.

The spooky old woman innkeeper shows the blonde to her room. It's the small bedroom—the same room I had been in. The blonde finds the lantern, same as me. She finds the dead bird. The key. The secret door. She hears the sound of distant chanting. Same as me.

Carrying the lantern, the blonde goes through the door and down a flight of stairs. She follows the chanting sound down a narrow corridor. The corridor is draped with cobwebs. There are statues and gargoyles in niches on the wall. The flickering light of the lantern makes the statues seem alive.

And some of them are alive. Some of the statues are really people. The people peel off from the wall after the blonde's gone past them. They come sneaking up behind her. One of them passes a gargoyle that is holding a long dagger in its claws. He takes the dagger and lifts it, the shadow of the blade wavering on the wall.

I was frightened now, really frightened. Not just because it was a scary scene but because I knew that, in Edgimond, I was trapped in the scene, doomed to play it out myself. I kept thinking: *They can't kill her, can they? She's the star of the movie. She's got to escape.*

The blonde reaches the end of the hall. She steps into a final room.

Here is the source of the chanting: a group of cowled witches, men and women, standing with their heads bowed. They surround a large stone altar table. A table of sacrifice.

As the blonde enters, the Chief Witch, standing at the head of the table, lifts his face to her.

It's the professor. Her professor from the college in Boston: the dark servant-priest. He smiles at the blond in welcome.

"You see my dear," he says. "It's all true."

The blonde's eyes widen in fear as she understands: Her professor is the Chief Witch who made the deal with the devil all those centuries ago. He's still alive because he is still sacrificing innocent victims to the devil. He has lured her here for that purpose.

Then they grab her. The people who have followed her down the corridor—they seize the blonde by the arms and lift her off her feet and carry her to the altar table. The blonde shrieks and struggles, but it's no use. They lay her, screaming and helpless, on the stone surface. They hand the long dagger to the professor-servant-priest-chief-witch.

The blonde begs for her life, twisting uselessly in the iron grips of the witches who hold her down.

"Please!" she shrieks. "I won't tell! I swear! I'll never tell! Please!"

My eyes filled with tears. The blonde was screaming the same words my sister spoke to me on the phone. And I remembered. That was why my father had made her watch this movie, this scene, over and over. She was a four-year-old child, shrieking in terror: "I promise I won't tell, Daddy! I won't tell!" But he made her keep watching so she would learn what happens to bad little girls who climb around in cramped corridors and learn secrets they shouldn't know.

The sweat ran down my temple. A tear ran down my cheek.

The witches hold the shrieking blonde on the altar table. They pull her white blouse open and give us a thrilling horror movie look at her lacy bra. The professor lifts the long dagger high. The camera follows the dagger up into the air.

"Please! Please! No!" screams the blonde wildly.

Then the dagger plunges down out of sight.

The screaming ceases abruptly.

The camera pans away and down, down to the base of the altar. Blood pours over the side of the table into a gutter made for the very purpose. We follow the blood along the gutter and through a hole in the wall. The hole leads outside into the fog.

The fog swirls around Horror Mansion.

Sick and pale, I sank back in the carrel chair. I stared at the monitor with hollow eyes as the movie continued. There wasn't much else to see. The rest of the picture was dull, standard B-movie stuff. It was just that scene. That truly horrifying scene. That scene my father had made Riley watch again and again.

And I had heard my little sister's pitiful screams of terror. I had crept into his study later that night and swiped the DVD and watched it for myself.

And then I had forgotten. Because I couldn't bear what I knew. I couldn't bear the fact that Riley screamed in hysterical fear at night because my father had subjected her to that mental torture in order to terrorize her into silence.

But silence about what? What had Riley learned? What had she overheard when she was sitting in the air duct where all the whispers of the house collected? What lay hidden in her crazy videos that made Orosgo feel he had to kill her? What lay hidden in her broken mind?

When the final credits rolled, I blinked back into awareness like coming out of a trance. I wiped my face dry with my palm. I reached out a shaking hand and unplugged the DVD player from the computer. I sat there, slumped in my chair, with the gizmo lying in my lap.

After a while, I sat up straight. I leaned in to the keyboard again. I called up the old feature story about Orosgo in *The New York Times.* I scrolled to the photograph again. I gazed at the wide-angle photo that showed the club members standing in front of the mansion.

That's where the answers were. In the 730 House. In the forest mansion that looked so much like the mansion in Edgimond, the mansion where I was trapped inside the movie. The answers, Broadstreet told my sister, were written in plain sight on the wall. I had to go and find them.

I was about to close the page on the computer when I remembered what I had seen last time. I felt compelled to look again at the photograph, to look again at the mansion, to look again at the upper window where the cowled figure of Curtin stood draped in obscurity.

I did look. But the window was dark, all dark.

Curtin's figure was gone.

25

I DROVE ALL DAY—ALL DAY AND INTO THE NIGHT. ON freeways up the coast, then on back roads into the interior.

I had stopped in San Francisco to buy supplies. Food, clothes, a backpack, a flashlight, a canteen, a handheld GPS, and some tools for a break-in. I even ditched Broadstreet's phone and got a new burner. I memorized Riley's number, then threw the old phone away. Then I was ready.

I drove and drove. Through northern California into Oregon. An indigo dusk spread from the empty east to where the sun burned fiery behind the clouds. Darkness fell. I drove. By midnight, I was on Route 27, winding up a mountain with nothing outside the windows but a jagged black tree line, a frowning forest of Ponderosa pines. At the peak of the rise, I saw the fire trail Riley had mentioned. I turned off onto a broad but bumpy dirt road. The road went on a long, long way, deep and then deeper into the woods. It grew narrower. Rougher. The trees closed around it.

In the middle of nowhere, I passed a turn-off. It was blocked with a metal gate and marked with a sign that said "*Private Property.*" I took that to be the main entrance to Orosgo's land. I went beyond it, following the GPS to the end of the dirt road. Best to walk in through the trees, I thought, and avoid any guards or cameras.

I pulled onto soft duff. Killed the lights, then the engine. Got out of the Passat. Worked my backpack over my shoulders. Hiked into the woods.

There is no night like night in the forest, no darkness like the darkness there. The autumn moonlight, silver through the evergreens, cast a pale glow over a landscape of hunkering mystery. There was a fractal-like sameness to the tangled depths receding from me in every direction. Whichever way I turned seemed a fantastic mirror image of every other. It was immersive, disorienting. After a while, I felt there was only this—this forest, no world beyond the wood.

The sky was clear now. Through the treetops, I could see the stars of the Milky Way spilled carelessly over the blue-black expanse. A gibbous moon bobbed in and out of view among the branches.

I headed slantwise back toward the main entrance. I picked out the path with the flashlight. I tromped slowly under the majestic and silent trees. They seemed to glower down at me and watch me pass.

I couldn't begin to describe how fantastic and grotesque it felt to come suddenly upon that mansion. I spotted the hazy glow of it through the leaves first and then reached the tree line and saw it in full. It stood in a broad clearing ringed with small spotlights turned down dim. Their beams cut into the thin forest mist and filled it with off-white illumination. After the dreamlike darkness, it seemed a dreamlike light.

But to see the house itself—it felt so impossibly strange—strange and frightening—to see that place, almost exactly the same as the house in Edgimond, which was almost exactly the same as the mansion in the movie. The sight set off a starburst of agitation inside me. The movie, Edgimond, Oregon. It was as if I had reached the junction where the three worlds met.

Hidden just within the trees, I lowered myself onto one knee. The cold of the forest dirt seeped through my jeans and chilled me.

I stayed there and watched the house a while. Most of the lights in the place were out. The interior was dim and gray. But at a window here and there, the outglow of a lamp was visible. As I watched, I saw a figure pass across a second story pane—a guard, it looked like.

I cursed beneath my breath. I wasn't sure I had the courage for this. If it weren't for the pitiful memory of my shrieking baby sister—if it weren't for the sorrowful sound of her voice on the phone—*I'll never tell*—I might well have run away.

Instead, I crept out of the woods into the clearing. A broad dirt and gravel driveway surrounded the place. Dead leaves tumbled over it in a soft night breeze. The leaves clattered, and the stones beneath them, stirred by their passing, rattled. I hoped those noises would cover my crunching footsteps as I approached.

There was only a pine or two here to hide behind. I hid behind one and scoped the surroundings. A broad dirt road—the main entrance I had passed—entered the clearing from my right. There were two Jeeps parked along the side of it. Did that mean there were two guards inside? Or four? Or more?

I crouched low and crossed the rest of the distance to the house until I was pressed close against the wall. I rose up to peek through a first-floor window. A single lamp was lit inside. In its dull yellow gleam, I made out a rustic reading room, bookshelves and stuffed chairs and side tables for wine. There were no guards in there, as far as I could see.

I took a chance. Switched on my flashlight. Shone it through the glass and examined the inside of the window frame. There didn't seem to be an alarm on it. I couldn't find one anyway. So I switched off the flash, slung my backpack off my shoulders, and rooted inside it for my tools. Then I went to work on the window.

It was remarkably easy to break in. A small jimmy pried the upper and lower frame apart. A flathead screwdriver worked through the gap between. I pushed the latch aside. I held my breath as I lifted the window, waiting for an alarm to start screaming. Silence. No alarm. So easy. As I climbed over the bottom frame into the reading room, I thought again of *The New York Times* article. *A listener finds himself swept up in the sheer prophetic scope of Orosgo's vision.* Right. Maybe Orosgo didn't need fancy locks and alarms to protect his secrets. Why should he? If he wanted to take over the world and put an end to "the fiction of human rights," the most powerful newspaper in the country seemed to feel, hey, go to it. Make the world a better place, you wise old billionaire, you.

I crept across the reading room. The floors were made of old wood, but rugs covered most of them and muffled my footsteps. I peeked out through the door and saw a long shadowy hallway running to the foyer. No lights. Only a misty glow leaking in through the windows. No guards in sight. Just a few stands with busts and vases on them. Some paintings on the wall. An indentation that might have been a doorway. That was it.

So all I had to do now was find the writing on the wall—before the guards found me.

I started down the long hall—and just as I did, suddenly, light bathed me. I froze. Two bright beams passed over me. Headlights coming through the hall window from outside.

I dropped to the floor like a sack of cement and lay there as the beams crossed the wall above my head. Then the corridor grew dark again. I crawled to the window and slowly lifted up until I could peek through.

My breath came out of me in a hoarse rasp.

The Cadillac Escalade had just pulled up at the front door. Its headlights snapped off and Slick and his muscle man Moses rose out into the spotlit mist.

Now I heard footsteps inside the house. Someone was descending a flight of stairs. A guard came into view in the foyer at the end of the hall. He was dressed all in black, black slacks and a sweater, but I could still see him in the dim lamplight.

I lay pressed to the floor and watched. Another guard came into the foyer from the hallway on the far side. Guard Two was carrying a small flashlight. Its thin beam danced over the black figure of Guard One. My heart beat hard against the runner. If that beam flashed down the corridor, it would pick me out easily. I looked for an escape route and saw a door right across from me. But I didn't dare try it. The risk of drawing the guards' attention was too great.

Now, anyway, Guard Two doused his flash. The hall was dark again. I lay and watched as Guard One opened the door to let in Slick and Moses.

I saw the four men gather in the dark, four shadows. I could hear them speaking clearly.

"Anything?" said Slick. He sounded brusque and relaxed, a competent professional at work.

"No," Guard One answered him. "We came out as soon as you called, but there's been no sign of him. Are you sure he's heading this way?"

Slick made an uncertain gesture. "We picked up a search for the place out of a library in Half Moon Bay. They were using one of Our Man's search engines. Anyway, the librarian described our guy, so we thought it was worth checking."

"Why don't you just put out a BOLO on him?" Guard Two asked.

"At this point, it'd be best if we can keep him out of the system. He has a lot to say for himself, and not everyone is on our side. Our Man would like him dealt with privately if possible." Slick sighed. "All right," he told the black-clad guards. "Let's just go through the house one more time and make sure he's not here. Then you can go home and get some sleep. Moses and I will take the second and third floor. You guys split up and cover the rooms down here."

They almost caught me right then and there. I was listening to them, thinking about what they said. Not only was there no alarm here, there hadn't even been any guards until Slick called them out.

Now they were going to search the house and leave. Clearly, my best move was to crawl back to the study, escape out the window and come back later when the guards were gone.

Which was exactly what I was about to do when they nearly got me. Because just then, the shadow of Guard Two moved to the wall and lifted his hand. I guessed what was going to happen one split second before it did. I rolled frantically across the floor, hid myself behind a vase stand, inches from the door there.

Guard Two flicked the switch on the wall and the lights came on all over the ground floor. No shadows left to hide in.

"I'll go this way," someone said—I couldn't see them anymore. The vase stand blocked my view. But one of them was going to come toward me for sure. I had to get out of sight, fast.

I drew my feet under me, rose up on a knee, and reached for the doorknob right by my nose. I could hear footsteps coming down the hall now. I figured I had about ten seconds before the guard reached me, saw me. If the door was locked, I was finished.

I held my breath. It wasn't easy with my pulse pounding. I turned the knob as slowly as I dared—slowly enough so that the bolt came back almost noiselessly. The door swung open. The guard's footsteps grew closer. Very close. Another second and he'd come around the vase stand and there I'd be.

I slipped through the door. And holding the knob tight, I closed the door silently and silently rolled the bolt back into place.

I was in a stairwell now, a back stair rising upward. I heard the guard as he continued his approach. Would he pass by?

No. He stopped right outside the door. Of course: he was going to check the stairwell.

I flew up the stairs on tiptoe so as not to make a sound. The stairs wound around in a slow arc that ended at a door on the second floor. Just as I reached the landing, I heard the door below open. I pressed against the wall, breathless.

The guard shone his flashlight up the stairs at me. If the beam had been a bullet, it would have left a scar; that's how close it came. But it didn't reveal me. The guard didn't see me there, trying to meld my body with the stairwell wall.

The flashlight beam swept away. The door below clicked shut. I stayed where I was a long moment, trying to will my heart to slow down. As I stood there on the landing, my cheek pressed close to the wall, I heard a soft jingling noise below. Keys.

The guard locked the downstairs door with a loud snap.

"Shit!" I whispered.

If the second story door was locked as well, I was trapped in here. But even if it wasn't locked, I couldn't carry out my plan of escape. I had to find another way out.

I tried the knob. To my immense relief, the door opened easily. I pushed it out about an inch and peeked through the gap. There was a short stretch of wall in front of me. A corridor of doors I could see off to my right. There was a railing to my left, running above the foyer.

The gallery lights came on. Slick and Moses were just coming up the main stairs, just coming into view.

I watched through the narrow opening as the two men paused on the landing to consult.

"You go upstairs," Slick said. "I'll look around down here." He brought a flashlight out of his pocket and switched it on.

"You got it," said Moses. He wound around the stairway newel post and headed up the next flight to the third floor.

I drew the stairwell door almost shut and watched to see which way Slick would go. I got a break there. He turned to his left, away from me, and went down the hall to the last door at the end. He opened the door and went through, out of sight into the room beyond. I saw his flashlight beam waving around in there.

There was no time to hesitate. If I stayed where I was, he would find me eventually, and with the door locked below, there'd be no way out. I had to get to the front stairs and go back down to the ground floor. Then maybe I could dash out the front door or out a window and get away.

I hurried down the hall toward the stairs. I passed one door, then another, then another. I was almost there, one more door away.

But now, I heard a noise from the farthest room. I saw Slick's flashlight moving back toward the hall. He was going to come out before I reached the stairs.

I did the only thing I could: I pulled open the nearest door, the last door. My heart leapt with hope. There was a stairway inside, a stairway down. I was about to step over the threshold when I realized: It wasn't a stairway in *this* house. It was the stairway in the house in Edgimond, the stairway out of the small bedroom with the dead bird in it. If I went through the door, I would pass through the veil of transition. I would be back in the wizard's clutches, back in the endless maze, back in the horror movie, heading down into the cellar where the movie-scene witches were waiting to grab me and carry me off to the sacrifice.

I froze where I was.

And Slick's flashlight hit me.

"Hold it right there, punk," he said with a laugh.

I gave a second's thought to going through the door—going back to the wizard's mansion. But I couldn't quite bring myself to do it. And anyway, the hesitation cost me the chance: it was already too late. Slick had his gun trained on me. He'd have blown me to kingdom come before I could take a step.

"Well, well, well," he said.

Gun in hand, he strolled toward me. His tall, lean frame in its blue suit was relaxed and casual. His long, cruel, handsome face was smiling.

He went on smiling right up to the moment he struck me down.

THE BLOW TOOK ME BY SURPRISE. A LEFT-FISTED PUNCH to the side of the head, quick and casual. One second, I was standing there with the guy grinning in my face, and the next, I was sitting on my ass with the stars circling around me like in an old cartoon.

Slick stooped down and grabbed me by the front of my sweatshirt.

"Upsy-daisy, punk," he said in a friendly tone.

He hauled me to my feet. My legs were wobbly under me. I felt cross-eyed. Slick's slick face swam in front of me, out of focus.

"I got him, Mo!" he called.

And Moses called back from upstairs somewhere. "Awright, Chief. On my way."

Still gripping my sweatshirt in his fist, Slick dragged me along the landing, back the way I'd come, my rubbery legs dancing under me, my head swimming. He slung me through a door. I stumbled over an open space until I banged into something: the edge of a table. I reached out to grab whatever I could. It turned out to be a chair. I managed to sit down on it, my butt landing hard on the seat.

"Toss me your backpack," said Slick, gesturing with his gun.

I was still dazed from being punched. It took me a second to understand what he was saying. During that second, Slick pulled the trigger.

The air exploded with the sound of the shot. The room seemed to quake with it. I fell to the carpet, uselessly covering my face with my two hands. Screaming at him: "Holy shit! Holy shit! What're you doing? Are you crazy?" I thought I must be wounded, but I didn't feel anything. I looked down over myself, searching for holes, for blood. There were no holes, no blood. I wasn't in pain.

"The next one goes in your kneecap," said Slick. "Now toss me the backpack, funny face."

In a panic, I fought to strip the backpack off my shoulders. It took me two tries before I could control my hands well enough to throw it to him. Still holding one arm in front of my face protectively, I peeked over it to see the mighty Moses strolling into the room. Slick lifted the backpack off the carpet and tossed it to him.

"Check that out, buddy, would you?" he said.

"Sure thing, Chief," Moses rumbled.

Still panting with fear, I grabbed hold of the chair seat and scrambled back onto it. Instinctively, I was looking around me to see where the bullet had gone. Scattered as my senses were, I began to get an idea of the room we were in. It was a big room, a banquet hall, with round tables set out on geometric carpeting and chairs set around the tables. There was a dais up front with a speaker's podium in the middle. The wall on my left seemed to be a sort of tribute wall with the words "730 Club" in enormous black letters at the top and wooden plaques with names on them in columns underneath.

That was all I saw at first. Most of my attention was focused on Slick—Slick and his gun.

The dirty cop stood in a casual pose, still pointing the weapon at me. He was waiting for Moses to finish rummaging through my pack. When the black man was done, he tossed the pack to the carpet and held my phone out to his boss.

"It's a burner," he said. "Nothing in it."

Slick took the phone and examined it. Keeping one eye on me, he poked in a number. Held the phone to his ear and waited.

My temple was beginning to throb where the bastard had punched me. I flinched and rubbed the sore spot, my gaze wandering back to the wall with the plaques on it. My eyes went idly over the names. A lot of names, a couple of hundred at least. They were in alphabetical order, the plaques fitted into metal slots so they could be moved and rearranged. I recognized some of the people, or sort of recognized them anyway. They were names I'd heard of but couldn't quite place. Chester Candy. Ron K. Pierce. Jonathan Broughton. Names like that: the sort of people you know are important, but you don't know exactly what they do. Businessmen or something, I guessed.

I heard Slick speak into the phone. "Yeah, it's me," he said. "We got him. What do you want us to do?"

It came to me with a sickening shock that he was talking to Orosgo, the Man himself. I began to turn back to him—but my eye stopped on one of the names on the plaques.

Charles Lively. My father.

"Yeah," said Slick into the phone. "Sure."

Seeing my father's name on the wall made my gaze linger on the plaques one more second. Something struck me about them now, something wrong, but with my head throbbing and my mind on my predicament, I couldn't quite figure out what it was.

Then I heard Slick say, "You got it, boss."

Boss. Yep, Orosgo. I was in big trouble here.

Now, out of the corner of my eye, I saw Slick hand the phone back to Moses. I didn't have time to think about the plaques anymore. I faced the dirty cop. He was slipping his gun into the shoulder holster inside his jacket. He was coming toward me. He was smiling again. I did not think this was a good sign.

"Hold on . . . " I said, putting my hands out in front of me to keep him away. "Listen . . . "

But he didn't hold on. He didn't listen. He just grabbed my sweatshirt in his two fists, hauled me up out of the chair and kneed me in the balls. It was a solid, straight-on blow. It made me feel as if the world had turned to vomit and I was drowning in it.

Slick tossed my body to the geometric carpet. I lay there, curled up around a pulsing core of pain.

Slick pulled my chair to him, turned it around, and straddled it. Hovering over me, he smiled down at where I lay groaning.

"My boy," he said to me, "this is not going to be a good day for you."

"I already guessed that," I managed to gasp back. I was clutching my belly, trying to breathe.

Slick laughed. "Funny man," he said to Moses. "You're a funny man," he said to me.

"He's a smart-ass, if you ask me," Moses said.

"Hear that?" Slick asked me. "Moses thinks you're a smart-ass. Moses doesn't like smart-asses. He doesn't like smart-asses, and he doesn't like dumb-asses either, and he's not nice to people he doesn't like. So that means if you're a smart-ass with Moses, you're a dumb-ass. You get it? You're two things he doesn't like rolled into one puling sack of shit curled up on the floor at my feet. It's not a good situation for you."

Curled up, puling on the floor at Slick's feet, I looked up at Moses. "Your friend sure talks a lot, doesn't he?"

That made Slick laugh out loud. But it wasn't a pleasant ha-ha-let's-all-be-friends laugh. It was more the sort of sound that would have made my balls shrivel and turn to ice if my balls hadn't currently been in the process of swelling up and catching fire.

Slick stopped laughing. "Here's what's going to happen now, punk," he said. "We're going to torture you, and then we're going to kill you. Okay?"

I rolled my eyes back toward him where he sat smiling down at me. His long, handsome face with its stylish sandy coif went in and out of focus. When I could see him, I could see he wasn't kidding.

He was smiling, yeah, but he wasn't kidding. He was telling me exactly what he was going to do: torture and kill me. Okay?

"Not really okay, no," I said.

"Well too bad, because that's the story," he went on. "We're gonna hurt you and then we're gonna shoot you, and then we're gonna bury your body in the woods. And that'll be the end of you. No one'll ever know what happened to you, and no one'll care that much either. You killed a man back at that motel, remember? You're wanted by the police. When you disappear, it'll be a mystery. But since you're nobody, it won't matter. A few people will wonder where you went. Your friends, if you have any. Maybe they'll talk about you from time to time. Maybe not. But they'll move on, sooner rather than later. Then they'll have families and lives and forget all about you. Eventually they'll die too, and that'll be it. It'll be as if you never even existed." He made a little gesture with one hand. "Sad, but true. Your life will have been brief and meaningless with a very painful and unhappy ending. Shame really. The way I hear, it didn't have to be this way. You could've had a good life. Am I wrong? A career. Money. Women. Maybe a family someday. But you made your choice, and this is the consequence. So now you're going to suffer and die and be forgotten, and that's all there is." Here, he scratched his nose thoughtfully. "You want my advice? Your best bet is to despair. I know: a lot of people think that's a mistake. You'll hear them say, you know, like: 'Where there's life, there's hope' or 'Never give up.' Shit like that. But that doesn't really make any sense in your case, does it? At this point, your life is really just a technicality. Your life is going to consist entirely of me and Moses cutting pieces off you with a dull knife until you tell us what we want to know. Under those circumstances, if you have hope, if you don't give up, you're an idiot, right? It'll only make the suffering last longer. I mean, Moses and me, we're not sadists. Sure, we'll laugh while you scream, but that's only because you'll look funny to us writing around on the floor and screaming. But we're not doing it for some kind of squirrelly pleasure. We're not sickos or anything. It's just our job. So my advice is: Abandon all hope. Despair and tell us everything. And then I'll put a bullet in you, and we'll be done. Take my advice, kid. Despair and die. It's your best bet, things being what they are."

So here's what I was thinking while this chatty psychopath yammered on above me. Actually, I was thinking two things. One, I was thinking that Slick was actually giving me pretty good advice here. I mean, the odds were incredibly high that he was describing my situation perfectly: nothing left of my life but suffering and death. And who knew what after that? A martyr's crown? A champagne brunch in heaven? Well done, thou good and faithful servant? That didn't seem likely somehow. Don't get me wrong. My mother and father had carefully raised me to believe that all religion was a manipulative lie, so it would not have surprised me one bit if this crazy killer put a bullet in my head and the next thing I knew I was standing before the throne of Jesus complete with angel choirs. What struck me as unlikely was the congratulatory champagne brunch afterward. I didn't think so—not if I got taken out now before I'd had a chance to build that hospital I'd never dreamed about building or give a beggar a crust of bread or do any damn thing to demonstrate I had the potential to be more than a polluted Hollywood loser who would've sold his soul for an assistant executive producer credit on a *Justice League* sequel.

But number two, I was thinking: kiss my rosy ass, you stinking pile of corrupt psycho horse manure. About Slick, I mean. Because listen, if there was one thing I'd learned in the past few insane days of dragon-fighting and thug-dodging and clue-hunting and mind-bending revelations, it was this: my life was full of liars, and all the liars lied. My mom, my dad, my brother, even my kooky little sister in her kooky little way; my memory, my heart, my sources of daily news—all of them had played me false in one sense or another. I no longer knew who I was or what was true about me or what was true about anything or how to find out what was true or how to know it was true when I found it. But there seemed one thing of which I could be completely certain. If anyone in any way involved with Serge Orosgo told me something, the odds were spectacular that that something was completely false. If Orosgo said he was trying to make the world a better place, I knew he had to be stopped. If *The New York Times* said he was amazing, he was garbage. If my mom and dad said there was no God, we were, every one of us, in big, big trouble come Judgement Day.

And if Slick the Corrupt Cop told me to despair and die, well then, "Kiss my rosy ass," seemed the only appropriate response.

"So here's the thing, Slick," I said. "You mind if I call you Slick?" My voice sounded like an unoiled hinge. It took me three tries before I could uncurl my throbbing bod and sit up on the carpet under the chair-straddling Slick's watchful gaze. "I take your point, all right? I mean, look at me. Do I look like a hero to you? I didn't think so. When you tell me there's nothing but suffering and death in front of me—that I ought to just despair and die—hey, that's my philosophy of life on a *good* day. So the whole torture thing doesn't work for me, and I'm happy to tell you anything you want to know . . . "

"Oh," said Slick mournfully, shaking his head. "I get the feeling you're about to say 'but.' Aren't you? Something like, 'But I don't know anything?' "

"But I *don't* know anything!" I insisted.

"Wrong answer, punk."

"You want to know where my sister is, right? If I knew where my sister was, would I be here?"

Slick went on smiling, but I got the feeling he wasn't smiling on the inside. "What about the book?" he said.

"Riley must have it, no? Isn't that why you're looking for her? That's why we're both here, right? If we knew where she was or the book was, we'd be there. But we're here instead."

Slick shook his head. He stepped away from me and exchanged a whispered word with Moses.

And I, meanwhile—well, I can say with all modesty that during this small pause in the general conversation, I did something that surprised even myself with its cool-headed alertness. Because it should go without saying at this point that I was in an absolute frenzy of panicking terror behind my hopefully snarky exterior. I was full of silent shrieking at the prospect of having these guys cut pieces off me and preoccupied with frantic imaginings about which of my favorite pieces they'd start with and so on. But at the same time, I was using that trick I'd learned in Galiana. Thinking past the fear. Acting, blank-minded, past the fear. And so, while Slick was exchanging whispered words with Moses, I shifted my own glance up to the name plaques on the wall behind him.

Why? Because it had occurred to me what was wrong with the names up there, what had been bothering me about them before. My father had a plaque. He was one of the "730 Club." But not my mother. Not my brother. Which meant there was something special about 730 membership, that not all of Orosgo's minions got in, only some. And that meant, if I could find the links among the names on that wall, it would tell me something about the club's nature, something I didn't already know. And that, in turn, made me suspect that maybe this—this wall of names—was the information in plain sight that Jason Broadstreet had promised to send to Riley.

I couldn't take a photo of the wall to refer to later—assuming there was a later, which by no means seemed certain—but in the few seconds during which Slick and Moses were murmuring to each other, I did what I could: I picked out a few names and tried to commit them to memory. Chester Candy. Ron K. Pierce. Jonathan

Broughton—the ones I'd seen before. And also Susan Roth, Gerald Hannity . . . and that was it. Time was up.

Because Slick was coming toward me again, smiling at me again, and I knew what he was going to say. In fact, I was counting on him saying it.

And he did say it. He said: "Sorry, punk. Not good enough. Maybe you're telling the truth and maybe you're not, but we won't be sure until we butcher you to the point where if you did know where the book was, you'd tell us. Then, when I'm tossing bits of you over my shoulder, and what's left of you looks like something the average man would barbecue, if you still tell me you don't know anything? Well, I promise to shoot you before we bury you. Which isn't much, I know, but it's the best I can do." He gestured with his head at Moses. "Take him down to the cellar."

That was the part I was counting on. The take-him-down-to-the-cellar part. I'd figured they'd do something like that before they really got started on me. It only made sense, right? They weren't going to cut me up right here and dump a gallon and a half of blood on the geometric carpet of the 730 banquet hall, were they? Of course not. They'd have to take me into the cellar or out into the woods—or somewhere. Which meant they'd have to take me to the stairs.

Which is what they did. With a couple of giant steps, Moses was standing over me. He reached down and grabbed me under the arm with a hand the size of—I don't know—a really big hand—I'm talking an enormous hand with enormous strength in it. He hauled me to my feet so easily I might've been a rag doll or just a rag. He practically carried me to the door like that, one-handed. My toes barely touched the floor as I scurried to keep up with him.

Out into the hall we went, and then along the corridor toward the stairs. But then came the part I was waiting for: because before we got to the stairs, we passed that door again, the door through which

I'd seen the portal back into the wizard's house in Edgimond, the stairs to the mansion cellar shimmering behind the veil of transition, that pathway that I knew would lead me down to my own sacrifice, à la *Horror Mansion.*

So that was my choice: let Moses carry me down to the cellar to be cut to pieces or try a fast break back into Edgimond—where, okay, yes, I would likewise be carried down to the cellar and cut to pieces.

Still, I chose B, for obvious reasons—obvious to me anyway. And even so, I wasn't totally sure I was going to be able to yank myself out of this titan's iron grip. I only had a second to figure it out, that one second in which he escorted me past the magic door. The way I figured it was this: there are small men in this world and there are big men, and then there are men the size of Moses. But they all have knees.

I lifted my foot and planted the side of my sneaker into the side of Moses's kneecap with all the force I could muster. Did he topple over? Hell no. It was like kicking the Empire State Building—if the Empire State Building had knees. Moses did have them, and his knee did buckle under the blow just enough to make him lose his balance and loose his grip on my arm, not entirely but a little.

That was my moment. I snatched myself from his hand using all the strength I had. And even as he spun toward me, even as his hand went into his jacket to draw his gun, I hurled myself through the door, through the veil, through the portal into another kingdom.

And that is how I narrowly avoided certain death in Orosgo's mansion and escaped into certain death in the mansion of the wizard.

27

SUDDENLY I WAS STANDING ON A DESCENDING STONE staircase, holding a lantern in my hand. Behind me was the little bedroom where I'd found the dead bird just like the blonde in the movie had. When I looked back over my shoulder, I could see it there: the bedroom, not the 730 House from which I'd just come. For some reason, I could only see through the portals in one direction, not the way back.

I faced forward, trying to reorient myself, trying to drag my mind out of Orosgo's mansion of horrors and back here into this one. There was no time to screw around about it. I could hear the church bell tolling in the misty distance. Time was speeding up in this crazy house. Dawn was coming full speed—dawn and torment eternal.

I drew a deep breath. Focused. Below me, down the stairs, there was darkness. Up out of that darkness came the distant sound of chanting, a soul-chilling sound full of cultic evil. I knew what was waiting for me down there. I had seen the movie. Demonic witches and their acolytes were preparing for the victim they would sacrifice on their stone altar table. Waiting, that is to say, for me.

But there was no going back. I braced myself. The light from my lantern was unsteady and weak, a dancing candle flame. It cast weird shadows on the dripping stone walls. Just like in the movie. I started down the steps, my heart pounding.

Why had I returned to this place—this place where time was running out, where the penalty for not escaping the mansion maze by dawn was an eternity of suffering, a forever trapped in this house of horror, lost in a dream of sick surrender, devoured by the dragon every nightfall. Why had I decided to take my chances with Curtin's deadly labyrinth rather than try to escape Slick and Moses back in the Oregon woods?

I'll tell you why. It was because whatever was going to happen with Slick and Moses hadn't happened yet. It was the future, unknowable, random, all surprises. But this, what was happening right here, right now—Curtin had manufactured this out of images he found in my own mind, images I had buried there when I had buried my memories of *Horror Mansion*, when I had made myself forget the movie with which my father had tortured baby Riley, with which he had taught her to keep her mouth shut, with which he had driven her nearly insane.

But the memory was buried no longer. I had seen the movie. I knew what happened next. Which gave me at least a chance—some chance—to stop it before it happened again, to stop it and to get away.

So down, down, down I went into the dark. Just like in the movie. Down to the bottom of the stairs and into the long corridor. The deep, rhythmic, demonic chanting was louder here. The lantern glow threw its dim and flickering shadows on the floor and walls. Just like the blonde in the movie, I crept slowly along the dark hall. Just like in the movie, I passed statues and a gargoyle set in niches along the way. And just like in the movie, I could feel the cowled acolytes detach themselves from the shadows behind me. I could feel them creeping after me, ready to grab me and force me to the altar table.

And now, just like the blonde in the movie, I spotted torchlight up ahead. I knew I was approaching the altar room where my sacrifice would take place. And just like that idiot movie blonde—that blonde as stupid as any character who ever walked down a dark cellar hall in a cheap horror film—I kept going. Going slowly, slowly toward the chanting, toward the torchlight, toward the altar table where I would die.

At last, it happened: just like in the movie. The acolytes surged out of the darkness. Two of them grabbed me, one by each arm. Even though I was expecting them, they took hold of me with such sudden violence, I dropped the lantern. It crashed dully on the stone floor and went dark. Everything now was lit by the torches. Every face was yellow with their light. Every eyeball rolled white in the glow of them. Every shadow spread like a dancing stain, enormous, on the walls.

The acolytes carried me through the doorway. The altar table rose large before me. The cowled figures surrounding it went on chanting their eldritch chant.

All of it just like in the movie.

Except for what happened next.

When the circle of cowled and chanting figures parted from around the altar to receive my body, it wasn't the Chief Witch standing there waiting at the head of the table.

It was the dragon.

I had not been expecting that. The sudden sight of that hideous creature rising up from the floor like a mushroom cloud sent a hot flood of terror through my core. The beast reared up, huge and strobic in the flickering flamelight. The corpses that formed its body flailed and pulsed along its flanks. The faces of the devoured dead—faces that had become its flesh—stared at me open-mouthed. Its roar—that shrieking roar that was a hundred murdered voices—filled the little chamber, deafening. The sound paralyzed my mind.

For a full second, I couldn't even struggle. I could only gape at the thing, helpless, as the chanting acolytes rushed me forward, carried me to the altar table, offered me up to the dragon.

That moment just then—that moment before they lay me helpless on the stone beneath the beast just as they had laid the movie blonde helpless beneath the witch's long dagger—that moment was a nightmare that had lived secretly inside me forever, the nightmare of what my father was, of what he had done to my sister, of what my sister knew that I did not want to know. And now the scene had come to life, just like in the movie.

Except the victim was me. Except the Chief Witch was the dragon.

And except for this: I had the dagger.

Oh yes. Oh yes. I'd seen this movie, remember? I'd seen where the long dagger was hidden along the corridor, clutched in the gargoyle's claws. I had taken it for myself as I passed by and quietly slipped it into my waistband. The witches' acolytes hadn't seemed to notice. Maybe they felt the dagger wasn't necessary because they were offering me up to the beast instead of the Chief Witch. But in any case, it seemed they hadn't thought about the long dagger at all.

But I had thought about it. And I hadn't come to this sacrifice a helpless victim like the movie blonde. I had come armed with a savage blade.

The acolytes had hold of me by the upper arms, their fingers digging hard into my armpits, hoisting me up on my toes. But my lower arms were free. I could bend my elbows. I moved my right hand to my waist. I gripped the hilt of the long dagger. The acolytes forced me toward the altar. But as they did, I drew the blade. I twisted my arm and jabbed the gleaming point back over my right shoulder. I felt it sink into soft flesh. I heard the acolyte's high-pitched scream. He released his hold on me.

Now, with one arm free, I spun to the left and stabbed again. This time, I saw the knife go in, straight in beneath the witch's cowl to lance the throat of this chanting dickhead who was trying to serve me up as dragon food. He gagged and reeled away—and I was free.

Startled and confused, the acolytes and witches backed away from me, their torchlit eyes wide and gleaming beneath their cowls. I didn't wait for them to recover their senses. I had only one chance—one second and one chance—and I seized them both.

I faced forward. The stone altar table stood about waist high to me. I grabbed the edge of it with my free hand. Juiced by a spurt of adrenaline and fear, I found the power to step high and lift my whole body up over the side in a single swift motion. I vaulted up onto the tabletop.

The dragon saw me coming. The beast filled the room with its hideous roar. I stood beneath him on the altar table, the long dagger gripped in my fist. The beast reared up high above me, ready to swoop down and rip me in half between its shark-toothed jaws.

It swooped. Its open mouth came toward me, already starting to snap shut like a bear trap. I swung the knife in a furious roundhouse, turning my body to the side as I did. The dragon's mouth shot past me, missed me. The dagger blade sank hilt-deep into the creature's enormous eye. The dragon screamed again, convulsing backward in his agony. I felt the hot breath of the beast blow over me, full of death.

I managed to hold on to the dagger hilt, and the blade came free as the wounded beast pulled away. It swiped at me reflexively with its tremendous bayonet-like claws. I saw the movement only at the last second and managed to leap back to the very edge of the altar table. I teetered there, about to fall, frantically pinwheeling my arms for balance.

Then I found my balance as the wind of the sweeping claw swept by, and I rushed forward again, stabbing again. The blade went into a dead man's face—a gaping face that formed part of the dragon's neck. A flood of green-black blood gouted out over me, stinking of human terror.

I wrenched the dagger free and stabbed again and then again as the beast screamed and screamed and its mucous-like blood spewed everywhere. The acolytes in the shadows below me were also screaming—reeling and screaming and grabbing themselves as if I were stabbing them too, not just the beast.

And I—I was wild now. Senseless with fear and fury. I kept stabbing and stabbing at the dragon, the blade chucking deep into its fleshly hide again and again. I was awash in goo and gore, but I just kept stabbing. And the dragon's shrieks became grunts and growls and agonized mutterings.

The great beast wobbled. Its titanic form began to sink down toward the floor. Then it collapsed. Its head—a head formed of other heads and various body parts—smacked against the altar at my feet. I stabbed down at it, roaring madly. Stabbed and stabbed. And then, still groaning in a dozen dead voices, the dragon slid off the table, and the whole room shook as its body hit the floor.

Gasping and sobbing, I spun around, expecting a dozen witches and cowled madmen to rush forward and launch themselves at me. But that's not what happened.

What happened was this:

As I stood on the tabletop, dripping and rancid, the dripping, rancid dagger still gripped in my gory hand, I saw the cowled figures around me begin to sink away. Their faces grew soft and dark and shriveled and then caved in to the center of their cowls. Their eyes dripped down over the running flesh of their cheeks, and the robes they'd been wearing fluttered to the floor, empty now, mere cloth.

Nearly senseless, half-deranged, I stared around me, then gaped down over the edge of the altar table. I saw the dragon lying on its side on the floor, breathing huge, hoarse, and dying breaths. It seemed to be deflating as I watched, the substance of it bleeding out across the floor stones, the shape of it collapsing into its own puddled carnage.

And then—then, as the beast liquefied, a gust of shadows blew up out of it, a supernatural wind composed of human shapes. The tangled smoke of it rose past me, past my eyes so that I saw within the haze the spirits of people that the creature had devoured, just shady glimpses of them, the diners from the banquet hall and the women from the pit and more, rising from the dead creature's final breath, specter-like, dissipating into the torchlit cellar air to enter what next dimension I just can't tell you, I just don't know.

The dragon died and shriveled away. The spirits of its dead rose free. The witches and the acolytes melted into the cobblestones, all of them connected, I suddenly realized, all of them part of one half-remembered horror in one miserable mind: my own. I had defeated them, as I only vaguely understood then, by simple virtue of the fact that I had remembered them at last, confronted them at last, fought them face-to-face at long last.

I don't know how long I would have stood there on that table, how long I would have stood there staring, wet with slaughter, dripping with death. But now, a new sound vibrated through the fog of my stunned consciousness: a slow, mellow bell tolling somewhere far away. It was tolling the time. The passing time. The time till dawn.

I blinked and panned my shocked stare across the altar room. Somehow, I had to get out of here before the sun rose. I had to escape the labyrinth.

And now, at last, I knew how.

Slowly, grimacing at my own stench, I climbed down off the altar table. I looked along the floor, and there it was, just as I remembered: the gutter. The gutter where the blonde's blood had run out of Horror Mansion in the movie, run out through the walls into the fog outside.

My gaze traced the gutter's path. And yes, sure enough, I spotted a round hole in the base of the cellar wall: a drain that would let the blood of sacrifice flow out of the cellar. Just like in the movie.

Would the drain get me out of here? Would it finally get me free of the seemingly endless mazes of this house? I didn't know. But I was going to find out.

I walked along the gutter to the wall, then lay down upon the stones. I worked my hand and arm through the opening—and with a tremor of half-admitted hope, I felt rain—I felt cold air on my palm and the refreshing patter of the misty rain.

I worked my head through the hole and then the other arm. I was still clutching the long dagger in one hand, so I drove its point down deep into the soft earth. Using the hilt for a handle, I dragged my torso and my legs out of the drain. I crawled a few more feet across the sodden ground and then collapsed in the mud.

Was I out? Was I out of the labyrinth?

I used my last drop of strength to lift my head and look around me. My vision blurred as my eyes filled with tears. I could see across the rain-washed lawn to the tree line of the forest, the Children's Forest, where the magician Natani, trapped in the water of the pond, was weeping for his Maud. The first light of day was seeping through the curtain of the rainfall and causing the autumn trees to emerge from their own silhouettes.

I had done it. I was free. Free of Curtin's Horror Mansion. The sun had not yet risen, and I had escaped the maze.

I collapsed onto the earth again, weeping with exhaustion, laughing with relief. I lay there limp, my cheek pressed into the wet dirt. I let the rain wash the stinking dragon gore off my face, off my body. I lay there a long time.

The rain slowed, then ceased. A line of yellow light inched across the land from the east, then swiftly shot out over me, a wedge of warmth. The touch of dawn seemed to infuse me with new life. I stirred. I pushed myself to my knees. I left the dagger sticking in the ground and climbed to my feet. My tired body slumped as I stood watching the swaying trees of the forest blooming out of the dark of night. Their last autumn leaves turned red and yellow and green as the daylight washed over them. I drew a deep breath of the clean air.

Finally, I turned—turned full around to face the mansion. Like a gladiator who had just won a duel, I wanted to confront the opponent I had defeated.

But to my dull-headed astonishment, the mansion was gone. There was nothing there at all but the slowly drifting mist, the dissipating mist with the sun shining through it. Beyond that, I could just make out a great expanse of blue grass on rolling hills.

Where was Horror Mansion? Had it ever really been there? Was everything I'd seen a fantasy cooked up by the wizard? Or was even the wizard—the wizard and Edgimond and Galiana and all of it—a massive hallucination projected out of a brain gone bad?

I looked down at myself. The last of the green dragon gore was still visible on my arms and my tunic, dripping down in globs. The stench of it was still there on the air around me.

It must have been real, I thought. It must have been.

I heard a sound, a snort. I lifted my head. A sheet of mist blew coldly over me. It coiled and somersaulted and split apart.

And there stood my black stallion. Snorting again. Lifting its head as if to greet me.

I smiled weakly. "How the hell do you do that?" I asked him.

The horse came toward me in a slow, slouching walk, its head hung down as if it was abashed at having deserted me this long. When it reached me, I put my hand on the side of its head, my nose to his nose. How good it was to see his friendly horse face, to feel his soft hair against me.

I whispered in the stallion's ear: "Let's blow this fun house."

The stallion snorted and nodded.

I gripped his saddle. I lifted my foot into the stirrup and swung up into the seat in one graceful motion—if I do say so myself. I snapped the reins and clicked my tongue and off we rode over the empty land—over the open space where Horror Mansion used to be.

28

I FOLLOWED THE RISING SUN. THE MIST SLOWLY dissolved and vanished. The sky turned blue. I was leaving Edgimond. I could feel it. I was entering another of the Eleven Lands, a country free of the wizard's influence. The air was balmy here. The birds sang merrily in the trees.

My heart grew full as I passed a clutch of farmhands working in an orchard. They were young men and women, real girls and real boys, nothing pretend about them, all of them laughing and flirting together, the girls blushing, teasing, the boys braggy and bold. One particularly pretty young redhead was reaching up into the branches and then bending over her basket in a way that showed off her fine, slim figure. I watched her as I came near, feeling the sweet warmth of natural desire flowing through me, bringing me back to life after my long imprisonment. The girl glanced over her shoulder and caught me watching her. She laughed a taunting laugh.

Life, I thought gladly. Sexy life.

"Excuse me, my friends!" I called out to them. "What country is this?"

"Why, it's Menaria," one lad called back. He seemed surprised I didn't know. They all seemed surprised.

One of the girls called to me, "Where are you coming from?"

"Edgimond," I said.

Now all of them gaped. The first lad shook his head. "No one comes out of Edgimond anymore," he said.

I smiled. "I did," I told him—and I rode on.

The blue fields stretched out around me. Thoughts crowded my mind. Questions. What had I learned? Where was I headed? Why had I been chosen for this quest?

I reached the banks of a river. I dismounted. I let the stallion drink, and I drank. I swam in the water fully clothed. I washed the last of the gore off me. I stood in the gentle current and lifted my face to the noon sun.

More questions. So many. Why had my father terrorized Riley? What was the meaning of the names on the wall of the banquet hall in the Oregon mansion? Was that really Curtin I had seen in the mansion's window? And how could I escape the mansion there as I had escaped it here?

I remounted. I rode on. I tried to figure out how I had gotten here. I tried to construct a new narrative of my life including what I'd learned. How could I even begin to know myself unless I could understand my own past? We live in time. Our lives are like stories, day after day like page after page, all connected, beginning to end. How can you make sense of any one moment without all the moments that make it fully what it is?

As I rode, as I tried to think about my past, my hand went reflexively to my throat. I was trying to touch the locket there, Betheray's locket. To see if it would take me back into my memories again.

But of course, I wasn't wearing the locket now, not here in this other kingdom. I was wearing the talisman instead, the talisman of Anastasius. And now, when I touched it, for the first time, it pulsed with warmth too, just as the locket had. Just like the locket, it seemed to sweep my mind off elsewhere. But not into a memory. Into a vision.

I saw a city. A white city turning red in the light of the sinking sun. I saw it as clearly as if it had actually appeared on the landscape before me.

I remembered Maud's instructions to me. *Follow the rising sun across the Eleven Lands, and the emperor will call you to him.*

That's what this was. This image coming into my imagination through the living heat of the talisman. This visionary city. It was the call of Anastasius. The emperor was drawing me to him.

Following the vision, I turned my horse to the right. A high tor blocked my view. We rode around the edges of it, a long journey. We emerged on the far side as afternoon began to draw into evening. I approached the edge of a cliff. Reached it. Looked over. And I felt a thrill.

There it was: the white city, the very city of my vision, a city of startling stone rising up out of the level grasslands. Towers and pinnacles, square apartment blocks and columned temples and great domes, all of it made of white granite and marble, all of it beginning to glow red as the sun went down behind my left shoulder and its yellow light deepened to crimson.

My stallion and I rode along the cliff until we found a switchback passage down. Then we descended.

THERE WAS STILL some daylight left when I came to the edge of the city. By then, I had grown wary of the place. Something was wrong here. Nothing was moving. Or that is, the place was so still that everything that did move drew my eye. Whenever I turned toward some sudden motion, I saw—what? A squirrel, a bird, a bizarre reptile, an alien creature shaped like a mantis but furry and mammalian. All kinds of living things, in other words, but no women, no men.

This was weird, but it soon got weirder. I approached the city limits. There were no walls, just a border formed by adjacent buildings. Where the buildings parted, streets ran into the heart of town.

The city's stone had lost its red glow as dusk grew deeper. Its walls and columns and spires and domes were all turning gray. It was getting dark, and it was even darker once I rode a ways, and the buildings rose around me, blocking the light of the sunset. In fact, it was so shadowy here that I traveled a good few yards before I noticed the statues.

The first one really gave me a start. I glimpsed it out of the corner of my eye and gasped aloud and spun in the saddle to look at it. It was a man carved in marble. A small, tubby bald man. A strangely commonplace subject for a sculpture. It looked as if the artist had caught him in a random motion rather than a pose. He had one hand resting on his belly, a self-satisfied smile on his round face. He was dressed like an ancient Roman, in a loose robe that draped his body in elaborate folds.

Even as I recovered from my first surprise, a pigeon-like bird, startled by my passing, shot out of a building loft. I gasped again and turned toward the movement. And there was another statue—no, two more—no, three. Three marble women in marble robes standing in the street, their baskets on their shoulders. Two of them stood face-to-face as if in conversation, and the third was just turning away from them, as if she'd said goodbye and was heading home.

I went past them, down the road. I turned a corner and approached a marble arch. Its massive pediment was carved with images of a military triumph: a cavalry parade. At the center of the march was the figure of a king riding the back of something like a rhinoceros. The broad and bearded rider wore a crown and held his sword upright like a scepter. Below, on the frieze, was what must have been a caption: symbols or runes etched into the stone. Obviously, I couldn't read the words. And yet, by some strange magic, as I looked up at them, I began to understand their meaning.

The Triumph of King Cambitus, the Not Altogether Wise.

Funny title for a king. Another time, it would have made me laugh. I did smile a little but, almost at once, I noticed the deepening shadows on the pavement, the last daylight fading there. This city—so silent, so still, and growing so dark—was becoming so eerie now it was oppressive.

I passed under the arch and came out into a paved, open square, surrounded by massive, official-looking buildings. There was a domed and church-like structure to my right, an arcade with a long colonnade to my left. Straight ahead of me, a tremendous complex of buildings rose against the dusk sky. There were at least half a dozen columned entrances, just as many zig-zagging stairways, and tiers of porticoed temples, their pediments surrounded and crowned with monuments to kings.

Below, in the square all around me, there were statues, statues everywhere, statues of men and women both. Everyday figures, all of them, who seemed to have been carved in a moment of everyday action. Talking, walking, buying, selling.

I crossed the square, weaving among the statues, moving toward the complex. That seemed the center of things. If there was anyone alive here, I figured that's where he would be. My stallion's hooves clip-clopped on the cobblestones. The sound echoed in the uncanny silence all around me.

I found a trough of water at the base of a flight of steps. I left the horse there to drink. I climbed the stairs, a long climb, two long flights, the second zigging right off the first. There were two guards at the top or, I mean to say, statues of guards, statues of soldiers standing at attention, holding their spears. I sidled between them.

Then I went along a high arcade past more statues of more soldiers. I passed through covered rooms, walled with marble, decorated with frescoes that were hard to see in the purple dusk. There were statues of noblemen and noblewomen here—and more soldiers—more statues of soldiers carved in the act of marching past or standing guard.

I climbed the stairs. At the top, in the deepening shadows of evening, I found myself in a rose marble courtyard. Some of the statues here were different from the rest. They were larger than life and set on pedestals. It was hard to make them out in the dark, but I saw a mounted horseman, a muscleman lifting a nude woman into the air, and a mythic, half-human beast among some others. Near the base of these larger statues, there were the usual smaller ones, life-sized, noblemen and noblewomen, and lots of soldiers.

Finally, on the far end of the courtyard, I saw an enormous marble doorway that led into a throne room. I could see this pretty clearly because there were braziers in there, iron dishes on iron stands, loaded with hot coals that gave off a red glow. The glow illuminated the marble throne at the center of the place. A little group of men in togas—statues of men in togas—clustered at the base of the throne.

And on the throne, there sat the king—the statue of the king—the same king, it looked to me, as was carved on the arch: King Cambitus, the Not Altogether Wise. Broad-shouldered, barrel-chested, bearded with a great beard. And there was something strange about his face—strangely familiar. I approached him, trying to remember where I'd seen those patrician features before.

It was growing darker by the second now. The coals in the braziers seemed to burn brighter. And still, everything—all the statues, the whole city—was absolutely silent, absolutely motionless. I felt utterly alone.

I walked across the court among the great statues and the smaller ones. I walked toward the final doorway, toward the glowing braziers, toward the throne.

And here's where things started to get crazy. As I stepped close to the throne room door, a strange haze appeared, like a white curtain over the archway. Through the haze I could see—not the throne room—but the mansion in Oregon. I could make out the side hall I had just flung myself into after kicking Moses in the knee. I could see the design on the red runner and the vase standing on the tall wooden pedestal to my left.

It was a veil of transition. For the first time, for some reason, I could see from this world into the other, into real life. If I stepped through that veil, I would be transported back to Oregon. Moses would be right behind me, Slick, too, probably, both men drawing their guns, ready to shoot me down.

I stopped on the threshold, as motionless as the statues. Looking at the scene through the veil, I thought maybe . . . maybe there was a way I could fight back against these thugs as I had fought the dragon in the mansion. It was a long shot, but it might work.

Then I thought: No. There was absolutely no chance I was going to do anything as stupid as walking through that veil.

Then that's what I did.

Here's why.

I glanced behind me, back over the court. I saw the life-sized statues of soldiers and the larger-than-life-size statues of mounted men and hybrid beasts all sinking into the shadows of night. Beyond them, I could see out through the courtyard entrance, out over the stairs, out over the great square below, to the sky above the city. I could see right out to the horizon where the first faint stars were appearing in the inky blue.

And then, a bright spot, a gleam of light, appeared down low, right at the place where the sky touched the ground. The gleam grew bigger, brighter, and I realized: it was the moon, the rising moon, a full moon. Even as the daylight finally died, the moon's glow spread like a pale silver mist over the city.

Someone coughed.

I stiffened. I froze. I thought: *What was that?*

Someone else cleared his throat. I saw something move at the corner of my eye. I turned to see what it was.

And then, suddenly, out of the silent city, someone let out a loud shout.

"Intruder! Assassin! Get him!"

With that, several of the white marble soldiers suddenly flushed with color and lowered their spears at me. Then several more did the same.

I stared at them, stupid-faced, my mouth hanging open. I must've looked like the simplest simpleton in Simple Town.

Because now, as the moonlight touched them, the statues began to come to life. Not the big statues, just the life-sized ones. The lunar glow seemed to paint their stone with humanity, and motion rose up out of the core of them to touch the suddenly fleshly surface. The noblemen and noblewomen blinked into consciousness, turning toward me in surprise.

And the soldiers—so many soldiers with so many spears and so many swords—with bronze helmets on their heads and breastplates on their torsos and leather greaves on their legs—and did I mention the spears and swords? There were an awful lot of spears and swords. And the soldiers began to move into action.

Now one guy, a particularly big and burly centurion, lifted his sword high in the air. His mouth twisted with warrior rage under his black, burly beard. His eyes grew hot and wild.

"Get him!" he shouted again. "He's heading for the throne room."

It took me another stupid second to realize: he was talking about me.

As one, the soldiers rushed together to form a phalanx. They lowered their spear points at me. They lifted their swords. I was suddenly looking at a wedge of sharp steel, blades flashing, moonlit, out of the shadows. The courtyard, shrouded with eerie silence just a second ago, was suddenly ringing with battle cries.

"Get him!"

"Assassin!"

"Protect the king!"

I lifted my hands up in surrender. "Hold on!" I shouted. "I'm not an assassin. I'm a story analyst!"

They charged.

There seemed no point reaching for my magic sword. There were just too many of them. Nothing less than a blast from a machine gun would even slow them down.

The floor beneath me shook with their thundering footsteps. My vision filled with their furious faces and their deadly blades.

I knew what I had to do.

29

I TURNED AND STEPPED THROUGH THE VEIL OF transition back into Orosgo's mansion. I knew I was only delaying the moment when the guards would wash over me and cut me to pieces. But at least delaying the moment delayed the moment, if you see what I mean. Also, it was part of the strange quality of this fantastic other world that I always half-believed each visit there would be my last. I always harbored a vague hope that once I was back in the real world, I would get some modern medical care and find a cure for this insanity, and Galiana and Edgimond and Menaria and all the Eleven Lands would become just bad memories, just symptoms of my former madness, a disease I used to have.

And then, there was this: I had no idea how I was going to fend off the blood-lusting charge of so many statue soldiers. But I did have at least the first glimmer of a notion about what to do next in Oregon. I had a plan. Sort of.

I flashed back into the mansion just where I had left it, dodging through the doorway into the short hall with Moses recovering his balance and going for his gun behind me.

Two running steps brought me abreast of the pedestal with the vase on it—a tall, thick pedestal made of some dark, heavy wood with carved brass inlays on its sides.

I glanced over my shoulder and there was Moses, his gun leveled at me. He was about to shoot.

I hurled myself behind the pedestal and dropped into a low crouch, just as the big thug fired.

His gun roared three times. I screamed in fear as the hall shook with the deafening blasts. I don't know where all the bullets went, but one of them must have hit the pedestal because the heavy wooden stand shuddered violently, and the pottery vase tilted off the top of it and spilled down through the air to shatter into shards on the floor beside me.

Now, this—ducking behind the pedestal—this had actually been the first part of my plan. But I couldn't remember the rest. The gunshots had totally scattered my thoughts. I could not for the life of me think of what I was supposed to do next. It was something really clever. Something like what I'd done in the altar room with the dragon . . . the long dagger . . .

For the moment though, all I could think about was whether I'd been shot. I was frantically examining my body, searching for blood and wounds. There were none.

Then it was too late. Moses charged into view. His gun was pointed straight at me where I crouched, cowering against the wall. He could have killed me right then and there, but he didn't. He just looked down at me and shook his head as if I were a pathetic fool. Which I guess I was.

"Get on your feet, asshole," he said.

A second later, Slick was there beside him. He'd come running at the sound of trouble. He had his own gun drawn in one hand, and my backpack dangling from his other. When he saw me crouched against the wall surrounded by pottery shards, he bared his teeth in a grin of raw anger. He tossed the backpack to the floor but held onto his gun. Stepping forward, he reached down and grabbed the front of my sweatshirt in his fist.

"You heard the man. Get up, punk!"

Suddenly, I remembered the rest of my plan.

Furious, Slick hauled me out of my crouch.

And as I went up, I seized hold of a sharp wedge of broken pottery. I grabbed the back of Slick's head with one hand and jammed the shard into his eye.

That was it. That was my plan. Well, originally, I was going to knock the vase off the pedestal myself and then hide the shard until I could use it as a weapon, the way I'd hid the long dagger in the cellar of Horror Mansion. But then, when Moses started shooting at me, I forgot to knock over the vase. I forgot everything. I forgot my own name. Luckily, the vase had fallen and broken anyway. So when my brain cleared, when my plan returned to me, I improvised. I grabbed the shard and used it on the spot.

You wouldn't have thought a tough guy like Slick would scream like he did: that wild, high-pitched squealing scream like a wounded rabbit. But the blow had struck him dead on, and the point of the shard had caused his eye to explode in a burst of jelly. It was ugly to see and must have been even uglier if you were on the receiving end of it.

Anyway, Slick squealed and reeled and dropped his gun and clutched his face with both hands. And the gun fell onto the hallway runner. And Moses was turning to look at his partner in round-eyed horror. And I swept Slick's gun up off the floor. And Moses saw me do it and turned and tightened his finger on the trigger.

And I shot him. Bang. Bang. Bang. Three times. The gun jolting in my fist.

He was a giant of a man, Moses was, a big target. I didn't get a chance to aim, and I wasn't exactly a sharpshooter anyway, but I hit him eventually. The first bullet went into the wall behind him, scattering plaster. The second bullet made his jacket flutter as a black hole appeared in his shoulder. His hand flew wide and his gun flew out of it. He staggered back against the wall. The third bullet hit him smack in the center of the chest. He looked surprised—and then he looked dead. He slid down to sit on the floor, staring at me, slack-jawed, empty-eyed.

I was already on the move. Still gripping the gun, I grabbed my backpack. Frantic, I ran back toward the door, back toward the second-floor gallery. All I wanted was to get out of that house.

But the second I stepped across the threshold, I heard shouting from the floor below. I cursed. I had forgotten about the other guards down there, still searching for me. They had heard the gunshots. They were charging into the foyer, charging up the main stairway to see what was going on. There was no escape for me in that direction.

I turned quickly, wildly, clutching my backpack, clutching Slick's gun. I ran for the door down the hall, the one that led to the back stairs that had brought me up here in the first place.

The next moment, I was in the stairwell, racing down. I reached the door at the bottom. I didn't bother to try to open it. I knew it was locked. I lifted my knee up high and kicked out, hitting the door just below the knob. The door flew open. I burst out into the downstairs hall.

I rocketed down the corridor like there was fire shooting out the back of me. I knew the guards must have heard my breakout. I knew they'd be running to the gallery rail to try to shoot me down from above. I had to beat them to the front door.

I got there. Seized the knob.

"There he is!" I heard someone shout above me.

I pulled the front door open. The cold air washed over my face. Then: the gunshot I was expecting. A sidelight shattered. They'd missed me. I plunged out the front door into the night.

Then I was across the drive and into the forest, running wild. Pines like specters loomed around me. The forest depths yawned black ahead. Here and there, the risen moon dodged in and out of view above the treetops. It made the white bark of quivering aspen glow in the shadows.

At first, I heard the men behind me, shouting, giving chase. I saw the beams of their flashlights dancing crazily over vines and branches. But not for long. A few swift seconds and I was deep, deep in the forest, impossible to trace in all that tangled darkness.

I ran until I tripped on something—a root, I guess. I spilled to the earth headlong, jarring my shoulder, bruising my rib, scraping the back of my hand. Even that didn't stop me. I leapt to my feet on the instant and, an instant later, I was running again.

There was no way for me to retrace my steps, no way to come out of the forest where I'd entered it. But I knew my general direction and kept the moon to the right of me. When I finally flew past the tree line and burst out onto an empty dirt road, I felt pretty certain that I wasn't far from the Passat. I was gasping for breath by then, hacking, sweating, but I still didn't stop. With my backpack slung over one shoulder now and Slick's gun still gripped in my hand, I hied it up the dirt road as fast I could go.

And yes, I found my car, there where the dirt road ended. I slid in behind the wheel fast, tossing my pack and the gun onto the passenger seat. I started the engine and swung the Passat around and hit the gas.

I'M NOT SURE how I got away from there, or why exactly. If the bad guys had come after me, if they'd come down the mansion's main drive in their Jeeps, they could have blocked the dirt road and stopped me cold—or forced me into a shootout anyway. But they never showed. I drove on, unimpeded. My guess is: they had more trouble on their hands than they could deal with back at the house. Slick and Moses were both badly wounded, maybe dead.

They needed emergency attention and help. In fact, after I reached the paved road again, I could hear sirens behind me, and I imagined a line of cop cars and an ambulance heading toward the mansion as I sped away.

And away is where I sped, all right. I drove and drove and did not stop driving. The woods went on and on, and I went on until the road seemed never ending. It felt unreal. Just darkness at the windows. Just trees, their silhouettes. Just night as if eternal and solitude and the deep quiet underneath the engine noise. It came back to me now: how alone I was. No texts, no email, no internet, no friendly faces. I couldn't even coax a song out of the radio. I felt again that i, the break in the golden chain of communication that binds us to the modern world, that makes us always together, never alone. It weighed on me, weighed heavily. I was thrilled just to see a street sign: a sign of life. I followed the arrow, and soon there was another sign and another and I made my way to the freeway, heading south. The traffic was sparse, but I was glad to see it. Glad to see there were other cars, other headlights, other faces in the dark. The world had not yet ended.

I drove. The moon went down. The stars grew dim. The sky brightened. Dawn.

My gas ran low. I got off the freeway to fill up. I found a little diner with a clutch of tractor trailers parked in the lot outside. I nestled my car among the big rigs, where it wouldn't be easily spotted. I stuffed my gun into my pack and as I did, I saw that Slick had dumped my phone back in there. It didn't mean much to me at that moment, but it would.

I shoved the pack under the passenger seat. Then I went into the diner and bought a sandwich, bacon on a roll. I brought the sandwich out to the car, but I was suddenly too exhausted to eat it. I set it on the seat beside me. I tilted back the driver's seat. I closed my eyes.

But I couldn't sleep, not right away. Images from the shootout kept playing in my mind. Slick's eye exploding. The gun bucking in my hand. Moses sinking down the wall. It's one thing to kill a dragon, but it's another thing to kill a man. I didn't regret it, but I didn't much like it either.

And what was I going to do now? I could not go on like this forever. I could not go on like this another day, in fact. With the cops after me for murder. With the murderers after me. My parents against me. My brother against me. My sister gone, hiding, terrified, in danger. No friends I could reach. No way to clear myself in a world Orosgo seemed to own. No way to stay alive beyond a day or two.

Despair and die, Slick had advised me.

I despaired and I slept.

I WOKE UP slowly, my body aching, my eyes glued shut with sleep. When I managed to pry my eyelids open, I saw it was bright day, the sunlight splashed on the windshield, blinding. I raised my arm to shield myself from the glare. I straightened in my seat. I remembered where I was. I slumped. I sighed.

I sat in the car and ate my cold bacon sandwich, chewing morosely, tasting nothing. Slowly, though, as I ate, my sense of my situation began to coalesce. Clues started coming together in my brain. Answers to my questions began to suggest themselves.

By the time I swallowed the final bit of bacon, I had an idea.

I wrestled my backpack out from under the seat beside me. I unzipped it and rooted inside until I found the phone. I looked in the call history and, sure enough, there it was: the number Slick had dialed when we were in the banquet hall.

I pressed the redial button and held the phone to my ear. I listened to it ringing, once, twice, a third time. My stomach fluttered.

Then a click, and a voice—that voice I had never forgotten, slick and smooth and ancient as a snake's, with a vague and vaguely romantic accent.

"Mr. Lively," he said. His tone was flat and menacing.

And I answered him: "Call off your dogs, Orosgo. We need to talk."

30

AT THE EDGE OF A CLIFF OVERLOOKING THE SEA STOOD a palace of stone and glass. Magnificent, it spread across my windshield as my car emerged from the trees. I approached it over a long and level drive. To the left and right of me stretched a green and treeless meadow. You could trace the ocean wind as it passed over its grasses. It seemed like the moving hand of an invisible god. The meadow ended suddenly at an arching edge of whitish stone. Beyond that was the water, still and calm and dark under a drifting morning mist.

I had prepared for this encounter as well as I could. I had driven all day from Oregon to Santa Barbara and then spent the next day in a small motel on a side road just outside of town. Once again, I had sat at the motel's public computer. I had worked through searches until I found what I needed to know. I had gone into the city and bought some fresh clothes on State Street. Tan slacks, gray polo shirt and blue sports jacket. I didn't want to take this meeting dressed like a kid in a sweatshirt and jeans.

The whole time I was preparing, I was watchful but more or less relaxed. I knew there was a chance Orosgo's thugs would come after me or the police would come after me or Orosgo's thugs who were the police or vice versa. But I didn't think they would. The old billionaire and I had made a truce on the phone, and I believed he wanted this meeting, wanted to hear what I had to say. That night, when I watched the TV news, there was no mention of me, no mention of the melee in Oregon or of Billiard Ball, none of it. I expected as much.

Finally, the next morning, I set out for the address Orosgo had given me. I'm pretty sure I was followed during the entire drive. The same three cars kept trading places in my rearview mirror. One of them was a California Highway Patrol cruiser. They kept their distance, but they never let me out of their sight. I tried not to let it bother me. We all knew where I was heading anyway.

I got off the freeway at the community of horse farms and estates known as Hope Ranch. I wound down a long country road under a canopy of autumn oaks. At the end of the road, I turned up a hill and climbed through residential streets until I reached a manicured hedgerow that didn't quite hide the stone wall behind it. There was a gate there and a gatehouse. Two armed guards stepped from the little cabin and a third stayed inside, watching through the big window. One guard approached my car and asked me to step out. He was smiling in that friendly way friendly fascists smile in California. I guess the sunshine makes our fascists mellow.

When I was standing beside the car, he patted me down, looking for a weapon. The other guard climbed into the Passat and searched in the glove compartment and beneath the seats, front and back. Then he popped the trunk and searched in there. I had left Slick's gun in my backpack in the motel, so there was nothing to find.

At last, the first guard nodded to his pal in the guardhouse. The gate swung open, its motor grinding. I drove onto the property, through a stand of trees, then out into the meadow.

I reached the house and parked next to the other cars already sitting at the edge of an enormous cul-de-sac under a low concrete balustrade. Riley's dented little Passat looked ridiculous between a classic Rolls and a brand-new Tesla. There was a Lamborghini nearby too. It looked like an orange rocket ship.

The half acre in front of the house was elegant and beautiful: a walking maze of low bushes with a fountain burbling at the center, vines with red and purple flowers climbing over the surrounding balustrades, a graceful front path to a graceful front stairway flanked by marble cherubim. This was the third of Orosgo's mind-bogglingly elaborate estates I had been to, if you counted the mansion in the woods and the one at the top of Beverly Hills. I wondered how many he had in how many cities in how many countries, all told.

And while I'm describing the landscape, I guess I should mention the gunmen. They decorated the place like lawn gnomes, if your lawn gnomes happened to dress in black and wear mirrored sunglasses and jackets that bulged at the armpit where they carried their gnomish semi-automatics. Mirrored glasses or no, I could feel their watchful eyes following every step of my approach.

I walked up the path to the house. It was massive, two stories but as long as several football fields, gabled roofs linked to circular bays and walls of enormous windows everywhere. Below the cliffs, the sea stretched out into the mist. I could smell the saltwater on the dancing breeze.

The front door opened as I came near. A butler stood at attention on the threshold. I assumed he was a butler. Half butler, half hooligan, whatever. He was clearly packing heat like all the others.

He led me through wood-paneled rooms, past a marble fireplace carved with crests, and finally through an all-glass door and outside again to the red slate patio in back. The patio sat on the very edge of the cliff, enclosed by another one of those graceful stone balustrades. The sea was all around it so that it seemed to be floating in midair.

And there he was: my old pal Serge Orosgo. The man who employed my mom and dad and brother and who had been trying to murder me for days. Seated at the head of the glass breakfast table, he had the misty ocean stretched out behind him like a backdrop. It was only a little while since I'd seen him last, but it seemed like forever. Passing back and forth between the real world and fantasy land had messed with my sense of time.

He was dressed like a tycoon villain in a spy movie, wearing a classic smoking jacket, ruby red with a black collar, a white shirt underneath, open at his wattled neck. His square head was topped with silver hair. His face—the nearly transparent skin on his weirdly unwrinkled cheeks, the unnaturally wide stare of his pale blue eyes—was the face of a baby perpetually startled at the fallen state of the world. He was using a tiny fork to spear berries out of a hollowed melon. He didn't look up when I stepped out of the house, just went on eating.

"Sit down, Austin," he said.

It was the tone a lordly father would use with a wastrel son. I sat down in the filigreed metal chair across from him. The butler-gunman hovered beside me, hands clasped before him.

"Can I offer you something?" Orosgo said. Still eating berries, still not looking at me.

"Coffee," I told him.

The butler shimmered away like Jeeves, if Jeeves was strapped with a Glock.

Then we sat there in silence, Serge Orosgo and I. No sound between us but the wind off the water and the hiss of distant waves. He went on picking out berries with his melon fork, examining them, popping them into his mouth, chewing them as if chewing them were the most fascinating thing a fellow could do, more fascinating, certainly, than conversing with me. I guess this treatment was supposed to make me nervous. No need. I was nervous already. There were no illusions between us now. I knew who he was, and he knew I knew. His gunmen were all over the place. He could snap his fingers and they'd snap my neck. I only had one chance to get this conversation right.

That said, there was something different about him—different from the last time we met. It was subtle, but I could see it in those weirdly infantile, weirdly reptilian eyes. It was revealed in the slight tremor of his fork hand, and even in this whole elaborate performance of his, ignoring me and so on.

Was he afraid? Is that what it was? It felt like that. But afraid of what? Of me? Seemed unlikely. Of something though. Last time we'd dined together, he had been confident—looney but confident, as you'd expect a rich and powerful madman to be. But now? Something had taken the confidence out of him. That was how it looked to me anyway.

I waited for him to start the conversation. Finally, he set the melon fork on the melon plate beside the melon. He slouched back in his chair, make-believe regal, his hands folded on his lap. He went on chewing the berry in his mouth until I wanted to shout at him to stop all the damn berry-chewing and get down to business.

Then he did.

"You've killed three of my men, Austin," he scolded me sternly.

"Have I? I've lost count."

"One of them, Moses, was a police detective. And his partner, Detective Jameson, has lost an eye."

"Sorry," I said.

"Are you?"

"No."

"And yet you come to me for protection."

"I come to you to make a deal."

"You do want my protection, though, don't you?"

"Well, you could stop trying to murder me. That would help."

"Perhaps. But there'd still be legal consequences for you. I'm not all-powerful, you know."

"You're powerful enough."

"I can't override the law."

"Oh, sure you can."

"Well . . . " He conceded the point with a shrug. "Still. I can't stop Detective Jameson if he wants revenge. An eye for an eye and all that."

"That is too bad," I said coolly. "Because you don't want me dead, Orosgo. I'm the only one who can help you now."

"So you said on the phone."

"So I did."

Man, I sounded suave and confident, didn't I? Even to me, who knew I was neither. But I figured he could see the fear in my eyes, same as I saw it in his. We were each playing a role at this point.

I reached into the inside pocket of my jacket and pulled out a sheet of motel stationery, folded in half. I unfolded it and held it out to him. He hesitated, watching the paper fluttering and crackling in the breeze between us. He seemed to think it was beneath him to do the work of reaching for it. But I waited him out and he finally did reach. I watched him carefully as he examined the page.

The results were very satisfying, very dramatic. I won't say he went pale because he was already white as a snake's belly. But an expression of purest terror came into his surprised-baby eyes. He tried to hide it, but his lips trembled and got wet at the corners.

I pressed my advantage. "That's him, isn't it?" I said.

He didn't answer. He handed the paper back to me. His hand trembled like his lips. I took the page and glanced at it myself. I wasn't a great artist, but I could draw a likeness all right, especially a likeness that had been burned into my memory like this one. The raisin face with its beady, gleaming eyes, the little tuft of gray hair on his head, the tuft of gray beard on his chin. It was a good drawing of the wizard Curtin.

"This is your guy, right? The cowled guy who came to you in your dacha all those years ago? After you'd pillaged your billions from what used to be the Soviet Union."

When Orosgo answered me now, there was no pretense. His voice trembled like his hands and his lips. He spoke to me with what seemed a new sincerity. And, sure, why not? I was the one person on earth who shared his secret, who believed him and understood.

"I thought he was a dream," he said in a soft tone of amazement—so soft the sea breeze nearly carried the words away. "I thought the whole thing must've been a dream. Even now, when he's started coming back to me, his shape, his shadow, in the halls at night, in the mirror behind me, I thought . . . " He laced his fingers on his belly to keep them still. They were shaking so badly it took him two tries to get them laced.

"I think he's like that here," I said, slipping the page back into my jacket. "In this realm, I mean. He's a mind-thing. Like a dream. Like a phantom. Even in photographs, he comes and goes. It's different there. In the other place."

"The other place," he said cautiously.

"Galiana. Edgimond. The places in the book: *Another Kingdom.*"

For a moment, I thought he was going to pretend he didn't understand me. But then he said: "You've been there? You've seen him?"

I nodded. "I've seen him. Clear as I see you. His name is Curtin."

"Curtin." He seemed to roll the word around in his mind to see if it fit. "And is he . . . ?"

He didn't finish. I thought to myself: Is he what? Horrific? A demon? The devil himself? I flashed back to the mansion in the Edgimond woods, the dragon in the mansion, the horrible, bloody end of that endless dinner there.

"He's kind of like you, Serge," I said brutally. "He works on people's minds to get control of them."

"I know," he said softly.

"He's powerful like you too. But also like you, he's not all-powerful. He can be beaten."

"Can he?"

"Yes."

"By you?"

"No. But I can help."

"There, you mean. In this other kingdom."

"Yes. But what happens there happens here. I've got the scars to prove it."

Orosgo didn't answer. He fidgeted with his hands. He licked his lips.

I leaned forward, toward him, resting my forearms on the glass tabletop. "What was your original deal with him?" I asked. "He offered you—what? Fame? Power? The chance to brand an era with your name. The Orosgo Age."

"It's so long ago," he muttered, his chin sunk on his chest. "Like a dream. I can't remember."

"Oh, sure you can. So all this time you got to shape the world. Run the world in some quarters. And what did he get? What did you offer him?"

This was really getting to him now. He was truly agitated. He lifted a quivering hand to his forehead, massaged the uncannily smooth flesh there. "Oh, I don't know, I don't know. Nothing was ever mentioned clearly. Nothing was spoken aloud. Like I said . . . a dream."

"Oh, it was no dream, Orosgo. You promised him something in return for this immortality of yours . . . " When I said that word—*immortality*—his hand fell, his eyes suddenly flashed up at me. I said: "Oh. Wait. It wasn't immortality, was it. Not real immortality . . . Is that what you're afraid of?" I asked him. "Dying?"

"No, no, no," he murmured, but I wasn't convinced.

"We all die, Orosgo."

"I know that," he said irritably.

"So what the hell did you offer him? Your soul?"

That made him even more irritable. He grimaced and waved his hand. "Don't be ridiculous. There no such thing as a soul. If I cut you open would a soul spring out of you? No! Just guts and blood. Atoms and void. That's all."

Yeah, I'd heard this routine already, in the *Times* article. And as I say, I wasn't convinced. I leaned back in my chair. "But he'll take the book instead, is that it? Bring him the book and you're squared away. Otherwise, the original deal stands. Is that it?"

He made exactly the same gesture as before: a grimace, an irritable wave, as if to erase my words from the air between us. "I told you: I'm not even sure he's real. In fact, I don't believe in him. Just shadows in the dark. An image in the mirror. This persistent . . . *urging* in my mind. It's some delusion of old age, that's all . . . "

"No." I remembered the photo in the *Times*, the vanishing image in the window of the house, there and gone. "He's real all right. And he wants the book. He wants *Another Kingdom.* It's the portal between his world and ours. If he can get his hands on it, he can control them both."

"Dah!" he said.

"But if I get it first . . . well then, who knows? Just the little of it I've already read gave me the power to flash back and forth between one place and the other. If I could read the whole thing, what could I do then? Control my passage? Do magic? Summon the Emperor Anastasius. Alert his armies. Restore Elinda to her throne? And isn't that what Curtin's afraid of? Isn't that why he wants you to stop me? Why he wants you to bring him the book? What he loses there, he loses here as well."

I watched him as I spoke. He averted his eyes guiltily. He knew something, or thought he did. But before he could answer me, his faithful butler-slash-assassin came in with the silver coffee service. Orosgo and I both retreated into the corners of our minds while Killer Jeeves set my china cup before me and poured. It gave me a chance to consider how insane this conversation was, two lunatics arguing over their delusions.

"Milk and sugar?" said the butler.

"Black," I said.

Out he shimmered. I stared at Orosgo. Orosgo stared down at the patio slates.

"I've had my people look into it," he said finally. "There are . . . ideas out there. Theories. On the dark web. You know the sort of thing. Very complex, very deep conjecture. It begins with the very origins of life. Even before the advent of DNA, the very process of replication that defines life involves the creation of a symbolic representation of the organism. You see what that means, yes? Life itself is metaphor, a link between matter and meaning. Every story—from *King Lear* to "Hey Diddle, Diddle"—is a bridge between those two. Every one of them rearranges the human brain to make that connection on a quantum level, channeling uncertainty out of the random and into . . . "

And so on. You know that scene in horror and science fiction movies where someone explains the completely ridiculous setup in pseudo-scientific terms that the screenwriter plucked out of a Wikipedia search? And you eat your popcorn thinking, *Yeah, yeah, yeah, just get to the mayhem, would you?* Well, this was that scene. Orosgo started talking in that way billionaires do, where they don't give a monkey's turd about what you have to say because they're the billionaire and you're not. And he just went on and on not to mention on about multiple universes and quantum mechanics and how just the right story could arrange the subatomic particles in just the right brain in just the right way to make the mind capable of passage from one of an infinite number of realities into another. On and on—I couldn't repeat it now if I tried—until finally, I just lost my patience. I slapped the glass table with my palm.

I said: "All right. Enough, Orosgo. Now let me tell you what *I* know. Okay? *My* deep conjecture." Startled, he stopped. He stared. Who the hell interrupts a man with billions of dollars? Me, that's who. "What I know? Is that you're an old and evil man. You're scared of dying, and I don't blame you. If there's anything—anything at all—even vaguely resembling a god at the helm of this blood-soaked universe, you are well and truly screwed through all the generations and beyond." I sneered and shook my head at him. "Rusty Winkelman! Did it begin with him? The old chairman of my father's department at Berkeley. My poor old Uncle Rusty. Was it my dad who poisoned him? No. My mom, I'll bet. Uncle Rusty always loved my mom. She could have talked him into drinking cyanide just to please her. My father then pretended to discover the body. Yeah, that sounds like the way they'd do it. Then my dad came home and told mom it had all worked out just the way they planned it. And that was what my sister heard when she was crawling around in the walls. That's why they terrorized her to keep her silent. And then, lo and behold, my father took over the psychology department and hand appointed the next chairman. That's why you put his name on the wall at the 730 Club. And he was just one of hundreds, wasn't he?"

Orosgo sank back in his chair. He frowned at me, a deep, angry frown. All that money he had. Everyone else kissed his ass and called it ice cream. He hated being forced to sit here and listen to the truth about himself as if he were some ordinary man.

I sipped my coffee from the china cup. Breathed out of it: Ah!

I went on. "That's who those people are, right? The names on the wall in the banquet room of the 730 House. Every one of them—every one I could remember, every one I could check—every one replaced a powerful man, a man who died or who got embroiled in a scandal or a man who just suddenly retired young for no apparent reason. Heads of departments at prestigious universities. Heads of TV networks and news sites. The editor of *The New York Times*—the guy who hired Charles Head to write that puff piece about you. The pope in freaking Rome, for all I know. At hundreds of places all over the country, and in Europe too. You murdered the person in charge or blackmailed him or destroyed him with a scandal, and then you installed your own guy, someone dedicated to spreading the Gospel of Orosgo: atoms and void, no human rights, no freedom. Just Orosgo calling the shots from on high. Orosgo and his scholars teaching his ideas and writing books about them. Orosgo and his journalists reporting the news from Orosgo's point of view. Orosgo and his politicians turning his policies into law. Even Orosgo and his movie studios and his streaming services and his social media platforms making Orosgo propaganda for the masses. All the world's Orosgo, and we're just living in it, right? It's brilliant. You don't even have to hide the fact you're taking things over. Because who would oppose you? The government? The news outlets? The academy? Hollywood? They're all you. They're all your guys or trained by your guys or hired by them. Because you killed or ruined everyone who might have stood in your way. You miserable toad. Thirty years. Thirty years you've been at it, filling the big positions with Orosgo mind-slaves like my mom and dad. My brother." I shook my head. "Man, oh man. I would have you arrested if you didn't own the police."

We faced each other across the breakfast table. He had gotten control of himself now—some control. He'd quieted his trembling at least. He lifted himself up in his seat and regarded me as if from a height, doing the lordly father over the prodigal son again. "What is it you want, Austin?" he said.

I set down my coffee cup. It rattled on the saucer, revealing my own unsteady hand. All the same, I stared right back at him, my teeth bared, my fury plain. "I want my life back, you son of a bitch."

For a moment, he didn't react at all. Then he inclined his chin, just slightly. I thought I saw a hint of a sour smile touch the corner of his damp, nervous lips. Of course. This was familiar ground to him, a game he knew how to play. Someone wanted something from him. Someone was ready to make a deal.

"Go on," he said, his tone more certain than it was before.

"I want your thugs to stop trying to kill me. I want your cops to stop trying to arrest me. I want your newsmen to stop putting my picture on the damn internet. I want the word to go out that I've been cleared of all charges. My sister too. Riley. I want her left alone."

He gave a huffy little snort. His baby blue eyes gleamed. "And what do I get? What do you have to offer me?"

The way he said the word "*you,*" I could tell he meant "*a worm like you.*" In answer, I drew myself up in my chair, trying to look as little like a worm as possible. "You get the whole world, Orosgo. Isn't that what you want? You give me my life, and you get the whole world. You want Orosgo government run by Orosgo experts spouting Orosgo ideas reported by Orosgo journalists and turned into Orosgo movies starring guys playing Orosgo? It's done. It's yours. Every bit of it. The whole world. Take it. It's no good to me. As far as I'm concerned, you and the world deserve each other."

He gave a soft, miserable laugh at that. Lifted his chest and shoulders in a shrug. "I don't need you to get that. I almost have it now."

"Almost. But not quite. And time is running out. Any minute now, the Big Hook will come and yank you off the stage of life and then . . . "

Whatever was left of his miserable laugh faded miserably into a miserable silence.

"That's right," I said. "Curtin. The Curtin call. The final Curtin. He's no dream, Serge. Whatever deal you made with him, he will collect, believe me. His power is in the mind, and when that's all that's left of you . . . "

"Stop! Stop! Stop!" He spat the words like venom, baby blue eyes full of terror. "This is all nonsense. Nonsense!"

I sat back slowly in my chair. I did my best to simper at him. I said, "Kill me then. If it's nonsense, kill me."

No answer. Silence. The sounds of the wind and the sea. Our eyes met across the table. He lifted an unsteady hand to his mouth and wiped the spittle from the edges of it. He took a long breath.

"What can you do about it?" he asked.

"I can defeat him," I said. "Or help to defeat him. I'm the only one who can. God alone knows why, but I'm the one Queen Elinda chose to do the job. Like you said: the right mind in the right story." I could see Orosgo considering what I said. I drove the point home. "That's why Curtin wants the book, right? To stop me. To give him the power I'm supposed to have. If he gets it, do you really think he'll keep his word and let you off the hook? But if I get the book, if I do what I'm called to do, if I stop him from taking over the Eleven Lands, he's done. And you're free."

So there it was, the whole bargain laid out. The deal on the table. I had said what I had come to say. Now the decision was his to make. He sat there, thinking it over. And I sat there thinking: *This is the single craziest conversation anyone has ever had!*

"Why should I trust you?" Orosgo asked me finally. "You said you could get me the book before. You lied."

"I lied so you wouldn't kill me. Now I'm telling the truth for the same reason. Our interests are aligned. I have to beat Curtin to fulfill my quest, and you want him beaten so he doesn't drag you down to hell where you belong. It's a clear choice, Serge. You give me my life back and you get the world. Otherwise, you die and Curtin takes your soul."

Once again: silence. We sat there face-to-face, and I felt the sheer googly-eyed nuttiness of our conversation enveloping us both. It occurred to me that only one of two things could be true right then: either we were a pair of maniacs raving at each other like drunken schizophrenics in a hobo camp or we were bargaining over every single thing that really mattered.

It seemed a long, long time before Orosgo said: "I need some time to consider your offer."

"How long?" I asked.

"Until you reach your car," he said. "If I haven't had you killed by then, my answer is yes."

I laughed out loud. I meant it to seem carefree and debonair, but it sounded a lot more like hysteria, even to me. My chair scraped on the slate as I pushed back from the table.

"Tell Mom and Dad that my last words were '*Thanks for the coffee.*'"

I started walking toward the house. My breath was suddenly short. My pulse was suddenly hammering in my head. Everything felt on the fritz inside me: short-circuited, electric, jumbled up. It was going to be a long walk back across the estate, wondering at every step whether I would reach my car or be dispatched into the netherworld by an Orosgo bullet.

I crossed the patio. I reached the house. The butler-gunman opened the door for me from within.

And behind me, Orosgo said: "What about the book?" I paused. I looked back at him. "*Another Kingdom.* How will you find it? You don't even know where it is."

"Sure I do. My sister has it."

"But she's vanished. Why do you think you can find her when all my people have failed?"

I gave what I hoped was a devil-may-care smirk. "Because I already know where she is," I said.

And that, I figured, was my cool exit line. So with my best cool-exit-line wink of the eye, I turned to the house again and walked right through the open door back into the marble throne room of Menaria, where a hoard of screaming centurions was charging toward me, spears lowered, swords raised.

31

I WAS SO SURPRISED I SCREAMED OUT LOUD, BUT MY scream was washed away by the battle cries of the onrushing army at my back.

That's the thing about the world, you know? Reality is very immersive. When you're in it, you forget there's anything else. I had been so involved in bargaining for my life with Orosgo I had forgotten that my life was seconds away from ending in Menaria, near the throne room of King Cambitus the Not Altogether Wise.

But that's all I had left now: seconds. Looking over my shoulder as I fled, I saw the soldier horde was maybe fifteen yards away from me and coming on full speed. The wedge of their bristling spearpoints filled my vision. The edges of their lifted swords glinted in the light of the risen moon.

And then, there was no more room to run. I was at the foot of the marble throne, my progress blocked, the marble image of King Cambitus looking down on me from above. I turned around and faced the army.

I had made no plan for this moment. I had been too distracted trying to stay alive in real life to figure out how I was going to stay alive in another kingdom. So I did the only thing I could. I reached for my sword. Not much hope there against such a multitude, but it was the only hope I had.

For a moment, my hand remained empty. I remembered how the sword had stopped appearing in Curtin's mansion, and my heart sank at the thought that maybe his curse was still in place.

But no, the next second, the weapon flowed out of nothingness into being as my fingers curled around the hilt.

The lead soldier, a centurion, reached me. His own sword was held high and descending swiftly toward my head. His bearded face was twisted with warrior rage. I drew my blade and slashed at his to block it. He grunted in surprise as the two swords clashed together inches above my brow. At the same moment, the flowing mercury of my magic armor poured out of my skin and covered me, top to toe. I knew it would not protect me long against so many spearpoints, but what could I do besides fight on to the very end?

And yet, amazingly—astoundingly—there was no need.

Immediately, the entire army stopped in its tracks as if they had turned to marble again. The centurion and I were nose to nose, our swords locked together in midair so that, close-up, I saw his expression change completely. As my magic helmet surrounded my head, I saw him staring at me, bright-eyed, open-mouthed. I sensed—then shifted my gaze and saw—the rest of the army, frozen in their tracks, staring the same way. For another half-second, the centurion's sword and mine pushed against each other. Then the pressure released as he stepped back and lowered his blade. The rest of the soldiers lowered their weapons, too.

I scanned their dumbstruck faces, dumbstruck.

Then the centurion said: "The sword of Queen Elinda. Her armor."

Still bewildered, I managed a nod. "Uh . . . yeah."

And a new voice—a deep, booming voice—came from behind me.

"Then you must be her chosen one."

I spun around to see the King—King Cambitus—suddenly made flesh and blood as the moonlight washed over him. He was stepping down from his high throne. One of his attendants, now also come to life, took hold of his hand to keep him steady.

The King came toward me, lit red on one side of his face by the glow from the throne room braziers and white on the other by the moonlight. He was a large man, taller than me by a head, broader at the shoulders, big and vital across the chest. He had a great black beard that covered much of his face. But even so, I could see again that his features were familiar to me in some way. Beneath his golden crown, around the eyes and nose, he reminded me of someone. I couldn't think who.

He towered above me majestically.

"Speak, boy," he commanded. "Answer me. Are you the one?"

Now you have to understand: I did not know what the right answer was. I did not know whom to trust. I had faced nothing but witchcraft and deception since I'd left Galiana, and nothing but killers and dirty cops back home. I didn't know what to say that would keep me alive. So I took the simplest path: I told the truth.

"I am. Yes. The Queen chose me. Sent me." And then it occurred to me to add: "Let wisdom reign."

The King frowned deeply. His eyes narrowed. What a look! Was he enraged? Was he about to command his soldiers to destroy me? I remembered what they called him: the Not Altogether Wise. Maybe my crack about wisdom reigning had insulted him. I held my breath, waiting for his response.

He lifted his gaze over me and looked out at his army.

"Let wisdom reign!" he thundered at them.

And all together, the soldiers smacked their fists to their breastplates in salute and called back to him with a single voice: "And each man go his way!"

I could have wept. I almost did. I had been so utterly alone for days, so utterly friendless. Had I really, finally come among friends?

My lips trembling, my voice shook as I lifted my damp eyes to the King and said, "You're of the Queen's party then."

The kingly frown cleared like summer showers. He broke into a broad grin behind the large black beard. He clapped his hand on my shoulder.

"I'm her father, lad," he said.

I started. Stared. Her father! Hot damn. No wonder he looked familiar.

"Do you have the talisman?" he asked me.

I slid my sword back into its scabbard. Sword, scabbard, and armor all melted back into nothing. I reached to the front of my shirt and parted it at the collar to show him the talisman hung around my neck. I could feel it throbbing there, and I remembered how the power of Anastasius had come through it to lead me to this city. To these friends.

Still grinning, Cambitus nodded. He glanced imperiously at one of his attendants. "Fetch him furs. He'll need them." Then looking at me again, he said: "Let us walk together."

At once, the soldiers parted to let us pass. They struck their breastplates in salute again and I realized: they were saluting me! Me, because I was Queen Elinda's chosen. So much relief and even joy filled me I thought my feet would leave the earth.

The King and I crossed the courtyard side by side. The courtyard was alive with movement now, soldiers and noblemen banging their breastplates or fingering the folds of their robes as they bowed to us. Looking out beyond the fluted columns of the gallery up ahead, I saw the entire square below, as well as the nearby streets, had become busy in the moonlight. Men gripping scrolls hurrying urgently, girls carrying baskets, housewives sweeping doorways, workmen pushing barrows, donkeys pulling carts, butchers driving cows, and citizens who bore the marks of rank gathered in small groups to argue, gossip, and chat. The eerie silence of the city had been replaced with a clatter of motion and a buzz of human voices.

As Cambitus and I kept walking, a detachment of soldiers fell in around us: a security detail, clearing our path.

"I wish you could stay among us," the King said. "But your mission is an urgent one. You must return to your journey right away."

My spirits fell at that. I would have liked to stay among friends for a while. But I nodded bravely, or what I hoped was bravely.

King Cambitus slapped my back. "We must help you while we live," he said.

"Yeah," I said. "This statue thing. What is that? Some kind of curse or something?"

His Majesty nodded majestically. "Curtin. In this city, we live only in the light of the moon."

"How'd that happen?"

He sighed a great sigh. "I was not altogether wise," he said.

"I noticed. The inscriptions, I mean."

"Mm, I had them done myself. To remind me. I was called King Cambitus the Wise before Curtin came. And had I not been at least somewhat wise, the country would be his completely, moonlit or no."

We emerged onto the gallery, walked along the columns toward the zig-zagging flights of marble stairs. A slavish attendant ran up beside us, carrying an armload of heavy fur-lined robes.

"Your furs, Your Majesty," he said breathlessly, offering them to the King.

Cambitus brushed him off with a regal wave of his hand. The attendant was forced to run along beside us, stumbling under the weight of his burden.

"Curtin was once first advisor to the Emperor Anastasius," King Cambitus said.

"Yeah, I heard the story. Anastasius gave Galiana to your daughter when they became engaged, and Curtin felt slighted and wanted revenge."

"He gained his first foothold in Edgimond. The people there are legendary for their greed and cowardice and stupidity." He gave a grim smile. "We even have an old saying: 'The truth is the truth even in Edgimond, where there is no honest man to speak it.' "

"Yeah, where I come from, they have that saying about Hollywood."

"Curtin's thirst for vengeance will not be satisfied until he is ruler of all the Eleven Lands," Cambitus went on. "Then he can amass the armies he needs to crush the forces of the Emperor. So far, only one thing stands in his way."

"What's that?"

His Majesty seemed to grow greater as he drew a great breath. "Me," he said. "Me and the land of Menaria."

We started down the broad stairway together. The protective soldiers marched before us. The poor toady, with his armload of furs, stumbled and tripped behind.

As we went, the King gave me a brief lesson in fantasy-land geography. Apparently, Anastasius's empire was a federation of eleven kingdoms. The twelfth kingdom, Galiana, was an independent ally, as powerful as all the rest put together. This kingdom, Menaria, with its capital city of Vagos, was a long narrow land that all but divided Galiana and Edgimond from the other ten lands, except for narrow corridors to the north and south. Because of that, it had served as a natural barrier to Curtin's conquests, and he had been looking for a way to take it over.

"He tried to corrupt the people, but they were loyal to their King," Cambitus said.

"So he tried to corrupt the King himself," I guessed.

Cambitus nodded. "Curtin can terrify and seduce and sometimes even sicken, but he cannot strike on his own. Even his monsters are made of men."

"I know," I said. "I killed one of them back in Edgimond."

Two of the soldiers leading us overheard that. They turned to glance back at me, plainly surprised and impressed.

The King eyed me narrowly. "The Beast of Sacrifice?" he asked.

"The late, lamented Beast of Sacrifice, yeah," I said. "I cut the bastard to pieces."

Cambitus answered nothing, but he clapped his hand on my shoulder again as we descended the stairs. And I, who was feeling a bit short of paternal support at the moment, was deeply moved by this gesture of fatherly approval.

We came down into the great square, and there was my black stallion waiting for me by the water trough.

"Is this your mount?" the king asked. "A noble Galianan beast. One of Tauratanio's, no doubt. They have his magic in them." To the toady stumbling and reeling under his pile of furs, he said, "Pack the creature with supplies and bring him to the end of Twilight Road."

The toady said something along the lines of, "Yes, Your Majesty," but he was gasping for breath at that point, and it was hard to make out his words.

The King and I walked on across the square. As we went, the men in the square stopped their business and bowed to him, the women dropped him curtsies. The gestures of respect seemed to me heartfelt but not obsequious. It was clear that here in the royal city of Vagos, Cambitus inspired admiration but not awe. The King glanced neither right nor left but merely acknowledged his people with a raised hand and went on speaking to me.

"Curtin laid siege to my mind," he said. "Hoping to win me over as he had won Lord Iron." He gave a slight shudder, remembering. "It went on for months. It was like a fever. I never knew who would act as his agent next. I never knew whom to trust, or even sometimes what was real and what was a dream or an illusion. Some men offered me treasure, some outlined plans to extend my dominion, and some, some women, offered me pleasures of the flesh. But I was wise. I was King Cambitus the Wise," he went on—wistfully, I thought—"and I refused them all and kept my people free."

Let wisdom reign, I thought, *and each man go his way.* Clearly, the two things went together.

"Even when the wizard sent a poet to immortalize me, I kept my head and hardened my heart and ruled justly," the King went on. "I knew my country was the barrier between Curtin and the rest of the Eleven Lands, the defense of Anastasius's empire, soon to be my daughter's empire too, and so I held to wisdom for the good of all."

We neared the far end of the square, the place where I had entered. There were people leaning out of windows here, men and women in the apartments and offices above us, waving down at the King and calling to him.

"Hail King Cambitus, the Not Altogether Wise."

He waved back to them and smiled, and they smiled. And I, watching the exchange, thought again of my mother's snarky response to the Queen's slogan. *What's wisdom, I wonder.* Well, she was right. Obviously, that was the big question, wasn't it?

"If you knew what was happening in Galiana," I asked the King, "why didn't you send someone to Anastasius yourself? He's your future son-in-law, right? Wouldn't he have listened to you?"

"He would have. And I did, more than once. But Curtin was already at work in the other lands, moving to them from beyond our borders north and south. And my messengers did not have the talisman to guide them. Either they never reached the Emperor or they never returned."

I nodded, feeling a twist of anxiety in my stomach as I remembered that I, too, might never reach my destination. For one thing, Orosgo might have me gunned down before I even reached my car. Then what would happen to Galiana and the Queen?

I wondered: had I been altogether wise?

We had left the square. We passed beneath the triumphal arch and headed down a street between two rows of buildings. The city's white walls were aglow with moonshine, the glow interrupted at intervals by the yellow candlelit rectangles of the windows. The windows were filled with the subjects of the King. Their faces flickering in the flamelight, they waved and smiled. When I looked over my shoulder, I saw a whole crowd of people was following us now, just sort of trailing after us because we were who we were, I guess—the King and his friend, celebrities.

I looked up at the King again. "The curse—the moon curse," I said. "Curtin must have gotten to you somehow. How'd he manage it?"

As Cambitus had seemed to grow greater when he drew a breath with pride, so now he seemed to deflate and grow smaller after a long sigh.

He said: "The devil! He went into my mind somehow and found the love I dreamed of there. The lady I had invented, you know, to think about before I went to sleep, to give me comfort in the lonely night. He made an image of her out of moonlight. And I fell." He glanced at me and went on defensively: "To be fair, she did seem beautiful. And good. And true. The very image of the Queen I had imagined."

"What about Elinda's mother? Where was she?"

"Ah, gone. Long gone. She died many years ago. I had been alone since then. That was part of it. I had been alone for a long time with only my dream. And then—then to see my dream in the woods outside the city, to meet her there, my dream made real, whenever the moon would rise . . . Well, she ensorcelled me. He, Curtin, ensorcelled me through her."

"What a scumbag he is," I said. And when he—and a couple of the soldiers—stole a glance my way, I added: "Well, it doesn't seem fair somehow to get at you that way."

He laughed once. "Fair!"

"Well, you know what I'm saying. Curtin created someone who seemed worthy of your love, and you loved her. I don't see why that should give him power over your mind."

"Neither did I, unfortunately. I had done no wrong in loving what I loved: her beauty and her goodness and her truth. But they were not real. They were made of moonlight, and they faded with the moon. I loved the thought of them in myself and saw them in her, as he knew I would after my years of lonesome longing. I was not, it turned out, altogether wise. Once she had me in her power, he had me in his."

"What did she do to you?"

"She did what Curtin's other agents couldn't do: she corrupted me. Slowly, always under the guise of her goodness and with rationales that sounded like the truth, she led me to all the evils I had resisted until then. She taught me to wield tyrannical power over my people—in the name of doing them good. To confiscate their money and property—in the name of doing them good. To luxuriate in the praise of poets—also in the name of the good. I realized what was happening but too late. I had become weak enough for Curtin to put his curse on me—me and the people who followed me. And curse us is what he did. A halfway curse, it's true. He is still slowed in his attempts to conquer the Eleven Lands because he cannot move freely through Menaria when the moon is high. But he moves when he moves, and he does what he can, and if you do not reach Anastasius with the talisman, we will all be Galiana soon, and Edgimond: all Curtin's slaves."

We walked on, past several intersections. And at every street we passed, new people joined the parade behind us. At last, we were leading a massive throng, crushed together between the buildings, a human tide. The soldiers surrounded us and made a space for us, but the mob pressed close. Their voices echoed off the walls and filled the air with a pleasant sound as if of celebration. It felt like Mardi Gras.

Now, up ahead of us, not far off, I saw where the street ended. The city itself ended and opened on the moonlit field beyond. I remembered seeing the workers out there in their orchards and farms.

I said, "The curse only affected the city. The people in the country still move by day, right?"

The great bearded head nodded. "Only the people of Vagos have to live by the moon. The country people follow their own ways, the old ways. They're loyal to me, but they don't really know me. It's the traditions they know, and they put my face on them." He laughed sadly. "They were lucky. They followed the King as they imagined him to be: a King who is wiser than the King as he is."

As we came to the city wall, the toady who had been following us before reappeared. He was holding my black stallion by the reins now. He had packed the furs onto the stallion's back, behind the saddle.

The King and I reached the end of the road, the end of the city. The toady, still breathless, bowed his head and handed me the stallion's reins. I took them with thanks.

"The furs are for me?" I asked the King.

"And food and water as well. You'll need them to cross the White Mountains. You must take the narrow pass through to the meadowlands of Kore. It's rough going, but the talisman will guide you."

"All right. Is that the only way?"

"It's the fastest, though it's not fast. And the safest, though it's not safe. The other passages are beyond our borders, and Curtin has more power there. His monsters haunt those places and so does he."

I nodded. I sighed. I did not want to chance an encounter with another beast like the Beast of Sacrifice. Over the White Mountains I would go.

"Well . . . " I said.

One more time, Cambitus laid his hand upon my shoulder. I felt again the warmth of his fatherly approval, the fatherly approval that was missing from my own life, my real life. The King looked down at me from his greater height, and his eyes were kind and sad.

"Do you know my daughter?" he asked me.

I shook my head. "Not really. I saw her once. A few days ago. On the street. In another kingdom. Where I'm from."

"This Hollywood you spoke of."

"Yes."

"A foolish place, you say."

"Don't get me started."

"But she was alive. She was well."

"As far as I could tell, yeah. She's on the run. She's hiding out. But she's alive and well."

"And she chose you to come here, to fight for her."

"I guess so. I don't know really. I read some of her book. Just a little, but it did something to me. It made me able to come here somehow. It put me on this quest."

The King considered this with great seriousness. Then he took his hand from my shoulder and gestured toward my horse: *Time to go.* I took hold of the pommel and swung myself into the saddle. I looked down at the King—and at his people too, all the people, the large mass of them who had followed us out of the city and were now gathered to see me off in the moonlight. The sight of them squeezed my heart somehow. The first friends I had had in days. I was sorry to leave them so soon.

The King saw the expression on my face. He grinned again, his teeth moon-white behind his black beard.

"She is a great woman, my daughter," he said. "Wholly wise—far wiser than her father ever was. If her book changed you, you must have some wisdom in you too."

"I guess I must," I said. "But it's news to me."

He reached up toward me. I clasped his hand. *A king's hand,* I thought, impressed. He gripped mine tightly.

"Let it reign," he said. "Let the wisdom reign."

And then, much to my surprise and embarrassment, a powerful wave of emotion washed over me, a powerful wave of loneliness and confusion and mourning. I felt oh-so-fatherless and oh-so-lost.

"I don't even know what it is!" I cried out to the King, my voice breaking. "I don't even know what wisdom is."

Still clasping my hand, King Cambitus straightened, surprised. "Wisdom?" he said, as if it was obvious to anyone. "Wisdom is to love the Good."

I blinked back tears. "Really? That's it? That's all?"

"That's it. That's all. To love the Good—the greater Good more than the lesser."

"Well . . . " I said, trying to recover some dignity. "All right then. All right. That's something. Great. I've been wondering, you know. Someone asked me once, and I was just wondering."

The King smiled again and shook my hand and let me go. The people gathered around him, waving at me and cheering:

"Let wisdom reign!"

I waved back. "And each man go his way!" I called to them.

I turned my stallion toward the silver dark. My heart was strangely full. I heard the cheering voices at my back as I began to ride away from them.

Wisdom, I thought to myself. *Wisdom is to love the Good. The greater Good more than the lesser. That's it. That's all.*

And for a few more of the stallion's steps, these words uplifted me and made me feel stronger inside. But it was only for a few steps—a few steps and no more. Because after that, a voice seemed to whisper in my ear, a soft, dry, hissy, loveless voice: my mother's voice.

Suddenly, with a little cry of dismay, I reined the stallion and brought his head around. I faced back toward the glowing white city, back to where the waving, cheering people surrounded their monarch.

"But Your Majesty!" I called to him "What is the Good?"

In answer, the great king extended his arms to either side of him, threw back his head and laughed—laughed long and loud with a kind of jolly nobility.

"Don't ask me, lad," he shouted back. "I'm not altogether wise!"

Oh terrific! I thought.

I turned my horse toward the moon again and rode for the mountains.

32

I RODE SLOWLY THROUGH THE NIGHT, SLEEPING IN THE saddle sometimes. As dawn came up, the mountains came into view, a jagged graph line behind a pale white curtain of mist. I touched the talisman around my neck. I felt the heat and life radiating out of it and into my fingers. I felt the call of Anastasius in my chest. I adjusted my direction slightly and rode on.

By noon, the White Range loomed above me, imposing, snow-covered. I brought the black stallion to a halt and peered into the distance. I could see the road narrow to a dirt trail that rose up the nearest slope, snaking through the pines that sprinkled the base. The pines died out around a third of the way up. If the trail continued beyond that, I couldn't see it.

My heart darkened at the intimidating sight—but it darkened even more a moment later. Because a moment later, I tried to nudge the stallion forward with my bootheels, and he didn't respond; he didn't move. He huffed once, steam bursting from his nostrils, but he just stood there, still.

The moment it happened, I knew what it meant. All the same, I tried again, spurring him harder. But it made no difference, as I had known it wouldn't. The stallion wouldn't budge.

This was the end of the journey for him. He would go no farther.

"Really?" I said. "Come on!"

It wasn't the prospect of climbing on foot that made me so depressed. It was the prospect of going on alone. I said I had had no friends until I came into the Menarian capital of Vagos, but that wasn't quite right, was it? The stallion had been my companion all this way. He had always been there when I needed him. No matter where I left him, no matter what I got myself into, he had guessed my movements before I even knew what they would be, and he had met me at the spot where I emerged.

My throat felt tight as I swung myself off him and alit on the ground by his flank. I gave his breathing hide a gentle pat.

"All right," I said.

Then, reluctantly, mournfully, I unloaded the furs from his back. I dressed myself in one of them and made a sack of another. I could feel the snowy wind coming down off the mountain's height. I pulled the fur hood over my head and clasped the collar closed at my throat. I tied up my food and water in the sack and slung it over my shoulder.

For a long while then, I stood beside the horse's head and looked up the slope, full of misgiving. Finally, I turned toward the stallion. I looked into his big, contemplative eyes.

"Well, listen . . . " I began.

The black beast simply turned and started walking back the way we had come together. Well, what did I expect? Mutual vows of eternal friendship? A promise he'd drop me an email from time to time? It's funny how you come to love animals. You never know if they care, if they love you back, or what love could even mean to them. Maybe you just love some character you've imagined for them, your own ideas superimposed on them, the way King Cambitus loved his moon maiden and the country people loved their King.

But all the same, I loved the stallion. I watched him walking, then trotting away, growing smaller as he crossed the fields of

Menaria, heading west toward Edgimond and Galiana and Shadow Wood, his true home.

On an impulse, I called out to him, "Tell Maud I'm still here! Tell her I will not fail her!"

But if the horse understood me or even heard me, he gave no sign of it. What did I expect?

I stood and watched him until he was nothing more than a dot moving against the blue horizon.

Then I turned and started trudging up the mountain.

IT WAS A miserable trek from the very beginning, and it slowly got worse. The trail began as a brown dirt line in a dusting of snow. Within half an hour, it was a mere indentation in a white blanket. The icy crust was hard, but now and then I broke through and sank to my shins so that my boots grew soggy and my feet were freezing cold.

The weather began to deteriorate. A heavy fog moved in and melded with the clouds. The clouds sank lower, grew darker. The wind rose. It started to snow.

Soon, I could barely see where to direct my steps. Uncertain, I reached inside my fur to touch the talisman. I had to open up the collar of my coat to do it. The icy air rushed in on me, bitter and biting against the flesh of my throat and chest. I gripped the medallion, felt its warmth. Its power put me on track again for a little while, but only a little. Within a few steps, I was lost once more as the snowfall grew heavier, the fog thicker, and the wind stronger still.

I climbed. The way grew steep and rocky. The furs felt heavy on my back. I grew hollow and weak. I knew I should eat, but I was too cold and unhappy to stop and take the time. I went on through the wind-whipped white.

Now, horribly, I began to catch glimpses of motion in the storm. Not just the blowing snow, not just the dipping shadows of branches, but other things. Half-seen shadows of half-seen creatures. Moving. Darting. Lumbering. They were following me, surrounding me, watching me, gauging: what was I? Was I dangerous? Was I edible? How should they attack? And when?

I got a clear look at one of them. It was not a reassuring sight. As I was trudging up the slope, using every mental trick I knew to forget my exhaustion and ignore my fear, I heard a branch snap, loud, like a gunshot, not far away. It sounded like a big branch. Whatever snapped, it must have been large and heavy.

I stopped in my tracks. I panned my gaze across the scene, peering through the blowing snow and the shrouding fog and the mist of my own breath. Nothing moved in the depths of the obscurity. I waited, watching. Still nothing. I convinced myself there was some other explanation for the noise: the wind breaking a branch off a tree, something like that. I faced forward, ready to start on my way again.

And at that moment, the wind strengthened, the fog thinned. There it was—right in front of me. Something like a monkey, but bigger than a man, but white and furry, almost like a sheep, but fanged and clawed and snarling. Its eyes glowed red.

A noise broke out of me: a pathetic animal noise, the noise that prey makes in the face of the predator. My hand fumbled frantically in my fur, trying to get to my belt, to reach for my sword. But before I could, the creature darted away with a leopard's astounding speed. There was a streak of white in the white—and it had vanished into the storm.

I stood there, panting hard, trembling, staring this way and that. I waited, dry-mouthed, expecting the yeti to burst, raging, out of the miasma and take me down.

But it was quiet on every side. At last, I clutched my fur tighter around me and climbed on.

The sparse forest was growing sparser now. I sensed I was nearing the tree line, but it was harder and harder to see my way. The fog tightened around me like a great cloudy fist. The snow seemed a solid streak of motion, close and cold as my own skin. After a while, I felt everything growing weirdly vague and distant. It took me a few minutes to realize: Night was falling. Soon it would be dark.

And they were out there again: the beasts. Or maybe it was just the one beast, that one fanged, wooly gorilla with its dagger claws and its red eyes. It moved so quickly—it was here, then there—I couldn't tell if it was alone or with its tribe. Under the noise of the wind, I heard it huff and grumble. I kept telling myself it was just my imagination.

It was not my imagination. It was real. It was out there. It was hunting me.

One more time, I braved the cold and opened my collar and touched the talisman. It was hot. Its force was strong. I adjusted my trajectory according to the pull of its power. I pushed on with renewed energy. The incline seemed brutally steep now. The sack on my back felt as if it were full of lead. The snow-wet wind was harsh on the crescents of flesh beneath my eyes, the spaces exposed between my pulled-up collar and my pulled-down hood. I felt my legs were going to give way under me, but I pushed up and on. I peered harder through the gloom.

There . . . something . . . what? Some darkness in the whirling white. It grew blacker and clearer with every step I took. A last effort and I was there.

It was an archway in the rock, the entrance to a cave. I charged in eagerly. At once, the walls cut off the wind. The sudden quiet and the respite from the battering cold was such a great relief I groaned aloud with pleasure. I stripped the sack off my shoulder and let it drop wetly to the cave floor. What a joy to let go of that weight. I stood there, breathing, wallowing in the relative warmth, the relative silence after the storm's freezing roar.

I tried to get my bearings now. I peered into the blackness ahead of me. As I did, I sensed, then saw, a faint orange glow. I looked down and discovered a preternatural light was shining out of my fur. I opened the collar and the light shone brighter. The talisman was giving off a flame-like red energy.

I fumbled the medallion out of the folds of the fur and held it up to illuminate the cave. It was only a small alcove. The rough gray surface of the rear wall was just a few yards ahead of me. All the same, I thought, it was deep enough to keep me out of the weather. I could make camp here. I could bundle the furs around me and sleep through the night and hope the storm would be gone by morning.

I took a step forward—and then stopped. I gaped at what I saw in the eerie red glow from the talisman.

There, set on the ground against the rear wall of the cave, was a pile of bones. Rib cages, limbs, and the strange, unnameable skulls of strange, unnameable beasts. They were stripped clean, piled high, the skulls staring with empty eye holes.

My brain was dull with weariness, hunger, and cold. It took me a second or two to make sense of what I saw. Then I did.

I had come into the lair of a predator, the home of a beast.

And just as I realized that, I heard it behind me.

It huffed and grunted. I recognized the sound of the yeti that had been stalking me up the slope. Through the sough of the wind, I could hear it approaching the mouth of the cave. Another moment and it would block the archway. It would have me cornered.

There was only one thing to do. I let the talisman drop back against my chest. I reached quickly into my fur. My hand went to my belt, and I seized the hilt of Elinda's magic sword as it came into being beneath my fingers. Under my fur, my body was suddenly coated with armor. The magic helmet grew up around my head.

This was not going to be fun, I thought.

I whipped my weapon free. Even in the shadows of the stormy darkness, the blade glowed silver. I bared my teeth. I let out a battle roar. I spun and charged through the murky blindness out into the freezing tempest and found myself suddenly in Orosgo's mansion, walking through the wood-paneled rooms with the butler-slash-gunmen following close behind me.

Well, that was a strange moment. It really was. My heart was still thundering with the rush of battle. My body was still expecting to come face-to-face with the Abominable Snowman out in the storm, but my mind was already beginning to comprehend that, no, I was here again in Hope Ranch, California, striding past the marble fireplace with Jeeves the Assassin hanging back creepily in my blind spot.

Oh right, right. I remembered now. Orosgo was about to decide whether to let me go or kill me. He was sitting out on the patio, toying with the last of his breakfast berries, trying to calculate whether it was worth it to keep me alive a while longer. Did I really know where my sister Riley was? Could I find the book *Another Kingdom*? Should he have me followed and snatch the novel from me and give it to Curtin in exchange for his soul? Or should he let me read the book all the way through so I could return to the Eleven Lands at will and alert the armies of Anastasius? Then maybe I could defeat Curtin altogether and stave off their reckoning.

Or should he just forget the whole thing and have Jeeves put a gun behind my ear and blow my brains out through my forehead?

We walked through the house, the killer and I. I could feel the butler's eyes on my neck. I kept telling myself I was Orosgo's best bet. If he killed me, he had nothing. Not the book, not Riley, not Curtin—nothing.

That's what I kept telling myself. But as I reached the front door, I heard a cell phone buzz behind me, and I felt as if my heart had seized up like a dry engine.

I stopped. I turned, slowly. The butler's eyes and mine locked as he reached inside his jacket and drew out his phone.

He held it to his ear. He listened.

"Very good, sir," he said solemnly.

He slipped the phone back into his jacket and hesitated a moment, hand in his armpit, out of sight. Would he pull his gun? End everything in the next second?

He didn't. He drew out his hand, empty. He walked past me to the front door. He opened the door for me.

"Have a nice day," he said.

I realized I had stopped breathing. I forced myself to start again. I walked past the butler, out the door, and into a morning that smelled of the sea.

33

MIDNIGHT, HAPPY TOWN.

The amusement park was closing. Stationed just off the freeway across the street, I sat in Riley's Passat and watched through the windshield as the people began to file out.

I was wearing a black windbreaker now. I could feel the weight of Slick's gun in the inside pocket, feel the shape of it pressed against my left side. Now and then, I nervously reached across and touched the hard bulge of the weapon through the jacket's fabric. Sure enough, it was still there. On my right side, I had a flashlight clipped to my belt.

Out in the park, the Ferris wheel stopped turning. The tinkly music died. The sparkling lights winked out, arc by arc, until the wheel became a great round shadow against the moonlit sky. The blue and red bulbs on the small roller coaster went dark in sections, the darkness climbing and falling with the loop-de-loop pattern of the tracks. The crowd, meanwhile, kept pouring through the gates in the surrounding fence, streaming into the grassy dirt parking lot. Headlights went on and engines started. Cars began to line up at the exit and putter off down the road. The carousel went dark. The horses became silhouettes. One by one, the lights on the shooting galleries faded and were gone.

The shutdown process continued a long time. The crowds streamed out. It seemed a large crowd for midweek. I reckoned it was the draw of the Halloween rides. I remembered the billboard outside Walnut Creek advertising the Horror Walk. People loved that stuff.

I sat and watched. I drew a long breath, impatient. Was I certain Riley was hiding in there? Not as certain as I'd pretended to be when I was having breakfast with Orosgo. Not as certain as I should have been with my life on the line. But kind of certain. Kind of.

They're all around me, Riley had said on the phone. *They can't see me, but they're everywhere.*

I figured she had to be hiding somewhere Orosgo's people would know to look: Happy Town, where she worked. But it also had to be somewhere big and complex, a place she knew so well that she could elude them even as they hunted for her: also Happy Town.

And there was another clue: that billboard outside Walnut Creek. It pictured a woman looking over her shoulder as she stepped into the clutches of a witch. It was the scene from the movie, wasn't it? It was the sacrifice scene from *Horror Mansion*. Maybe Riley had helped design the attraction this year. Maybe she hoped I'd figure it out and find her there. Or maybe she'd just gone there by instinct, haunted by her own haunting past.

In any case, that's where she was. I was certain of it. Kind of.

I was kind of certain I was alone here, too, that I had not been followed. After my breakfast with Orosgo, I had returned to my motel. I had waited there a full day to make sure no one was watching me. The next day, I had gone out into the parking lot and checked under the Passat for tracking devices. I had ditched my old burner and gone into town and bought a new one, a smart one this time with an internet browser, though I didn't turn it on. I had bought yet another outfit, including the black windbreaker. I had waited in stores and coffee shops until evening came. Then I left town. I took my time getting on the freeway. I wove elaborate routes through the hills to make sure there was no one on my trail.

Finally, I headed north again. Walnut Creek. The park. I was certain no one was following.

Kind of.

Now I sat and watched. The crowds continued to file out. The headlights in the parking lot continued to flash on. The colored lights and spotlights in the park continued to go dark. The disc of the Tilt-A-Whirl. The cars of the bumper rides. They all became shadows, gray ghosts in the crowded landscape.

After another forty-five minutes or so, Happy Town was quiet. I went on sitting, watching. I could see the last workers in the moonlight, sweeping up, shutting down. The final few of them brought bags of trash out and tossed them in dumpsters set at the edge of the parking lot. More headlights went on. More cars drove away.

Finally, the park was empty. No one left—except for Riley. Or so I thought. So I hoped.

I got out of the car.

IT WAS EASY to see why she had chosen this place to hide in, assuming she had. There was no security guard. Not even a watchdog. And while the chain-link fence was topped with three rows of barbed wire, it was the work of a few minutes to dig in the dirt at the base of the fence until I could slip under. Riley would have been able to leave here whenever she wanted. She would have been able to find food and use restrooms. During the day, she might even have gotten into costume and mingled with the crowd, unseen.

I rose up from under the fence and dusted myself off and began walking among the deserted attractions. The dark rides loomed above me on every side, weird, twisted shapes, enormous. The boarded galleries stood in long lines. Huge plaster monsters reared and grinned and stared. It was like being in a field of fossils, hulking beasts that had gone extinct in ancient days and turned to stone. Their shadows were etched clearly by the autumn moonlight. They seemed weirdly poised to come alive at any minute.

I walked in the chilly silence, searching for the Horror Walk. It took a long time to find it. Then there it was, up ahead, near the fence at the far side of the park.

The entrance to the attraction was a gigantic head of Satan. It was tall as a house. The devil's mouth was agape in a hungry, toothy grin. The mouth was the doorway through which the customers could enter. I approached it nervously, my eyes flicking this way and that, watching for danger.

I had seen so much real horror at this point, you might have thought I could enter the maw of a make-believe devil pretty calmly. Not so much, it turned out. As I came near that huge, horned head in the breezy darkness, I grew truly afraid. I felt my guts go hollow, and I reached again to touch the shape of the gun at my side. Something in my blood expected Satan to actually swallow me here. I stared up at the devil's sharp teeth as I walked into the blackness of his mouth.

I waited until I was deep inside before I unclipped my flashlight from my belt. I turned it on. The beam immediately struck a gargoyle, a gaping beastie grinning down at me from the wall. The effect was as if the thing had jumped out of the shadows at me: *boo!* I gasped aloud. My heart raced. I shook my head, annoyed by my own cowardice.

But the whole long walk was like that, every step I took. Every time I swung the flash to light my way, it lit something terrifying. A snarling werewolf. A skeletal zombie. A dragon head, eyes flashing down at me.

I told myself it was ridiculous to be afraid of these imaginary things. After all, I had faced them in reality—or I had faced something like them in something like reality. I had battled monsters in the Eleven Lands, where they might have killed me. Some of them had tried pretty hard. Any minute, in fact, I could walk through a door and find myself fighting yet another one of them—the Abominable Snowman—in the midst of the storm on the side of the White Mountain. So why should I start and gasp every time the flashlight hit some plastic imitation?

Just as I asked myself that, my flashlight beam hit the green, warty face of a witch—and I started and gasped.

I felt like an idiot. The witch—a wax dummy—wasn't even all that frightening. It was a ridiculous cliché: black-robed, black-hatted, standing over a stout black kettle. Rubber bats hanging above her beside a pale green phosphorescent moon. Wispy ghosts painted on the wall behind her.

All the same, the sudden sight of her had scared me to my toes. I clutched my chest and felt my heart rabbiting crazily.

"Damn it!" I said aloud.

I let the flashlight play over the tableau. There were other figures behind the witch, and these were more mysterious, more frightening. Cowled acolytes hulking in the deeper darkness. A gargoyle clutching a plastic dagger in a spindly hand.

The sight chilled me. It was the movie scene. *Horror Mansion.* Same as on the billboard.

I moved my flashlight around some more, exploring the surrounding area. Ghouls and ogres and zombies stared at me, their eyes glittering as the beam hit them. But none of them moved.

"Riley?" I called, my voice barely more than a whisper. "Riley!"

But there was no answer. Silence.

Was it possible she wasn't here? Had I guessed wrong? Had I misread my sister's clues and signals?

Desperate for inspiration, I shifted the flashlight into my left hand and my right hand went into my jacket, into my shirt. I felt for Betheray's locket there. Touched the hot metal. Gripped it.

Once again, with the force of a crash-cut in a movie flashback, I was suddenly in the past. Sitting on Riley's bed again with the book in my hand. *Nobody Listens.* I was right where I had been the last moment I'd seen myself like this. I was lifting my eyes from the children's book to look across the room. To see someone there. A face. An image.

I saw it clearly this time. It shocked me.

It was me. It was my face. My face from when I was a child. There was a dresser against Riley's bedroom wall. A dresser with a mirror. I was looking at my own reflection there.

And I knew that face, that boy. It was the boy who had led me out of Edgimond to Menaria. Guided me out of the Eunuch Zombie Cave of Female Sacrifice. Helped me find my way through the *Horror Mansion* maze. It was the same boy.

I stood in the funhouse darkness—and sat, at the same time, on the bed of my memory. I stared at that face—my face—gaping.

And then—a ghostly voice whispered: "Austin."

Horrible creatures leapt out of the darkness at me and vanished again as I spun around, bringing the flashlight's beam in an arc around with me. My free hand snapped from the locket and sank inside my jacket pocket to grip my gun. But by the time I finished turning, I had recognized Riley's voice.

All the same, it was a shock to see her standing there, her small figure only an arm's length away.

My little sister. She was dressed in a witch's costume, a voluminous black robe, a black wig, a conical black hat with a big round rim. It made her look even smaller than usual, even more like a child than usual, a little girl dressed up for Halloween. Her round cheeks were sunken and shaded, as if she hadn't eaten for days. Her pale eyes were big with fear. Her face was white with it. It wrung my heart to see her like that.

We stood there for a moment, frozen by the sight of one another. Neither of us able to speak.

Then, her voice breaking, she cried out, "Aus!" and threw herself into my arms.

I held her. The beam of the flashlight in my hand danced around wildly, catching the grotesque faces staring down at us. Riley sobbed into my chest. Her body quaked violently, fluttering against me like a butterfly. There never was much to her, and what there was was frail.

The stupid witch hat was poking me in the face. I pulled it off her. The black wig came with it. I dropped the rig to the floor. Her pigtails were pinned up on top of her straw-blonde hair. I kissed her head tenderly and patted it with my free hand.

"It's all right, sis. I got you. You're safe."

She sobbed and shook. She felt so small in my arms. Just like when she was little.

It was a long time before she grew still against me. Then she drew back, lifted her eyes. Her cheeks glistened with tears in the outglow of the flashlight. Her lips trembled.

"I knew you'd come, Aus," she said.

I smiled. "Of course I came." I brushed a strand of hair off her forehead. "Don't I always?"

She nodded. She sniffled. She laughed at herself, a desolate laugh. Then, with a sudden hint of her old mischievous energy, she said, "Did you find my clues? The flip-picture? The movie in the passageways?"

"I found them."

"They were always listening, see. I knew I wouldn't be able to say anything on the phone, so I left them there for you. Wasn't that smart of me?"

"It was. Very smart."

She straightened, proud of herself.

"I had forgotten all about that movie," I confessed.

She blinked, surprised. "Did you? We watched it together."

I shook my head. "We never did. You watched it with Dad. He showed it to you."

"Dad? No. Wait, really? Wasn't it you?"

"Think about it, Riley. Would I ever let you watch a movie like that?"

"Yeah, but . . . Why would Dad . . . ? Why would *he* show it to me? I mean, jeez, it scared the shit out of me. It traumatized me for years. I always thought you and I . . . "

But she fell silent. She blinked, confused. She'd blocked the memory, too, same as me. She'd changed it around, I guess, to keep herself from remembering who our parents really were.

"It doesn't matter now," I said. "I'll explain it to you later. Let's just get out of here. Do you have the book? *Another Kingdom.* Do you have it?"

"Yes. I hid it. Over here."

She gestured with her head, pointing deeper into the funhouse. I nodded. I aimed the flashlight beam down the Horror Walk path. She started off just a step ahead of me, reaching back to hold my hand.

"Are you sure no one followed you?" she asked.

"Pretty sure. But it doesn't matter. I cut a deal with Orosgo. For now, at least, he needs me."

"Why does he want it so much? The book. I read it. I skimmed it anyway. It's just some story."

I sighed. "It depends how you read it, I guess."

Like storybook children lost in the woods, we walked hand in hand, past paper trees and wax monsters. We passed a scene of hideous torture. A man writhing on a hook, the point thrust fully through him, spine to belly. I thought of Riley, hiding in here for days with all these horrors. It must've been like hiding inside her own mind.

"Was it you who sent it to me?" Riley asked. "It just showed up at my door one day. Wrapped up in brown paper. There was no return address. Just a note: 'Keep this safe.'"

"It wasn't me. No. It was . . . a friend. She wanted to give it to me, but Orosgo was already on my trail. I think she was hoping I'd see it on your shelf when you called me. And I did, but I didn't know what it was. I think Orosgo's guys may have hacked the call. They saw it instead of me."

"I'll bet that's it. Richard called me after that. He told me to give it to him. He said he would come and pick it up. But it wasn't him who came. It was strangers. A white guy and a black guy."

"Slick and Moses. Right."

"That's why I ran. Richard is part of it, you know. I think Mom and Dad are too."

"Part of . . . "

"The Illuminati."

Right. Her crazy video conspiracy theories. Only it turned out they weren't so crazy, were they?

"You're not going to give it to them, are you?" she asked. She turned her big, frightened eyes back on me. Her tiny hand gripped mine more tightly. "If they want it so badly, they shouldn't have it. That's what I figured anyway."

"You figured right, sis. I'm not gonna give it to them. I just need to read it through, then it'll be in my head. Then we can burn it and be done."

"But won't they come for us?"

"Probably. Eventually. But for now, like I said, Orosgo needs me. If I can just—holy shit!"

My flashlight beam had just hit the dragon.

It was the last monster before the funhouse exit. It was big. Really big. Big around and tall. Its head scraped the black ceiling. And while it wasn't exactly the same dragon I had killed back in Edgimond, it was enough of a twin to give me the scoobie-doobies. Not your ordinary lizard-like kill-the-maiden creature from the old chivalric tales, it was fat and ghastly, colored the same sickly greenish-white as putrid flesh. It wasn't made of body parts, no, but it was bulky and gooey and distorted enough in form that its outline and the outline of the Edgimond Beast of Sacrifice were more or less the same.

How had Curtin's dragon been transported here, I wondered. Or maybe the question was: how had my secret fears been transported to Edgimond? But then, while we were at it, how had Curtin traversed the gap to seduce Orosgo back in Russia all those years ago? I probably should have listened more closely when the old man was explaining about quantum universes and whatever it was. Now I could just feel—sense—the uncanny connection between that other kingdom and this one. Maybe reading the book would explain more.

"Scary, isn't it?" Riley said, looking up at the dragon with her big eyes. I nodded, licking my lips. "The way it works: you come into this pitch dark space just as you reach the exit. Then you cross a sensor and it lights up and roars. All the girls scream. Even some of the boys."

"I'll bet they do."

"Wait here," she said. "You have to be careful. I keep the sensor turned on at night as an alarm."

She let go of my hand and moved toward the dragon. I felt a foolish urge to pull her back from the thing, keep her out of its clutches. God, I hated that monster.

She took a big careful step as she moved under the beast, lifting her feet high so as to avoid the sensor. Then she kneeled down directly under its burning eyes. I held the flashlight beam on her and watched, nervous, crazily afraid the thing would suddenly come to life and snap her head off.

It didn't. She wrestled up a floorboard at the creature's feet. Reached into the space below and brought out the stack of pages bound with twine. I held my breath as I watched her in the flashlight beam. There it was, at last: *Another Kingdom.*

She carried the manuscript back to me, taking the same big step away from the dragon as she had when she went toward it. She obviously knew every inch of this funhouse like the back of her hand. She'd been clever to hide here. No one could have found her unless she wanted them to.

She stood in front of me now, holding *Another Kingdom* against her chest, like a girl carrying books to school. I couldn't stop staring at the package. What was in it? What would happen when I read it? If a mere glance at the beginning had given me the power to pass between worlds, what would a full reading do to me? What would happen after that?

"Aus? You with me?" Riley said.

Her voice brought me back to myself. I straightened, my eyelids fluttering. "Yeah. Yeah. I'm fine."

"We should go," said my sister. "They lock this exit, but we can get out the front way, the way you came in."

"Yeah," I said vaguely. "Sure."

"Let's go." She started past me.

I took a deep breath, rousing myself. "Right."

I pivoted around to follow her, bringing the flashlight beam around as I turned.

Riley's shrieking scream filled the shadows as she stopped short. Terror turned my blood to ice.

I had become so accustomed to the grotesque and hideous faces springing out of the darkness at me that it was a long second before I realized that this grotesque was real. Its features were twisted. Its mouth was a corkscrew snarl. Its teeth were bared. One eye socket was horribly gutted and purple and webbed with fresh scars. For a moment, my brain simply could not take in the impossible.

Then it did. And I whispered: "Slick!"

In the movies, he would have made some speech. He would have expounded on his plans and rigged up some terrible long-form death that would have given us a chance to escape at the last second. But this wasn't the movies. All he did was level his .45 at little Riley's head as she stood clutching the book to her chest. Her scream dwindled to a frightened pant. Slick's twisted grin got twistier. His one remaining eye seemed to pulse in his head like a living blob.

He said: "That's what I came for, bitch."

And he pulled the trigger.

What mighty force of mind set me into motion between his first word and his last, I'll never know. It felt as if time slowed down while my body turned to a streak of fire. I hurled myself at Riley and carried her into the shadows as the gunshot exploded, a blast so loud it seemed to erase the world.

I left my feet, carrying my sister with me through the air. The flashlight fell from my hand and hit the floor and went out. The funhouse was plunged into blackness so complete that with my ears deaf from the gunshot and my eyes blind, I felt as if I were whirling, lost, through infinite space.

Then the two of us, Riley and I, crashed to the floor and were thrown apart by the impact. At the thick, thudding sound we made, Slick fired again in our direction. The flame from his gun barrel was an obscene red-hot tongue in the darkness, there and gone. Riley screamed again. Was she hit? Was she dying? Was I?

Slick fired once more at the sound of her voice, but I was still tumbling away from her with the force of my first leap, rolling, deaf and sightless, into total obscurity. I didn't know where she was. I didn't know where anything was.

My body came to a stop. There was silence—or if there was sound, I couldn't hear it with my ears still pulsing from the noise of the gunfire. I lay absolutely still, knowing the slightest sound would draw another shot. I tried to hear if Riley was breathing, but I couldn't hear anything. I couldn't see anything. I remembered how I had lost Betheray, how Iron had killed her as I chased after him, helpless. I thought if I lost Riley now, I would never forgive myself. My heart would be my hell forever. I lay where I was, drowning in nothingness thick as seawater.

I don't know how many seconds passed. Not many. Maybe two or three. My mind had started working again, clickety-click. I was trying to assess the situation. I'm sure Slick was doing the same. He must have known that I had a gun too. It was his gun, after all. So he couldn't turn a flashlight on, could he? I'd shoot him dead if he did. He couldn't make a move or make a sound any more than I could. So he was just as blind as I was, and probably just as deaf as well.

All the while I was thinking this through, my hand was slipping slowly, slowly into my windbreaker. Taking hold of the pistol grip. Drawing the gun out. Slowly, slowly.

One of us—Slick or me—was going to make a noise eventually. One of us—Slick or me—was eventually going to give himself away. One of us was going to die in the next few seconds.

As God was my witness, it would not be me.

Now, as the clangor in my ears subsided—and his ears, too, I guessed—I began to hear something. I thought it must be Slick. I thought he was moving slowly, carefully in my direction, hunting me. But I could still see nothing, nothing at all. I clutched my gun in my sweaty hand, but I didn't fire. If I missed, it would give my location away, and he would blow me to pieces. Losing an eye had probably thrown his aim off, maybe even way off, but he was a practiced killer, and I imagined he'd adjust. I could not afford a mistake. I just lay there, and now the clammy sweat broke out on my face as well.

A floorboard creaked. I held my breath. The killer was closer—very close. I pointed my gun at where I thought he might be. But I was still totally blind, too blind to fire.

The next time I heard his footstep, he seemed only a few yards away from me. My finger tightened on the trigger. Should I risk a shot? Not yet. A miss and I was dead. I was afraid to take the chance.

One more footstep, I told myself. *If I hear one more footstep, I'll do it.*

But the next thing I heard was not a step—and it wasn't close to me. It was at a distance somewhere in the pitch darkness off my left shoulder. It was a soft metallic chink. The sound of keys dropping to the floor.

And then a whisper—Riley's whisper: "Shit."

I held my breath. I was at once thrilled with relief that she was still alive and terrified that Slick would fire at the sound of her voice and kill her.

But he didn't fire. No. He knew I had my gun just as he had his. He had to make his next move just as carefully as I did.

But then came his next step. And he was moving away from me, moving toward her, toward the place where Riley had revealed herself. A floorboard creaked off in that direction. Of course. He didn't need to shoot and give himself away. All he had to do was grab her. Once he had her in his clutches, he could use her as a shield. I'd be helpless.

Another soft footstep in the dark. Slick was moving her way relentlessly.

It was only then—then, at that last moment—that it dawned on me what Riley had done. That strange, sad, crazy, clever little sister of mine. As lost and loopy as she sometimes seemed, she had been ahead of everyone from the beginning. She had outsmarted all of Orosgo's hunters. She had left a trail of private clues to lead me to this place. She had even found the path through her own broken heart and mind to expose the truth of a vast conspiracy.

And now she had created the chance I needed to survive.

Because she had given herself away on purpose, to draw Slick toward her—and toward the dragon. In the next second, he tripped the sensor. The enormous beast at the funhouse exit blazed to life and roared. Its great body, captured in whirling spotlights, reared and shuddered, its eyes flaring red, its mouth spitting make-believe fire.

And there was the killer outlined clearly against its nightmare brilliance.

I think Slick got it at the end. He didn't look for Riley. There was no point. He looked for me. He knew I had the gun, and he knew I could see him clearly. So he spun around in my direction, pulling the trigger even as he turned. As the dragon reared and roared behind him, his gun spurt flame and death. It all happened very fast.

But not fast enough, Slick. Not half fast enough.

In that last moment before Slick had tripped the switch, I had guessed Riley's stratagem. I was ready the instant the dragon came to life. Lying on the floor, I pulled the trigger of my gun and kept pulling it again and again until the hammer clicked on nothing and the weapon stopped jerking in my hand.

I saw Slick's shadow go reeling back toward the roaring beast, his arms wheeling, his gun flying off into darkness as the creature spat fake flame. Slick half-turned in the dancing spotlights and toppled down to the floor so hard I thought he would keep toppling right through it, down and down forever.

I, meanwhile, was pushing up, screaming through the noise of the dragon. "Riley! Riley! Riley! Are you there?"

Dimly, through the ringing in my ears, I heard a circuit breaker give a humming thunk. The dragon vanished. The roaring ceased. The funhouse went black again.

"Baby! Baby! Baby! Are you hit?" I was screaming wildly. "Are you hurt, Ri? Are you wounded, sweetheart?"

I rose trembling to my feet, searching the blackness for her, screaming and screaming. "Ri! Are you hit? Baby! Baby! Where are you?"

The empty gun slipped from my fingers. I stepped forward. I kicked something. I heard it roll. The flashlight. In the next second, I had swooped down and scooped it up. I shook it and the beam shot out and struck her where she stood. My little sister. Dazed and blinking and distant with shock. Swimming in her black witch's robe. Touching her tiny frame with both hands, checking for blood and pain.

She looked at me then with a look of wonder, almost exactly the way she used to look at me when I would lie in her bed beside her and tell her stories to help her sleep. She spoke to me with the same sweet, childish affection and awe as she did then.

"I think I'm okay, Aus. I don't think I'm shot. I think I'm okay."

I cried out and pulled her into my arms and held her. I was all love, and all rage, both love and rage together. I pressed her against me as hard as I could and cursed my father for driving her mad, cursed my mother for wanting us dead, cursed my big brother for abandoning us and cursed Orosgo and all his minions for every moment of fear and danger they had put us through. The fools, I thought. The fools, fools, fools, the lot of them. If they had just come after me, they would've beat me. I was no hero. I was just some guy. They could've scared me off. They could've run me down. But I would kill every single one of them before I let them hurt my little sister.

I heard her speak weakly against my chest. "What do we do now, Aus? What are we going to do now?"

I sighed. I lifted my eyes to heaven, blinking away tears.

"Grab the book, baby," I said. "Let's blow this fun house."

AS WE WORKED OUR WAY BACK THROUGH THE HORROR Walk to the entrance, my biggest worry was that I would step through Satan's mouth and find myself in the blizzard on the White Mountain again, rushing into the swordfight with the Abominable Snowman. I didn't have another battle in me. If I'd had to fight that thing right then, I'd have been dead in seconds.

Some providence protected me, though. Right hand on the flashlight, left arm around Riley's narrow shoulders, holding her dazed little figure close to me as she clutched the manuscript to her chest, I stumbled out of the devil's maw into the moonlight. Both of us were shocked and staring as we staggered across Happy Town toward the fence.

"Do you think we should call the police?" Riley asked me. I heard her voice trembling. I felt her body trembling too.

"No," I told her. "We're not going to call anyone."

"But they'll find that guy's body in the morning. They'll see I'm gone."

"It'll be all right."

"But how? How will it be all right, Aus?"

I didn't answer. I didn't know. I only knew this: I had to read the book. Before anything else happened, I had to read *Another*

Kingdom. That was what Queen Elinda wanted. That was what she had wanted from the start, and that's what I was going to do. The wisest queen in all the world had chosen me to be her hero, so that's what I would be. That had to be the best thing, I thought. Because if she was the wisest, she must love the good, the greater good more than the lesser. So what she wanted must be the most good thing, and I would do it if I could.

Riley and I crawled under the fence, first me, then her. We stumbled across the street to where her Passat was waiting.

"Can you drive?" I asked her.

"I don't think so," she said.

"Well, you have to."

"Okay."

I handed her the key and took the manuscript from her. I held the door while she sank wearily behind the wheel. Then I closed her in and carried the manuscript around to the passenger side and got in beside her.

Riley was still just sitting there, just staring out through the windshield. "Where are we going now, Aus?" she asked me.

"Back to LA," I said.

She nodded, dazed. She started the engine. But she didn't put the car in gear.

"What's going to happen there?" she asked.

"I don't know," I told her. "I guess we're going to find out."

"There's so many of them," she said. "And they're so powerful. Is it just going to be us against them? Just us against the whole world?"

I wagged my head a little. She looked so small and frightened. I had to tell her something—something to give her hope.

"Not just us," I said. "We wouldn't have gotten this far if it was just us. We have friends. We have allies."

Her wide eyes swept across the moonlit night outside the windshield. "Where, Aus?" she asked me.

"In another kingdom," I said.

I could see she was still trembling—still trembling and forlorn—as she looked down at the manuscript I was holding in my lap.

"Let wisdom reign," I told her. "And each man go his way."

She nodded without comprehension. She took a deep breath and put the car in gear. We started out of the parking lot.

As the Passat rolled along the road back toward the freeway, I took out my new phone. I turned on the internet connection. I signed in. At once, all of my texts and emails appeared on the screen. My friends from LA. Old friends from school. And Jane—Jane Janeway. Five emails from Jane. Three texts. Was I all right? Where was I? She was worried about me.

The world had not yet ended.

I had to drag my sleeve across my eyes then so I could see clearly. Then, when I could, I put the phone away. I reached up and turned on the reading light above my seat. I undid the twine that bound the pages. I removed the title page from the top and slipped it to the bottom of the pile.

Riley silently guided the car through the night.

I read the opening lines of the manuscript:

The truth is? By the time everything went crazy, I was pretty much crazy already. Edgy, anxious, hypochondriacal. Thirty years old and I hardly recognized myself. I mean, there was a time I used to be somebody. Not somebody famous, just a dude, but somebody. I used to be able to look in the mirror and say, that's me, that's Austin Lively . . .

Acknowledgments

This novel reached its first audience in the form of a podcast, an intense labor that involved more people than I can now name. Michael Knowles brought the words to life with a brilliant performance. Jonathan Hay led a perfect and perfectionist production team that included Mathis Glover, Austin Stephens, Mike Coromina, Cynthia Angulo and Rebecca Shapiro. Jeremy Boreing and everyone else at the *Daily Wire* made the whole project possible.

In novel form, Robert and Mark Gottlieb at Trident Media found a wonderful publisher at Turner, and everyone there—Todd Bottorff, Heather Howell, Kathleen Timberlake and the whole team—did a great job.

As for my wife Ellen Treacy, I have been thanking her in my books for many decades now, and it's still not enough.